DROW ROYALTY

DROW ROYALTY

GOTH DROW UNLEASHED™ BOOK TEN

MARTHA CARR

MICHAEL ANDERLE

DISRUPTIVE IMAGINATION

LMBPN Publishing
PMB 196, 2540 South Maryland Pkwy
Las Vegas, NV 89109

First US Edition, June, 2021
(Previously published as a part of the megabook *The Drow Grew Stronger)*
eBook ISBN: 978-1-64971-845-7
Print ISBN: 978-1-64971-846-4

THE DROW ROYALTY TEAM

Thanks to the JIT Readers

If we've missed anyone, please let us know!

Angel LaVey
Daniel Weigert
Deb Mader
Diane L. Smith
Jackey Hankard-Brodie
John Ashmore
Kerry Mortimer
Larry Omans
Paul Westman
Peter Manis
Veronica Stephan-Miller

Editor
The Skyhunter Editing Team

DEDICATIONS

From Martha

To everyone who still believes in magic
and all the possibilities that holds.
To all the readers who make this
entire ride so much fun.
And to my son, Louie and so many wonderful friends who
remind me all the time of what
really matters and how wonderful
life can be in any given moment.

From Michael

To Family, Friends and
Those Who Love
To Read.
May We All Enjoy Grace
To Live The Life We Are
Called.

CHAPTER ONE

This can't be real. None of this is actually happening right now, is it?

Cheyenne Summerlin stalked through the corridors of black stone, blinking at the bright code scrolling across the walls. Grimacing at the distraction, she reached behind her ear and ripped off the silver activator coil. The code flickered and disappeared with the buzzing pinch that still made her eyes water. She jammed the activator into her coat pocket and kept moving.

Beside her, L'zar Verdys moved with long, purposeful strides away from the Heart at the center of Hangivol. The drow thief stood tall, his hands clasped behind his back and a daring, infuriating smirk on his dark-gray lips.

"Look at this," he muttered, gesturing toward the crowd of snarling magicals gathering in the wide archway of a branching corridor on their left. "They look happy, don't they?"

Cheyenne stared expressionlessly at the Crown's servants and attendants cramming into the archway, who were shoving each other against the black walls. "Happy enough to jump out and try to rip us to shreds."

"Oh, they could *try*, yes." L'zar raised his eyebrows at the sneering, hissing magicals glaring at them, a multitude of races, skin colors, and facial features. He didn't even bother to lower his voice when he passed a foot from the archway. "Then they'd find themselves at the foot of the deathflame with nothing but oblivion to greet them there."

A slavering rat-faced skaxen drew her head back and spat violently at L'zar. The drow's fingers flicked toward the furious servant in a fraction of a second, sending the foamy wad of spittle flying back toward its owner, where it landed with a grotesque smack. The skaxen screamed and reeled away from the corridor, clamping both clawed orange hands to her eye and pushing through the crowd to withdraw the way she'd come. No one else said a word.

L'zar clasped his hands behind his back and kept up his brisk but unhurried pace through the Crown's inner fortress in the center of Ambar'ogúl's capital. "You know, for the first time, I think I like the way things are headed in this place."

On the other side of Cheyenne, Ember Gaderow snorted. "Because no one can do anything to stop you."

The drow chuckled and cast the fae girl a sidelong glance. "They wouldn't have been able to anyway. The only difference is they know it now. It's about time the willing slaves in this place pulled their heads out of their beloved Crown's ass and opened their eyes to the truth."

And he thinks the truth is that he's much better than she is. I'm still not buying it.

Cheyenne and Ember shared a quick glance, and the fae girl shrugged.

They followed L'zar down too many twisting corridors for Cheyenne to count until they finally stopped at two broad metal doors the same black as the walls, stretching a full twelve feet up to the equally black ceiling. The drow turned toward his daughter and her fae *Nós Aní* and dipped his head in acknowledgment. "Ladies, I believe our reception awaits."

"What are you talking about?" Cheyenne stopped when he slammed both hands against the doors and pushed them open into the room beyond. *The Crown might not be able to do anything to him, but I sure as hell can.*

L'zar marched into the room as the massive doors thumped against the walls. Dozens of low black metal tables lined the wide, tall room, each of them with matching benches like picnic tables. Every surface was cluttered with every type of magical and non-magical weapon imaginable, daggers, maces, clubs, swords, throwing stars, axes spears. Mixed in with these were the same floating metal orbs the Crown had sent out into the city's multiple rising levels, both for the affluent and the lower-class citizens alike, to keep her not-so-loyal subjects in line. Cheyenne's fingers slid around the cold metal coils of the activator in her pocket, but she didn't need to put it on again to know that these pieces of weaponized tech were dead. *For now.*

Standing around all the tables and benches, either cleaning the weapons or testing them or simply hefting them in their hands, were at least fifty O'gúl soldiers, all orcs. Some looked like they'd been a part of the fight in the Heart's courtyard less than twenty minutes ago. Others were fresher-looking as if they'd joined the party in the weapons room and had missed all the fun before Cheyenne returned her drow coin to the altar. All of them glared at L'zar, practically skipping down the center aisle between the metal tables toward the double doors on the opposite end of the room.

The first orc they passed thumped a metal club against his meaty palm and snarled. *"Nilsch úcat."*

L'zar looked quickly at the orc and feigned insult, leaning away and placing a mocking hand to his chest. "Who, *me?*"

"Nobody wants you here, Weaver."

"She'll grind you to dust before the end."

"Blood and fire, *nilsch úcat.*"

3

"The next time any of us see your face, it'll be in the halls of the unmarked dead!"

The snarling, growling curses flew faster from the orcs' mouths, growing in volume until they were all shouting after L'zar, spit flying from between their protruding tusks with the force of their hatred. The drow didn't change his pace across the room, meeting many of the soldiers' gazes and dipping his head in approval, grinning as if they were congratulating him for his efforts instead. One orc at the far end of the room got so worked up, he swung a wickedly sharp ax back in a wide arc and sent it crashing into the metal table in front of him with a roar. Sparks flew, and the table dented significantly beneath his blow. By the time L'zar reached that table, the orc's chest was heaving as he scowled at the drow, thick spit flying in strands around his tusks.

L'zar stopped, looked the orc over from head to toe, and dipped his head. "Nice arm."

The weapons room echoed with unintelligible curses and O'gúleesh obscenities. Cheyenne and Ember stopped behind L'zar as his gaze wandered over the other set of doors in front of him. The halfling turned to glare right back at the enraged soldiers and raised an eyebrow. "They're gettin' worked up over this. Over *you*."

"Ah." L'zar passed his hand over a section of the metal doors, then looked over his shoulder at his daughter. "This is nothing. Wait 'til we get outside."

Great.

Cheyenne glanced at Ember, who flinched when another orc pounded some heavy metal weapon into a table or a bench with an echoing clang. Then she looked at the halfling with the ghost of a smile. "Even *you're* not this much of a sore loser."

"At least we can make that distinction."

An unseen heavy metal lock slid aside within the doors' mechanism, and L'zar pressed his hands against the metal surface before leaning back to peer at the screaming, roaring soldiers behind them. "You only have a fortnight. Don't waste it."

Then he shoved open the doors, and the mid-afternoon light from the open streets of Hangivol's inner circle spilled into the weapons room. The instant L'zar, Cheyenne, and Ember stepped outside, the orcs launched their weapons at the heavy doors that were slowly swinging back inward. The blades smashed into the slabs, glancing off with deafening echoes of metal on metal. A spear struck the door and stuck fast, the shaft quivering at the impact. The deadly blade of a war ax stuck into the very edge of one slowly closing door a second before a black metal dagger whistled through the air, spinning hilt over point as it passed through the last four inches of space between the doors and sailed over Cheyenne's shoulder.

On instinct, she slipped into drow speed and turned slightly to snatch the suspended dagger from the air. When she returned to normal speed, the doors of the Crown's fortress shut with a resounding boom behind her. She scowled at the dagger in her clenched fist.

L'zar glanced at it and raised his eyebrows. "Feels like you just reached into a frozen body and ripped out an icy heart, doesn't it?"

"Quit saying crazy shit like that." Cheyenne chucked the dagger at the ground and stuck her hand in her jacket pocket to hide her urge to wipe it on something.

"Honor, *Cu'ón!*" A drow man in a dark-blue, shimmering suit cut at weirdly sharp angles lifted a fist in the air and shot a blast of silver and black light toward the magical dome stretching high above the entire city of Hangivol. The spell raced toward the dome and the gray-filtered light and crackled against the shielded wall with a muted hiss.

L'zar met the other drow's gaze, stepped forward on his

heel with the toe of his borrowed Earthside shoe pointing straight up, and spread his arms in an exaggerated bow.

The other drow chuckled as his cry of recognition was taken up by the dozens of other drow stepping out of dark, shimmering doorways. They each sent a blast of their magic into the dome until the filtered light dimmed beneath the hissing crackle of impact and the dark streaks of magic racing across the curving wall of the shield for every citizen of Hangivol to see.

Cheyenne's mouth popped open at the sight of so many other drow gathered in the square outside the Crown's fortress. She immediately forced it shut again but couldn't help but stare at all the glowing eyes and bone-white hair and slate-gray skin like her own. They were all well-dressed, standing tall and dipping their heads toward L'zar and his daughter as the *Cu'ón* led the way through the square. *I had no idea there were this many.*

A drow woman with white hair falling past her hips, wearing a gauzy dress so low-cut it might as well have been a halfway-open robe, grinned at Cheyenne. The feral hunger in the drow woman's gaze made the halfling look quickly away. *Apparently, L'zar's not the only one who's mastered that look.*

The drow in the low-cut dress slammed the heel of her fist against the closest wall with a metallic clang. One by one, the other drow took up the weird greeting, wordlessly striking dark fists or open hands on the metal walls, doors, and door-frames. It wasn't nearly as unruly and chaotic as the other times O'gúleesh had gone full-creepy on Cheyenne by banging on metal. The magicals here struck over and over in a slow rhythm as they grinned at the two drow and the fae crossing the square to make their way to the outer rings of the capital.

L'zar threw his head back and laughed. Then he stepped sideways away from Cheyenne and spread his arms again, gesturing toward her like a crier clearing the streets in front of some medieval lord. "The *Aranél* returns!"

The other drow took up the cry.

"Honor, *Aranél!*"

"She is seen!"

"*Mór úcare!*"

Cheyenne frowned when she heard the last one. "Why are they calling me that?"

"That's what you are." L'zar grinned. "Cheyenne, the Weaver's daughter. Dark child returned. Princess of Ambar'ogúl!" The drow spread his arms and pranced across the square, turning in a slow circle as he moved and laughing back at all the drow who'd come to see them both.

Ember grimaced. "He's much crazier than I thought."

"Tell me about it." Cheyenne frowned at her father and snorted when he delivered bow after exaggerated, moronic bow to the drow in every direction. "The loyalists called me that. *Mór úcare.*"

"I'm guessing that's the 'dark child returned' part."

The halfling scrunched her nose and watched her drow father's crazed antics as they reached the other side of the square. "And *Aranél* is 'princess.' They keep throwing these words around in front of me, and I'm too dense to pick up on any of it."

"Oh, *that's* right." Ember rolled her eyes. "You should've spent more time learning the language so you could've picked up on all the secret messages. I bet there's a whole section on O'gúl history at the library."

Cheyenne gently elbowed her friend in the side and kept walking.

The fae girl squinted in thought and glanced slowly around the square. "And I'm just noticing for the first time how weird it is that everybody here speaks English with random O'gúleesh tossed in."

"Huh." Cheyenne blinked at the realization. "Guess we'll have to ask about that one."

When they reached another wide archway of dark, shimmering metal on the other side of the square, L'zar spun again to face the gathered drow. They still pounded in unison. The slow, steady rhythm vibrated through the ground and the air, and Cheyenne clenched her jaw to keep her teeth from feeling like they were rattling around in her head.

"Brothers! Sisters!" L'zar spread his arms, his golden eyes wide and glowing with a sharper light than usual. "A new Cycle turns in fourteen days. Be ready for the end. I know *I* am."

A collective, wordless shout rose from the other drow, and L'zar took a deep breath as he grinned at his people paying tribute to him right outside the Crown's lair. Both hands shot up to his head as his long, slender fingers smoothed the hair away from the sides of his face and his forehead. Then he spun smartly again and raised his eyebrows at Cheyenne, gesturing toward the arch. "This is the beginning, Cheyenne. There's so much more than what you've seen."

Cheyenne glanced at the dozens of drow keeping up the pounding rhythm on the metal walls. "Am I supposed to be impressed?"

"Not in the slightest." L'zar leaned farther toward the dark archway and waited for Cheyenne and Ember to pass through ahead of him. "I'd be quite disappointed if you were."

CHAPTER TWO

The passage leading through the wall around the Crown's inner city containing nothing but drow subjects was so long, Cheyenne couldn't see the other end of it. The noise coming from both ends of the dark tunnel was quietest at the very center, though she was more focused on the erratic flashes of yellow and blue light streaking through patterned grooves in the tunnel's walls and ceiling. "What's that?"

L'zar gazed at the blips. "No activator to answer that question for you?"

"I don't need it for everything. Unless you have no idea, and I should write you off as clueless."

The drow laughed and ran a hand along the grooved wall. "You're still in a touchy mood, I see."

"I just found out I'm the O'gúl Crown's niece and that I have to come back here in two weeks to order her off the throne of a world she's been poisoning for who knows how long." Cheyenne cocked her head and shoved both hands into her jacket pockets. "'Touchy' is a bit of an understatement."

"Let it go for now." His voice was surprisingly soft when he said it, and she almost turned to look at him in surprise. Then he chuckled and slapped a hand on the wall, which resulted in a cracking echo up and down the tunnel. "You've earned your right to feel however the hell you want, Cheyenne, but moping about it is a waste of everyone's time. I'm not a fan."

"Sure, let me just change my moods to suit you."

L'zar gave her a small, amused smile and pointed at the flashing lights along the ceiling. "And *that*, by the way, is the city code rewriting itself."

"Wait, what?"

He nodded once and clasped his hands behind his back. "All part of the interim hold on magic if you will. The Crown's preparing in whatever way she can for your next meeting in two weeks. So are all her marvelously expendable subjects. *Her* words, once upon a time. And this is Hangivol, the most technologically advanced city and the heart of Ambar'ogúl, preparing for the new Cycle."

Cheyenne gazed at the crackling flashes across the otherwise dark surface. *The activator's staying in my pocket for now. I don't think I could handle reading a bunch of crap about myself, if that's even included.*

The metallic banging coming from the drow inner city behind them faded, replaced by a growing ruckus from up ahead. Cheers, shouts, bawdy laughter, and much more chaotic pounding in sporadic bursts came from whatever circular level they were about to enter at the end of the slightly declining tunnel. "Why do they do that?"

"I *know* you understand what a celebration is, despite the fact that I haven't yet seen you participate in one."

She gave her father a deadpan stare, and he shrugged before turning away from her. "I'm talking about all that banging. They did it at Rez 38 and then in Peridosh. *You* did it the day I came to talk to you about—"

"The traitor in the FRoE, yes." L'zar's head bobbed from side to side as strange, ululating O'gúleesh music filtered through the tunnel toward them. "It's a sign of immense respect, Cheyenne. They're paying tribute."

"To *me?*"

"Unless they're staring at someone else while they're doing it, yes."

She frowned at the bright end of the tunnel quickly approaching. *I guess all the Earthside O'gúleesh won't have much of a problem with me ruling over there. If I even do. Seems like they already approve.*

When they stepped out of the tunnel and into the dazzling light reflecting off every bright, shining surface, Cheyenne recognized Upper Tech. It wasn't the same courtyard she'd visited with Persh'al, but it was definitely the same district. And the people here were unhinged.

Magicals of every race danced in the glistening streets, their fine jewelry and expensive clothing whirling around them in bright flashes and ridiculous patterns. An incredibly tall, thin woman with skin the lightest shade of pale blue and four arms twirled between high-flying leaps, slamming her hand against a metal bench every time her bare, hand-shaped feet touched the ground. An orc with a high, stiff collar on his black dinner jacket and five gold rings inlaid in each tusk swung his head from side to side, kicking the metal walls of a building in rhythm to the strange music.

Expensive scarves and capes swirled in a kaleidoscope of shimmering patterns as the once entirely proper denizens of Upper Tech danced and whooped and roared in victory.

Cheyenne straightened, glancing back and forth across the square at the maddened celebration. "This place was a *lot* different the last time I was here."

Ember backed away from a goblin who lunged toward her, his tongue hanging out of his open, grinning mouth as he shook his head wildly and snatched the odd-shaped top hat that was split down the middle off his head. The fae girl widened her eyes as he cackled and whirled away again, throwing his weird hat into the air, not caring where it landed as he danced across the square. "What was it like last time?"

"Like everyone had a stick up their ass."

Ember chuckled wryly. "Maybe the sticks finally made it up to their brains."

"That does sound like an accurate assessment."

"L'zar!" A skaxen man wearing a sparkling green bodysuit limped toward them, spreading his arms in greeting. "Took you long enough, eh? We all thought you'd been rotting in the ground for the last two hundred years."

L'zar gave the skaxen a tight-lipped smile as they passed. "That's hardly long enough to cause concern."

The skaxen did a little jig in his delight, his bad leg making him look like he was trying to skip on one leg as he shook his clawed orange fists in the air and kept dancing.

Cheyenne forced herself to look away and caught up with L'zar. "Who was that?"

He looked slightly over his shoulder to raise an eyebrow at the dancing magicals. "I have no idea."

Ember floated beside them, unable to decide between frowning at the strange celebration or laughing at it. "You know, after everything I've heard about the shitty direction things have taken over here, I honestly expected this place to look a lot worse. Is the whole city like this?"

L'zar barked a laugh. Cheyenne ignored him and shook her head. "No, Em. Upper Tech's like Windsor Farms, with slightly more sticks up asses."

"Okay." Bobbing her head, Ember gazed around and blinked against the glare reflecting off the glittering white metallic surfaces everywhere. "So, this is the fancy level without drow."

"Pretty much."

L'zar turned toward another tunnel leading out of Upper Tech and paused when a fae man with violet skin and dark-blue hair falling over his shoulders floated into their path. Ember took a sharp breath and stared at the first of her kind she'd seen in this world, but she quickly covered her surprise.

"You shouldn't have returned." The fae man's expressionless face and his calm, even tone were totally at odds with the celebratory air spilling through Upper Tech, and his shimmering violet eyes were cold. "Nothing good will come of this."

The prodigal drow pointed at the fae and squinted. "I'm trying to place your name."

"The last thing I'm giving you is my name, thief."

"If we're throwing names around, I prefer 'Weaver' while I'm here." L'zar spread his arms and offered the fae man a flashing grin. "*Cu'ón* does fairly well too."

The fae man pointed across the square in no particular direction but away from the tunnel he currently blocked.

L'zar chuckled. "Come now, that's not very celebratory. If not for me, you can at least step aside for the *Aranél*, can't you?"

The only reply he received was a slow blink from the fae's luminous eyes and a highly judgmental glance up and down.

The drow thief winked at the fae, then stepped aside and gestured for his daughter to enter the tunnel. "Cheyenne."

She studied the fae man, who only gave her a brief and dismissive glance, then looked at the rest of the dancing square again. *I'm not about to start fighting magicals who don't appreciate L'zar Verdys in their city.* "There's more than one way out of this level."

"No." L'zar's grin disappeared, and his golden gaze bored into the fae's violet eyes. "You step aside for no one, Cheyenne. Not today. Enter the tunnel."

The warning in her father's voice sent an involuntary shiver down the halfling's spine. She exchanged a quick glance with Ember and blinked slowly. *We're doing things differently than the last time I was here.*

"Excuse us." Cheyenne nodded at the fae man and slipped

around him into the bright tunnel leading out of the district square.

Ember followed, smiling briefly at the other magical until the fae man turned his gaze on her and narrowed his eyes. She swallowed and raised her eyebrows as she floated past him into the tunnel.

L'zar dipped his head toward the fae, a smile flickering across his lips before he followed his daughter and her *Nós Aní*. The blue-haired fae turned slowly to watch the trio make their way down the tunnel and out of the upper level beyond the drow inner city. His silver-slippered feet didn't touch the ground once.

When L'zar caught up to walk at Cheyenne's side again, she shot him a sidelong glance. "Apparently, not everyone's happy to see the rebel Weaver return to Ambar'ogúl."

"That brooding fae is one of the outliers. I think." L'zar shrugged. "It doesn't mean he's loyal to the current Crown or that he won't celebrate the new Cycle when it turns. The second he steps inside his opulent quarters on the top floor of some high-rise penthouse, he'll be dancing himself into a purple fae sweat."

Ember leaned forward to look at him. "So why'd he try to block us?"

"Not us, just me." L'zar brushed his hair away from his face with a nonchalant chuckle. "I probably did something a thousand years ago to piss him off, and he's still holding a grudge. That happens a lot."

Cheyenne snorted. "Doesn't sound like he's just 'one of the outliers,' then."

"I'm talking about total numbers in Ambar'ogúl, Cheyenne." The drow lifted his chin with a sneer and clasped his hands behind his back as they moved through the tunnel. This one also sparked and crackled with visible light in the grooves in the walls. "Most of the magicals here are only too happy to see change, even if it comes merely because I stepped back over the Border from the human realm you and I love so much."

The halfling's eyes widened, but she kept walking straight ahead without turning to look at him. "They don't like that you were over there for so long."

"Mostly, they don't like that I was over there at all. Or that anyone goes Earthside, though it's been happening for as long as any of us can remember. By the way, let's keep that little nugget of truth to ourselves for the time being."

Cheyenne glanced at the flashing ceiling of the tunnel in exasperation. "And what little nugget is that?"

"The one about where you come from. It's not common knowledge, as I'm sure you've noticed by now." L'zar hummed a humorless chuckle. "We have to approach it gently when the time is right."

"Oh, yeah? As gently as you approached barging through the Heart so I could throw myself off a balcony for that stupid coin?"

"Naturally. That's about as gentle as we get, isn't it?" He shot her another grin and raised his eyebrows.

Cheyenne shook her head. *More secrets about who I am. I guess it's better to be keeping them this time instead of being the clueless one.*

"Stop." The urgency in L'zar's voice made Cheyenne and Ember spin to look back down the tunnel. He ignored their surprise and reached a hand straight out in front of him, eyes wide, before whirling around and slapping his hand against the wall on their left. The tunnel echoed with the smack of flesh on metal, then the wall flashed yellow light. A section of metal burst out of the wall two inches in front of Cheyenne and Ember, making them both jump back before a hollow clang signaled the sliding metal hitting the other side of the tunnel and blocking them.

Cheyenne glared at her drow father, who merely grinned

and stepped away from the wall he'd slapped, hands clasped behind his back again. "What the hell are you doing?"

"Testing my memory." He scanned the ceiling and the solid obstacle in front of them. "I'd step back if I were you."

Ember quickly did as he said, and Cheyenne narrowly avoided dropping through the hole that opened in the floor a second later. She leaped away, slamming a hand against the wall to steady herself as the metal floor shifted and folded in tiny clinking squares. When the movement stopped, the trio found themselves standing at the opening of a short stairwell leading into the underbelly of the city.

The halfling peered down the dark staircase. "A heads-up would have gone a long way, you know?"

"I told you to step back."

"Yeah, *after* you almost took my face off when you cut the tunnel in half."

L'zar clicked his tongue. "The surprise is half the fun."

"Okay, agree to disagree." She gestured toward the stairs. "Why don't you go ahead and meet all the other surprises first, huh?"

"With pleasure." The drow thief stepped forward with a little jig, gave his daughter a mocking bow, and headed briskly down the staircase.

Ember bit her lip to stifle a chuckle and shrugged when Cheyenne shot her a warning look. "At least his memory works."

"I'm not sure I trust that either." With a snort, Cheyenne stepped down after her father, followed closely by Ember. The second the fae girl's head descended below the level of the tunnel's floor, the small metal squares unfolded and sealed themselves back up to cover the hole in the floor. Cheyenne glanced at the ceiling. *Why do I feel like he doesn't have any idea where we're going?*

CHAPTER THREE

L'zar led them through a confusing series of twisting corridors and descending stairwells. Twice, they passed open chambers where magicals had gathered under Hangivol's various city levels in private. The first time, L'zar paused outside the chamber entrance and gave the three ogres inside a full bow, sweeping low over the upturned toe of his forward foot.

None of the ogres were amused by his antics. The closest one glared into the corridor and snarled before waving a huge, thickly scarred hand at the chamber entrance. A metal door slid out of the wall and cut off L'zar's view of the room with a sharp clang.

"Hmm." He chuckled and kept moving. "I expected more of a reaction."

Cheyenne rolled her eyes. "You almost sound disappointed."

"You know, I just might be."

The second chamber they passed was visible only through a narrow slit in the wall, but the magicals' enraged voices filtering through it into the corridor made it easy for Cheyenne and L'zar to pinpoint where this second gathering was held. The halfling noticed the narrow opening in the passage wall immediately. *Nobody considers drow hearing down here when all the drow have been living the high life in the inner city.*

"I say we put an end to this *now!*" A hissing, snarling skaxen woman pounded a fist into her clawed hand. "I won't stand for seeing that low-life piece of *nilsch úcat* scum sitting on the throne when the Cycle turns."

L'zar came to a silent stop in the narrow underground passage when he heard those words. He cocked his head toward the slit in the wall and turned that way.

"Shut your mouth, Raesh." A huge magical stepped in front of the opening and blocked the rest of the chamber from view. "That's bordering on treason, and you know it."

Cheyenne wrinkled her nose at the stench of rotting meat and body odor that wafted into the passage. She looked at L'zar and pointed down the hall.

The drow lifted a finger for her to wait and faced the chamber opening, folding his arms while listening intently to the argument.

"It's only treason once the new Cycle turns, Folreg," the skaxen hissed in reply. "You were singing prettily about the unending rule three days ago. Don't tell me you're changing your tune *now.*"

"I don't sing." The massive shadow covering the slit in the wall moved aside again, and the thin light from inside the chamber threw a yellow line down the center of L'zar's grinning face.

"You two need to pull yourselves together." The high, nasal pitch of the third speaker's voice made Cheyenne think of nails on a chalkboard. "I'm as prepared to see the new Cycle turn as the rest of us. The Crown's had Hangivol on its knees for longer than anyone wants to accept anymore. If L'zar Verdys truly returned to take the throne for himself, I say we sit back and watch the threads unfold."

"If L'zar Verdys came here to sit the throne, he brings the

deathflame for all of us!"

The huge magical named Folreg growled. "Just because he set you back a few hundred years with that flight scheme of yours doesn't mean he's here to kill his own."

"Set me back? Set me *back?*" The skaxen leaped across the chamber in a flash of orange flesh and snarled. "That blood traitor took *everything* I had! For what? So he could power some fell-damn experiment he stole from the tinkerer in Qi'woc."

"He must have had his reasons."

"He only needs one! His own greed and insatiable desire to watch the rest of us flail while he skirts by without consequences."

"Raesh, I said—"

"So it's treason! I have nothing left to lose." The skaxen woman pointed a glinting claw at the unseen magical with the nasal voice and shouted, *"You've* been spending too much time in the Goldsmile dens, Hivara. As long as those stay open, you'd be happy with a *radan* sitting the throne. If I see that Weaver scum in this city before the Cycle turns, I'll show him a side of O'gúleesh loyalty he's never seen before."

L'zar chuckled and raised a hand toward the thin opening in the wall.

The magicals in the chamber fell silent, and more than three bodies shifted uneasily inside the room. "What was that?"

Cheyenne leaned toward him to mutter, "Don't."

"I can't help it." L'zar waved his hand at the opening, and the narrow slit widened as both doors slid slowly apart to reveal the chamber beyond. "My name's been invoked."

When the doors stopped opening with a shudder and an echoing boom, the trio in the passageway looked on a gathering of over a dozen magicals, all of them crouching in surprise and wariness. Half of them had summoned attack spells in their hands, and all but one of them immediately killed their magic when they saw L'zar Verdys standing in the corridor, his arms spread wide as he gave them that feral grin that had given him such a reputation even in prophecies.

"You called, and I answered." The drow scanned the shocked faces in the corridor. "I wasn't aware there was a side of O'gúleesh loyalty I haven't had the chance to examine, but I have to admit I'm remarkably curious."

The huge magical who smelled like rotting meat—a cross between the gargoyle-like Golra and a rhinoceros—grunted. "You skaxen moron."

The skaxen woman's yellow eyes widened at L'zar, her entire body trembling as she raised a handful of hissing orange sparks in her upturned hand. "How *dare* you?"

"Me?" L'zar gestured toward himself and chuckled. "I merely want to give you the opportunity."

The skaxen hurled the ball of sparks at him, intentionally aiming for the space beside his head and the far wall of the passageway instead of the drow's grinning face. Her spell exploded against the metal wall disguised as stone and crackled across the grooved lines spanning the hallway. Cheyenne and Ember stepped toward each other in the middle of the corridor and stared warily at L'zar.

The drow cocked his head and blinked. "Come now, Raesh. That's no way to greet an old friend. They were only minor damages. I hear you recovered quite nicely."

The trembling skaxen woman shrieked in rage, her open mouth lined with fangs contorting her already rat-like face. Then she lunged toward the drow in the passageway.

L'zar danced away from her and cast a spell with a quick, one-handed gesture. Raesh careened into an invisible wall before she could set foot out of the chamber and shrieked again, ignoring the dark blood spraying from her broken nose as she clawed at the shield he'd cast around her. "I'll kill you! I swear it. I'll kill you myself! Do you hear me?"

"In a fortnight, my dear, you can do whatever you want." L'zar headed down the corridor again with an extra spring in his step. "Until then, I'd be careful about making promises you aren't sure you can keep."

The skaxen shrieked again, fighting both the shield and her fellow conspirators, who were trying to draw her back into the chamber as someone inside activated the doors to slide shut again. L'zar looked over his shoulder at Cheyenne and widened his eyes. "And everyone thinks *I* have anger issues."

The halfling slowly shook her head and shot a final brief glance into the chamber before the doors fully shut. Some of the magicals stared at her, their faces lined with a mix of disgust and fear. Then the doors clanged shut, muffling Raesh's furious screams on the other side.

Ember floated beside her as they continued after the drow thief, intent who was on stirring up trouble. "That was intense."

Cheyenne snorted. "Yeah. *That* is why everyone wants to kill him."

"Not everyone, Cheyenne." Ten feet ahead of them, L'zar thrust a slender finger in the air but didn't turn around. "Just those who think they're better than the rest of us."

"Like you?"

He laughed. "Oh, don't be so dramatic. I have a special set of skills, and it takes a rare mind to fully appreciate their scope. I most certainly don't fall into the category of O'gúleesh who want to kill me."

Chuckling softly as they came upon another branching set of corridors, L'zar pointed at various places in the walls, illuminating bright flashes of yellow and blue in the grooved metal before doors and walls in places Cheyenne couldn't see opened and closed and responded in whatever way he commanded. Frustrated shouts rose from one branching corridor on their right, followed by bursts of raucous laughter from a passage coming up on their left.

"Get back here and face me, Weaver!"

"The Crown should have killed you when she turned the Cycle!"

"Rot in the abyss!"

Cheyenne looked straight ahead as the shouted curses of enraged magicals echoed after them down the hall. The laughter on their left came from a group of yellow-skinned gremlins streaked with black grease and soot. They raised tankards of a thick drink that looked like blackened oil in a toast as L'zar danced past them.

"About time someone closed off that bridge."

"Honor, *Cu'ón!*"

"Where you goin', L'zar? You missed two other lounges back down that way."

L'zar stopped in front of the snickering gremlins and pointed behind him. "The doors to the safes are wide open. It would be a shame to leave them unattended for so long."

The gremlins started cackling, spilling their oozing black-sludge drinks all over themselves as they fell into each other and tried to raise more toasts at the same time.

Ember laughed with them, and the gremlins raised an indecipherable shout with something about a fae at the end. She elbowed Cheyenne in the side and stuck her thumb over her shoulder as they followed L'zar away from the gremlin celebration. "That sounded a lot like he was telling those yellow guys to go rob the magicals who hate him."

Cheyenne glared at her father's back as he pointed randomly at different areas in the wall and hummed a careless tune. "He can play drow Robin Hood all he wants. I'm not buying it."

L'zar laughed. "Such a warm welcome home, don't you think?"

"Not really. Do you have to screw with everybody like this?"

He whirled around and pointed at her. "Yes. Yes, I do. You

have no idea what I've done and how long I've waited for this day, Cheyenne. Stop trying to ruin it for me."

She peered behind her at the still-echoing shouts of the angry magicals behind them. "This isn't how you get people excited about you being back and your daughter challenging the Crown."

L'zar blinked slowly and stopped before a final turn in the hallway. When he turned, his smile was gone. "Stop talking about any of this like you understand a fraction of it. This is *my* city, Cheyenne. It'll be yours soon if you want it enough, but I wouldn't blame you if you didn't. I certainly don't, but I suggest you embrace what's happening. You don't want to make them think you're ungrateful, do you?"

"What?"

Holding her gaze, L'zar cast another spell on the wall in front of him. It shimmered with green and orange light that converged into the four-pointed star symbol. The illusion covered by the wards fell away, and two massive metal doors studded with two-inch bolts down either side stood at the end of the corridor. "They're waiting. I did all this for you, *Aranél.* Don't forget."

Leaping backward, L'zar threw his full weight onto the metal doors, and they burst open into the main room of his secret bunker below the capital city of Ambar'ogúl. Without another word, he turned and strolled through the open doors like he owned the place.

Technically, I guess he does.

Ember peered through the doors at the short staircase leading into the room beyond. The dozens of voices inside faded into an eerie, expectant silence. "That last part sounded pretty genuine."

"He's had thousands of years to practice sounding genuine, Em. Come on." Cheyenne headed through the doors down the staircase. "We better be done with surprises today."

CHAPTER FOUR

When Cheyenne and Ember descended the short, wide staircase into the room beyond, the entire crowd of L'zar's rebels stared up at them in silence. The doors swung shut on their own with a boom.

Maleshi Hi'et raised a fist into the air and shouted, "The heir returns!"

The room exploded with voices echoing the cheer and shouting greetings of their own. Ember laughed and floated down the rest of the stairs toward the celebrating crowd. Cheyenne stood frozen on the second-to-last step and stared at the dozens of bruised, bloody, battle-torn rebels pounding their fists on the giant metal table in the center of the bunker's main chamber. "What?"

"Don't just stand there, kid," Corian shouted, waving her forward. "Get your ass down here and join us. It's *your* party."

She took a halting step down the stairs.

"First real O'gúl win, huh?" Laughing, Lumil stepped onto the stairs beside the halfling and clapped a hand on Cheyenne's back to guide her down the stairs. "I remember my first battle, halfling. Didn't think I'd be able to move again. I mean, it didn't help that I got stuck right here by a fell-damn spear, but hey." The goblin woman thumped a fist against her side below the ribs and laughed again.

"I didn't get stabbed," Cheyenne said blankly. *I didn't even fight.*

"Of course you didn't! It's shock. That'll clear out in no time." Lumil led Cheyenne toward the other rebels, who gathered around L'zar Verdys' daughter to clap her on the back and thump their fists to their chests.

"Well done, Cheyenne."

"You did what you had to do, and you did it right."

"This is the start, *Aranél*. The chains are broken and the Cycle will turn, with you at the helm."

"Wait, no." Cheyenne shook her head at the orc nodding vigorously, his bottom lip pulled down as he grinned around giant tusks painted with black rings. "I'm not at the helm of anything."

"Ha!" The orc snorted and pounded a fist into his other hand. "You already are."

Staring blankly at the far wall of the main room, Cheyenne swallowed and tried not to flinch away from all the congratulatory pats and thumps and shakes of her shoulders. *If they don't stop touching me, I'm gonna lose it.*

Standing back from the crowd beside the metal table, Maleshi watched the halfling barely putting up with all the attention. The nightstalker raised her hand again and shouted, "Sakrit! Last time I checked, you had a hundred barrels stashed in this dump."

"You been counting my supplies, General?" A huge light-gray ogre with dried blood streaked down both bulging arms turned away from the crowd and pointed at Maleshi.

The nightstalker dipped her head toward him, the stiff collar of her military jacket rustling with the movement. "You can't expect me to come back to this shithole and not seek out the most important part first."

"Yeah, you came back for the swill. That I'll believe." Sakrit laughed and stalked across the wide room. A quick spell from the ogre opened a door in the stone wall barely big enough for him to squeeze through into the tiny hidden room beyond, but he did.

Maleshi's closed-lipped smile grew as she turned back toward Cheyenne, who hadn't moved an inch while nearly every member of the Four-Pointed Star gave her a congratulatory thump. *We'll start a brand new battle in here if somebody doesn't save her from all that.* "Cheyenne!"

The halfling blinked when Maleshi called her name and bent forward through the wall of jeering, shouting, beaten-up magicals to get a better view.

"Get over here." The general waved her toward the other side of the table. "We'll celebrate this victory in what little style we have left, huh?"

"Right." Cheyenne grunted when a rebel she recognized from her last visit materialized beside her in a swarm of tiny black flecks before grabbing her forearm for some kind of comrade's handshake.

"This is where it all starts." Only a deep blackness existed within the hood of his black cowl, although his black hand was clenched tightly around her forearm. "With L'zar Verdys's daughter. I had my doubts, sure. We all did in one way or another. You proved us wrong."

"Thanks," Cheyenne muttered. "Excuse me." *I'm done. I gotta get out of here.*

She shouldered her way past the circle of rebels gathered around her, all of whom reached out again for a thump on the back or a fist nudged into her shoulder.

A goblin woman stepped in front of Cheyenne to get her attention, still cackling at a wartime joke from the snickering orc behind her. "That's something for the *Aranél* to decide, isn't it?"

"I saw you jump off that wall, kid. Wouldn't have been my first choice, but impressive all the same."

"You've already put your terms together, haven't you? The Crown won't stand on her mountain of skulls for much longer."

"See this right here, Cheyenne? Bull's Head bastard stabbed me right in the thigh. I knocked him over the balcony seconds before those walls went up. Stings worse than an imp bite, and I'll show this scar to every young pup born to my line after today. You can count on *that*."

"Like you could find a mate willing to put up with you long enough for that to happen, you big-mouthed greenskin."

Laughter erupted around her as she tried to march through the bodies pressing in on her and shoving each other too. A flare of extra heat churned in Cheyenne's belly and raced up her spine and across her shoulders, mixing with her intense physical discomfort. She clenched both fists, and a flare of purple light blazed behind her eyes. Without knowing what she was doing, the halfling unleashed a wave of dark, shimmering energy all around her. The shockwave knocked the raucous magicals away from her in a wide circle, sending those closest to the Crown's challenger barreling backward into their neighbors and clearing a ring of space around her.

The main chamber fell silent again, and Cheyenne took a deep breath. She caught a glimpse of Maleshi standing on the other side of the table before her gaze fell on the surprised expressions of the other Four-Pointed Star rebels. *I should explain that one, right?* She cocked her head and centered her gaze on Maleshi again. "I don't like being touched."

A roar of approval and victory-drunk laughter filled the chamber. Every magical standing within striking distance of a metal surface started banging on it again, and those who had been blasted into their friends were jostled around, jeering at each other and themselves.

Maleshi dipped her head toward Cheyenne in acknowledgment, and the halfling chuckled. *Not the reaction I expected, but at least I can breathe again.*

"Hell of a way to kick off the toasting, eh?" A dark-purple troll with a blood-soaked bandage wrapped around his throat pumped a fist in the air. "Where's the fell-damn grog when we need it?"

"Deathflame take your grog, Kayal." The ogre Sakrit squeezed back out of the magically hidden pantry with two large dark-green glass bottles in each hand and a massive metal barrel strapped to his back with coils of hardened rope. "If you're gonna mention that swill in my presence, I say whoever started to slit your throat should've finished the job!" Another round of laughter rose at that as Sakrit trudged across the chamber and clinked the four bottles down on the table. The metal keg followed shortly after with a heavy clang. "Don't tell me you brainless mutts need to be told to get the tankards."

"I've got you covered there, friend." L'zar appeared again from some other area of the bunker, wheeling a heavy metal trunk behind him in each hand. "Who else thinks all this would be much easier if we took down the tech-eaters?"

"Ha! Never thought I'd live to see the day when you made yourself *useful*, L'zar."

"Never thought I'd hear intelligence fall out of your mouth, either. I guess only one of us was surprised today."

L'zar's rebels roared with laughter as the drow hauled one huge trunk up onto the metal table, slid it away from the edge, and thumped the second down beside the first. He flicked his fingers at the trunks' latches, which flashed briefly before flying open. The trunks' open lids hit each other with a loud bang, and the magicals gathered around to pull out empty metal cups, tankards, and goblets.

Cheyenne reached Maleshi as the drinking vessels were passed around with more playful insults and friendly scuffles. After shrugging out of her backpack and setting it on the floor against the wall, she brushed her drow-white hair away from her forehead and turned to watch them from beside the nightstalker general, folding her arms. "The ogre brought out four magnum wine bottles and a keg. Doesn't seem like nearly enough."

Maleshi snorted. "That's more than enough fellwine to last us a week, kid."

"Oh, shit." Cheyenne stared at the green glass bottles and chuckled. "Seriously?"

"I wouldn't turn my nose up at a barrel of Bloodshine either if I were you." The general shot Cheyenne a sidelong glance and subtly nodded across the chamber toward Ember, who had been pulled into a conversation with Lumil, Byrd, and two battered orcs. "Sakrit made a good call on that one too. You might not know about it."

"Fae don't drink fellwine." Cheyenne pressed her lips together to keep from laughing and nodded. "We already figured that one out."

Maleshi grinned. "Aren't you just privy to all the nuances of O'gúleesh drinking customs?"

"Spent a lot of time in Peridosh. Where else am I supposed to go out on a weeknight to get in a barfight or two?"

"Earthside?" The nightstalker shook her head. "I couldn't tell ya. *Here*, though, for the next two weeks, you can go just about anywhere to get the same results, and you won't find a single O'gúleesh reveler trying to fight you. No war machines tunneling into the marketplace, either."

Cheyenne watched the cups being passed around and finally let herself smile. "Promise?"

"Ha. Once those bottles open, kid, I won't be able to promise you a damn thing." Maleshi leaned toward her and lowered her voice, though no one would have heard her over the rowdy conversation and the rising shouts coming from Byrd and Lumil as they argued about who slashed up more Crown soldiers. "Good way to deflect from the *real* issue, though."

Cheyenne looked slowly across the chamber. Almost all the rebels had a drinking vessel of one kind or another, but Sakrit still hadn't popped the corks to let the O'gúleesh liquor flow. "I have no idea what you're talking about."

"Have an issue with large crowds, huh?"

Cheyenne focused on Ember and the goblins again and slowly exhaled through her nose. "I do when the whole crowd's touching me and shouting my name."

"Who else's would they be shouting, kid?"

The halfling swallowed. "I don't need to be put on a pedestal, Maleshi. I didn't fight those magicals, and I almost didn't finish what I came here to do."

"Bullshit." Maleshi straightened the front of her military jacket, sending a shower of dust and what looked a lot like flecks of dried blood to the floor around her. Then she lifted her chin and clasped her hands behind her back. "You put yourself on the line as much as the rest of us to get to the Heart. Every O'gúleesh in this ridiculous bunker would make the decision to stand behind you and fight a thousand times over just to get to where we are at this moment. It might not seem like much right now, Cheyenne, but what you did today was impossible until a few hours ago. They were ready to give their lives to make the impossible happen, and they'd do it again in a heartbeat, no questions asked." The general turned to face the halfling princess and raised her eyebrows. "So would I."

Cheyenne shook her head and had to look away. "How many of them did?"

"Two." Maleshi didn't skip a beat in answering. "They'll be

sent off in O'gúl warrior fashion before the end of the week. Thanks to you, it wasn't any more than two. I can't say I enjoy losing the use of my own body for an extended period of time, but it was quick thinking."

Cheyenne snorted. "I told her to call off the fighting, not freeze the whole damn courtyard."

The general threw her head back and let out a deep, unhindered laugh. "That drow bitch wants every thinking mind in this world to believe she's got everything under control, but she's as fond of stretching the truth as her brother."

Catching sight of L'zar beside the open and almost empty trunks of metal drinking cups, Cheyenne wrinkled her nose. "Still weird to think of that connection. I did *not* see that coming."

"If you'd known all that before you agreed to come here and return your *marandúr*, would it have swayed your decision?"

The halfling blinked quickly and shook her head. "I don't know. But I should've been given all the facts first."

"I agree, you should have. You deserved to know the truth like the rest of us." Maleshi dipped her chin and took a deep breath. "But we couldn't take the chance that telling you would drive you away from your birthright. That's part of being a leader, Cheyenne."

The halfling snorted. "Being lied to?"

"Letting what you deserve take a back seat to doing what's right for those you're responsible for protecting."

"Wow. You sound almost as philosophical as Corian right now."

Maleshi's smile tightened as she turned toward Cheyenne and shot her a quick wink. "I've had thousands of years to ruminate on my choices, kid."

"And last but not least!" The huge orc with the black bands of paint around his tusks stomped toward them with a metal goblet in hand. "For you, *Aranél*."

Cheyenne gave him a deadpan stare as he bent low in a semi-mocking bow, delivering the goblet with his other hand behind his back. He chuckled and stared up at her with narrowed yellow eyes until she took the thing and turned it over in her hands. Made of black metal, the goblet seemed to suck away the light around it and funnel it into what looked like rubies studded all over the cup above the long, thick stem. "I get the fancy cup, huh?"

The orc's laughter rumbled through his chest. "It's a replica. The gems are fake. Sorry to disappoint."

"Wonderful."

"So feel free to smash it at the end of the night. It's been done before."

Cheyenne couldn't help her wry chuckle as she stared at the dark goblet. *Not that many times if they've been waiting this long for something to celebrate.*

The orc straightened and fixed his gaze on Maleshi. A hush fell over the bunker's main room when the other rebels realized what was happening. Some of them nudged their neighbors to interrupt the conversation and point out the next interesting moment.

"And for the Hand of the Night and Circle," the orc's lower lip turned down as he grinned around his thick tusks, "a token of our undying gratitude for the spark of this fell-damn revolution."

Maleshi lifted her chin and stared him down. Despite the orc having at least six inches on her, the general could have been the tallest magical in the room. "Well?"

He whisked his other hand out from behind his back and thrust a mangled, glinting silver shape twice the size of his palm under her nose. Maleshi blinked. The quiet rebels around them sniggered and tried to fight back their amusement. It took Cheyenne two seconds to realize the unusual shape was a creature's skull with the bottom jaw removed.

Maleshi's nostrils flared as she looked up from the silver skull and scanned the tensely waiting magicals scattered around the chamber. "Which of you brainless morons went through my personal effects when I made my great escape?"

No one said a word. On the far side of the chamber, L'zar cleared his throat and nodded toward Corian, who was standing behind him. The nightstalker blinked in surprise at the skull in the orc's outstretched hand, one tawny, tufted ear twitching above his light-brown hair. Then he laughed and slowly pressed a fist to his heart as he met Maleshi's gaze. "My blood for the Hand of the Night and Circle."

"In battle or the bedroom, *vae shra'ni?*" jeered a goblin with his arm in a makeshift sling.

The rebels exploded in boisterous laughter again, pointing at Corian and falling over themselves in their mirth. Feet stomped on the stone floors as the rebels pushed each other around and laughed harder. Corian grinned at Maleshi, and she snatched the silver skull out of the orc's hand with a half-joking hiss. "And you sent Jara'ak to return it to me for you."

"I wasn't planning on returning it at all," Corian shouted above the howling laughter and the pounding echoes. He turned slowly toward L'zar, who looked at his nightstalker *Nós Ani* with a mocking shrug.

Maleshi laughed and stormed toward the bottles of fellwine and the metal keg on the table. "Dahal would be rolling in his grave if he saw this skull empty in my hand. What are we waiting for?"

The rebels lifted their mismatched metal goblets, tankards, and simple cups in a cheer of agreement. The general snatched one of the fellwine bottles, ripped out the cork with her teeth, and spat it onto the floor with a roaring cheer. The shouts and snarls of approval rose in a deafening roar as General Maleshi Hi'et poured a splashing stream of fellwine into the overturned silver skull in her hand. Sloshing the sparkling green liquor all over the place, she handed the bottle off to the magical beside her and raised the skull, whirling to face Cheyenne. "To the *Aranél!*"

The rebels lost it when she guzzled from the silver skull, fellwine splashing down the front of her military jacket and bubbling in small pools on the stone floor. The other fellwine bottles were snatched up and uncorked, and Sakrit cranked open the spout on the metal keg before filling whatever goblet was thrust his way to catch the shimmering golden Bloodshine spilling out of it.

Cheyenne's eyes widened at the unbelievable amount of fellwine Maleshi put away, and she forced herself to shut her mouth when she realized it had been hanging open. *Yeah, Mattie Bergmann and Maleshi Hi'et are two different people, all right. Shit's about to get real.*

CHAPTER FIVE

Once every cup was filled and the real party got started, Cheyenne found herself staring at the golden liquid poured from the keg into her fake-fancy goblet. Ember laughed at a toast one of the rowdy rebels tossed her way and approached her friend's side, grinning from ear to ear. "Honestly, I thought the fighting was crazy, but this?"

Cheyenne said, "I know, right?"

"It doesn't even seem real."

"Tell me about it."

Ember peered over the lip of Cheyenne's black goblet. "No fellwine for you either, huh?"

"Are you kidding?" The halfling snorted and gestured at the revelers with her drink. "These guys make everything we did at Peridosh look like a bunch of kids on a playground. And Maleshi's drinking out of a freakin' *skull*."

"You think it's real?" Ember lifted her heavy metal tankard of Bloodshine and raised her eyebrows as she slurped.

"I mean, it could be, for all we know. Dipped in silver or something. Or it could be a gag."

"You should ask her."

Cheyenne laughed. "*I* should ask her?"

"Don't look at me like that. No way in hell am I going up to the psychotic nightstalker warlord to ask if her drinking skull is the real deal or a prop."

"Ha. You're forgetting one important detail, Em."

The fae girl cocked her head and shot her friend an exasperated look. "Enlighten me, then."

"You're *Nós Aní* to the *Aranél* of Ambar'ogúl." Cheyenne fought back a shudder. "You can ask anyone anything you want, and they can't do a damn thing about it."

"Oh." Ember found Maleshi in the crowd of drinking rebels. The general had propped one blood-splattered boot on the closest pulled-out chair and leaned forward over the table, laughing and drinking out of her silver skull with the others. "Still, *you* should ask her."

"I think you care a lot more about the story behind that one than I do. Might as well use your high status while you can. Your best friend's drow royalty, apparently." Cheyenne snickered and lifted her goblet in a sarcastic toast before taking her first drink of Bloodshine. She wrinkled her nose and sniffed at the burst of tingling bubbles sailing both down her throat and somehow up to her head. "I don't know what to say about this stuff."

"Like champagne on steroids." Ember took another long drink and smacked her lips. "I love it."

Cheyenne laughed and looked at her friend in surprise. Then she caught sight of Foltr for the first time and lowered her goblet.

The gnarled old raug had made his appearance at the celebration without anyone noticing his arrival through one of the dozen archways leading into the bunker's main chamber. He shambled toward the partygoers with a heavily wrinkled scowl on his gray face, orange-brown eyes blazing beneath the thick ridges of his furrowed, hairless eyebrows. The heavy walking stick in his clawed hand clacked on the stone floor, but it wasn't loud enough to draw anyone else's attention. When he stopped at the end of the huge black table, he propped both wizened hands on the top of his stick and lifted his chin. Then he cracked the base of the stick against the floor and sent strobing orange light in every direction.

The rebels turned toward him with their smiles frozen on their faces. Foltr lifted his stick and pointed at the table. "It's been a long time, but I assumed you lot were smarter than a pen of bare-assed pups still sucking on their mothers' teats. Clear the table. Give the seats to those who earned them. And somebody better pour me a drink before I have to come after it myself."

Laughing, Sakrit grabbed the last tankard from the open chest before hurling the empty box behind him. It clattered to the floor, quickly followed by the second, and he grabbed a half-empty bottle of fellwine to fill the tankard to the brim. He turned back toward Foltr with a grin. "For the ancient one."

"The ancient *sleeping* one," a troll man shouted, raising his goblet. "You missed all the action, raug!"

"I miss nothing." Foltr snatched his drink from Sakrit's hand with a grunt and moved toward the closest chair beside the head of the table. He took a moment to upend his drink in a long guzzle, then slammed the tankard to the table before lowering himself into the chair. "But the lot of you seem to be missing the point entirely. Don't make me say it again."

A cheer rose from the surrounding magicals as a select few removed themselves from the crowd to head toward the table. Maleshi slid her boot off the chair and sat where she was. Corian and L'zar approached the end of the table, where the drow sat at the head beside Foltr and the nightstalker took the chair on L'zar's other side. Jara'ak, the buzzing magical made of swarming black specks, Lumil, and Byrd joined them.

"Cheyenne." Foltr stretched his arm toward her and nodded. "I would be honored if the *Aranél* sat beside me. Both of you, of course."

"Right." Cheyenne and Ember exchanged confused glances before making their way toward the table. The halfling sat in the chair beside the ancient raug, who sniffed and nodded curtly before propping one hand on the top of his crooked cane and grabbing his tankard with the other. Ember sat on her other side and gazed at the others at the table while the rest of the magicals stood or lounged about on stacked crates, drinking and laughing in their own private conversations and ignoring the little meeting the raug had called.

The troll woman Elarit Masharun took a seat directly across the table from Cheyenne. The silver chains draping across her purple nose from one eyebrow to the other were flecked with someone else's blood, and she widened her eyes at the halfling with a small, approving smile.

Cheyenne nodded back and took a sip of her drink. *She's sitting right next to Corian like nothing ever happened. No idea Persh'al's been lying to all of them.*

"Foltr." L'zar sat back casually in his chair at the head of the table and smiled at the raug. "I know you're a stickler for details, but I'm sure this can wait until we've all had our fill of victory."

"You've already *had* your fill, Weaver." Foltr looked the drow thief up and down. "You've been having your fill since you opened your mouth for your first lie. Do us all a favor and shut it now unless someone asks you a direct question."

"Your bite hasn't aged a century." L'zar laughed and thumped his fist on the table. "I've missed you."

"That makes one of us." Foltr grunted, but a small smile

flickered at the wrinkled corners of his gray mouth. "The last time the *Aranél* sat at this table with a less complete assembly, she was clueless about her part to play in this grander scheme."

Cheyenne choked on her Bloodshine and tried to play it off as choking on a laugh. "Thanks. It was that obvious, huh?"

Across the table, Elarit leaned back in her chair with a knowing smirk. "Glaringly."

Foltr waved aside the troll woman's comment and fixed Cheyenne with his scrutinizing gaze. "You walked through a river of fire to be here for our city. For this world, which is the only world most of us in this room have ever known. You know another, Cheyenne. Whatever knowledge you carry with you of our kind on Earth differs vastly from what you know of Ambar'ogúl and its history. Which is next to nothing, it would seem."

She pointed at the wizened raug and raised an eyebrow. "I *do* know the Crown is my aunt."

L'zar chuckled. Corian dipped his head and stared at the black metal surface of the table, unsuccessfully hiding a small smile. Maleshi slurped fellwine from her silver-plated skull.

The old raug grunted. "That discovery was by necessity, yes. A good thing to know. It changes nothing." He thumped his stick on the stone floor again and settled both gnarled, clawed hands over the round knob on top. "Tonight, you'll learn what you're fighting for, *Aranél*. Not because you asked, but because you are owed the truth. After what you've accomplished today, *we* owe you the truth."

While the rest of the rebels drank and laughed and got into half-playful skirmishes, an expectant silence hung over the magicals sitting at the central table. Foltr gazed at each of them with narrowed orange-brown eyes, daring anyone to challenge the decision he'd made for everyone.

"I'll start then, eh?" L'zar steepled his fingers and rested both hands on the table, leaning forward with a feral grin. "I never had my doubts that we'd reach this moment."

Corian barked out a laugh. "I believe the raug wanted to start and end this conversation with the truth."

"If you're looking for a heartfelt confession from me tonight, brother, you'll be disappointed. I don't lie and tell."

Corian rubbed his mouth, his tufted, catlike ears twitching as he shook his head. Elarit rolled her eyes and buried a smart remark in her tankard of fellwine.

Maleshi's chair scooted backward with a screech of metal on stone before the general stood, swinging her skull cup to the side to avoid spilling it on the line of magicals sitting at the table. Hooking her boot around the metal chair leg, she pulled out the empty chair on the other side of Ember and thumped down into it. She narrowed her eyes at the other members of the Four-Pointed Star across the table, then leaned forward to peer past Ember at Cheyenne. The silver curve of the skull-shaped cup didn't leave her hand. "I think we should start at the beginning."

"For the love of everything I despise, General!" L'zar thumped back in his chair. "I didn't come all this way to listen to how Ba'rael Verdys filled her throne room with shit."

Ember snorted, and when L'zar turned his golden eyes to her, she stared at the table and hid her smile with another long drink from her tankard.

Maleshi fixed her gaze on the drow at the head of the table and cocked her head. "And *I* didn't come all this way to listen to you tell me what I can and can't say in your royal presence, *Cu'ón*. Keep at it, and there *will* be another battle tonight. And you won't have your daughter to do the heavy lifting for you."

L'zar raised an eyebrow and nodded once.

"Prince among thieves, huh?" Cheyenne muttered. "Literally."

Foltr hissed and raised his tankard to his lips. Only when he'd finished drinking did she realize he'd been laughing too.

Slurping from her skull again, Maleshi met Cheyenne's gaze. "The only true beginning to the story that has anything to do with anything these days is how the Crown turned the new Cycle herself and put all this into play."

"To be clear," Corian added, "L'zar's always been a dick. That goes all the way back to the beginning."

The table erupted in laughter. Foltr thumped his cane on the floor as he chuckled in grunting bursts. Maleshi and Corian raised their drinks toward L'zar in another toast and drank. The drow joined them, his golden eyes glowing as he gazed at every face at the table.

Except mine. Cheyenne smiled with the others as they made their infuriating leader the brunt of more jokes. *He hasn't looked at me once since we sat down.*

"The drow Crown K'laht sired two offspring," Foltr began.

"Two fell-dawn spawn," L'zar added quickly with another toast to no one.

"L'zar's the baby brother." Maleshi swirled the dregs of her fellwine around and around in the bottom of the silver skull. "Which explains quite a bit, when you think about it."

"I've earned my titles, thank you very much."

"Dark Smiling Weaver." Cheyenne stared at her father, who gave her a sidelong glance for half a second before dipping his head and taking another drink.

"That's one of them, sure. *I* was referring to Royal Bottomfeeder. The Scoundrel Prince."

"Endaru's balls, L'zar. Don't hurt yourself." Maleshi shook her head and shot the drow's feral, predatory look right back at him. "This conversation isn't about *you*, anyway. Give it a rest."

"I've suddenly lost interest, then. Should I excuse myself?" L'zar scooted back in his chair like he meant to get up.

Maleshi leaned sideways against the edge of the table,

barely sitting in her own chair anymore. "Ask the raug. I don't give a shit."

L'zar eyed Foltr and gave the old magical a mocking half-bow from his chair. "By your leave, Aged One."

"If you need my permission to remove yourself from that chair, you'll be sitting here all night," Foltr grumbled. "I'm not giving you a fell-damn thing."

With a low chuckle, L'zar ran a hand through his hair and sat comfortably back in the chair again. "Lovely to be surrounded by such loyal friends again."

The magicals around the table chuckled and raised a silent toast. Once everyone had set their cups back down on the table, expectant glances passed between L'zar's core group of rebel leaders.

"Don't look at me." Foltr set both hands on the knob of his cane again and shook his head. "I'm just here to correct the embellished *carako* waste bound to spill out of one of your mouths."

"You've made your point, Grandfather." Maleshi turned in her chair and thrust her silver skull in the air. "Dahal's thirsty again. Don't make my predecessor come after you. Where's the fellwine?"

Lumil turned from the group of magicals swapping battle stories and raised another cheer when she hoisted a sloshing green bottle in her fist. She trudged toward Maleshi's outstretched empty skull and poured the fellwine from so high, it spilled over the edge of the skull and splattered to the floor in a glowing green fizz. "For the general. And the general." The goblin woman gave Maleshi a mocking bow, then thumped the bottle onto the table and spun. "Where were we? Oh, yeah. Blood and glory!"

The magicals cheered as Lumil returned to the small group, one of many around the chamber.

With a self-important smirk, Maleshi took a sip from her

skull, smacked her lips, and turned toward Cheyenne again. "It's our lucky night, kid. While they talk about blood and glory, we get patricide and shitty life skills."

The halfling sputtered into her goblet, then forced herself to swallow the small bit of Bloodshine left in her mouth. "Sounds like fun."

L'zar grinned and lifted his tankard. "You have no idea."

CHAPTER SIX

"As the oldest, Ba'rael was next in line for the Crown's new Cycle," Maleshi continued. "If your Weaver father ever had plans of ruling, those plans were screwed from the moment he entered this world."

L'zar thumped a fist against his chest. "With a full head of hair and an already honed sense of how to take what's mine."

"You mean, how to take what's everyone else's," Corian corrected, raising an eyebrow.

The drow shrugged. "Same thing."

Maleshi snorted. "Knowing he was born with that sense of entitlement, kid, I'm sure you can imagine your father as the little shit he was in his formative years so very long ago."

"Yes, General. Because you spent so much time studying me in my formative years."

"I did," Foltr grumbled. "She's not far off the mark."

Another round of laughter rose at that, and L'zar dipped his head toward the raug. "Well-played."

"K'laht Verdys served as the O'gúl Crown for centuries," Corian added. "As far as drow go, he had a good head on his shoulders. To this day, I still can't fathom how he sired two of drowkind's most disappointing specimens."

"I blame our mother." L'zar raised his tankard. "To Ulahel and her final journey through the deathflame."

The magicals around the table ignored the drow's spiteful comment. Corian's smile faded somewhat, but he looked at Cheyenne with his silver nightstalker eyes and nodded. "Ba'rael always knew she would turn the new Cycle as the next Crown. It was her right from the beginning, and there is little that can stand in the way of a rightful heir claiming what's theirs. Or at least there was, back when Ambar'ogúl was a world I recognized."

"Save the self-pity for after the real party." L'zar stared at his *Nós Ani*, and Corian's upper lip twitched in irritation.

"So." Maleshi thumped a hand on the table and raised her skull, fellwine spilling over her hand in streams. "While L'zar was off screwing over every poor bastard who crossed his path, Ba'rael grew impatient. It's an interesting thought, isn't it? To have absolutely everything at your fingertips, nothing withheld, and *still* want more."

"The bitch will stay true to her nature 'til the very end." L'zar shook his head. "I remember it like yesterday. The day my rotting sister told me she didn't intend to wait for the Cycle to turn on its own. As many times as I've tried to drink myself into oblivion, hoping *that* memory would be the one siphoned out of my head by morning, I've apparently been cursed into never forgetting that excellent gem."

Cheyenne glanced quickly around the table. "You think you should be joking about curses right now?"

L'zar fixed her with his golden eyes, which were narrowed in warning. "It was a figure of speech in this instance, Cheyenne."

Corian leaned away from the drow at the head of the table and eyed L'zar. "But in another instance?"

"We can talk about that later."

The nightstalker looked at Cheyenne next, who gave him a small shrug and barely shook her head. She didn't miss it when Corian and Maleshi shared concerned gazes as well. *Right. It's all fun and games in the rebel bunker until somebody brings up the literal curse L'zar failed to mention. That'll be a fun conversation.*

L'zar took a long drink of his fellwine and sucked in a hissing breath, cocking his head as the strong liquor burned down his throat and swam up into his head at the same time. "We *were* talking about me. Briefly. And my rot-hearted sister coming to me personally to try to draw me into her secret and highly unnecessary plan."

At those words, the multiple prophecies Cheyenne had heard from Oracles and in her own dreams came back to her. *Cut out the heart. Cut out the rot. Christ, it's all tied together even as we sit here telling stories.*

"What did she say?" Ember asked, her luminous violet eyes fixed intently on the drow.

"She wanted to challenge our father before her time," L'zar replied simply, "Ba'rael had convinced herself she could do much better than the unprecedented era of peace under his Cycle."

"She thought K'laht was too soft on our people." Maleshi snorted. "Too content to let Ambar'ogúl run itself unless the Crown's intervention was absolutely necessary. Hell, that's how I got *my* job."

"You served under L'zar's father." Cheyenne gazed at the war general. "For how long?"

"Longer than any of us care to think about right now." Corian raised his tankard toward Maleshi and drank.

"Wait, wait." Ember pressed both hands on the table and glanced for a second at the silver skull in Maleshi's hand before looking back up at L'zar. "I still wanna hear about this plan of hers. She told you she was going to overthrow your dad?"

"No." A thin smile tugged at the corners of L'zar's lips. "She told me she meant to challenge him. By the old laws, of course. Her *marandúr* hadn't yet been returned to the Rahalma altar, and, I suppose, she wanted my full support."

Elarit snorted, the thin silver chains draping across the bridge of her nose jingling when she shook her head. "It worked out so well for her."

Sitting beside her, Jara'ak chuckled and widened his eyes at the troll woman's rare facetious comment. "You have a way with words, Lady Masharun."

"Don't call me that." Elarit buried her face in her goblet but looked up at Cheyenne.

"She's not wrong." L'zar sat back in his chair and looked at the ceiling of the bunker. "It didn't work out anything like what she'd planned."

Ember nodded. "Because you didn't support her."

"Ha." Corian waved his hand over the table, shaking his head. "Ba'rael didn't give a shit whether or not she had L'zar's support. She assumed giving him that information would goad him into making a fool of himself."

"Which I'd already done a thousand times over at that point," L'zar added dryly.

The magicals chuckled and kept drinking like their cups would never empty.

"She goaded him all right." Maleshi raised her silver skull toward L'zar. "Right into making herself look like an idiot."

Cheyenne frowned at her father. "What did you do to her?"

L'zar rolled his eyes. "Trust me, Cheyenne, if I'd wanted to physically hurt my sister, I would have done it centuries ago. Psychological damage, on the other hand, is a different game, at which I naturally excel."

Jara'ak thumped a fist on the table. "You've been building up for centuries is what you've been doing. Give the damn punchline."

Ember's eyes widened as she gazed from one magical around the table to the next. "This is a joke?"

"Only in the sense that I still find it highly amusing," L'zar replied blankly.

Corian blinked, swaying forward in his chair before turning toward the drow and pointing a fur-tipped finger at L'zar. "If you don't tell her, I will."

"Everyone's in such a hurry." L'zar set his drink on the table and tipped his chair backward on two legs, smoothing his long white hair away from his face. "I ruined all her plans, Cheyenne, by returning my *marandúr* to that altar before she grew enough of a spine to do it herself."

Ember shook her head in disbelief. "Why?"

L'zar grinned. "Because I could."

Jara'ak barked out a laugh. "Just to fuck with her head. She should've been used to it at that point, eh?"

Maleshi took another long drink. "It gave L'zar first right to challenge K'laht for the throne and turn the new Cycle for himself if he so chose."

L'zar pointed at her. "That was never my intention."

"Anyone with half a brain knows that," Foltr added with a grunt.

Cheyenne narrowed her eyes at Maleshi. "You said patricide."

"I did." The general gestured toward L'zar and raised an eyebrow. "I'll leave that elaboration to your royal drow ass."

Cheyenne's father gazed around the table, then rolled his eyes. "Ba'rael doesn't have half a brain, and she never did. To keep me from the throne I never wanted, she snuck into the Heart like a coward in the middle of the night and returned her *marandúr*, then slit our father's throat in his sleep and turned the Cycle by force."

"Jesus." Cheyenne slumped in her chair and grimaced at the

Bloodshine in her goblet. "And that was it? No one tried to stop her?"

"There was no one *to* stop her. I certainly wasn't going to."

She looked quickly at L'zar again. "But it was your fault."

"Oh." He feigned surprise and gazed around the table, chuckling. "I didn't realize you had any interest in defending the Crown's actions, especially not after you defied all the odds stacked against you in the very fabric of fate by challenging her yourself."

"I'm not defending her." Cheyenne's fingers tightened around the black metal stem of the goblet. "I'm saying you should have taken responsibility."

Elarit's high laughter filled the bunker. "That ship sailed long before the last Cycle ended, Cheyenne."

"And it doesn't weigh on you even a little?" The halfling's hands slid off the edge of the table into her lap as she stared at her father. "That your own father died because you wanted to screw with your sister's head?"

"In a perfect world, that would seem abhorrent, wouldn't it?" L'zar grinned back at her and spread his arms. "As you so aptly put it about a week ago, Cheyenne, I dropped a coin on a table. Ba'rael did the rest. I didn't challenge the Cycle, and I most certainly didn't guide her hand when the tip of the blade it held pierced K'laht's throat. I have my own crimes to pay for if the day ever catches up with me, but that is not one of them."

Cheyenne clenched her jaw and couldn't bring herself to say anything else about it. *L'zar's always looking out for number one, and that's it. He seriously doesn't care what he's done.*

"What about, like, trying to get vengeance or something?" Ember asked, staring blankly at the table as she tried to make sense of the situation. "For your dad. You didn't even try to step in and fight against *that?*"

"It comes down to their respective feelings about me, little fae."

"Watch it." She pointed at him, the tip of her pink-tinged finger glowing with violet light.

"I'd listen to her, L'zar," Maleshi said through a full-throated laugh. "Every magical in this room has seen what that one can do."

The rebel leaders gathered around the table fell into another fit of laughter, raising their glasses toward Ember this time both in jest and as a sign of respect.

"Look at that," Jara'ak roared. "A *Nós Aní* who has no issues taking a bite out of L'zar Verdys if she has to!"

"I'm assuming that's meant to be an affront to my honor," Corian muttered as the orc howled with renewed laughter. "Nice try."

L'zar leaned toward Corian and clapped a hand on the nightstalker's shoulder. "This one only bites in private."

Corian scowled at the drow and shrugged L'zar's hand away.

"And I'm pushing all the wrong buttons today. Damn, this *does* feel like home." Chuckling, L'zar smoothed his hair away from his face again and turned back to Ember. "As I was saying, the rest of my royally obnoxious family did have one thing in common. They were finished with me long before I ever returned my *marandúr* to the Rahalma altar. The only difference is that my father never made his lack of love for me anywhere near concrete with an official banishment."

"You banished *yourself*," Foltr grunted.

"Yes, it was all voluntary. Until a few hours ago." L'zar's wide golden eyes roamed around the table, drinking in the reactions of his loyal followers as each of them realized what he was saying.

Cheyenne didn't look away from him. *He's loving watching the truth sink in and ruining the mood for everyone. Dude's got serious issues.*

MARTHA CARR & MICHAEL ANDERLE

"L'zar." Corian set down his tankard and shifted in his chair to face the drow squarely. "Did she really?"

"Cheyenne was there too, you know. This is *her* party, after all."

The halfling closed her eyes in irritation. "I wouldn't want to steal your spotlight."

L'zar threw his head back and roared with laughter. "You *are* my daughter. Yes. Yes! Ba'rael banished me from Ambar'ogúl and made it official with her fancy little curse. That's neither here nor there."

"Of course it is." Maleshi's smile had vanished. "That's an important piece of information we all deserved to know the second you stepped through those doors."

The drow chugged the rest of his drink and slammed the tankard on the table, shaking his head. "This is a *celebration*. And no, I don't feel bad about *this*, either. How you choose to feel about what's happened is on each of you, not me. When I make the crossing again, I'll be happy never to return. I fell in love with the other side on the very first trip, and since we're all being honest and fucking open with each other, I despise what this side has become. I always have, and this has been a phenomenal reminder of why I stayed away as long as I did."

With that, the drow prince lurched from his chair, sending it flying away behind him and clattering across the stone floor. He swayed a little and steadied himself by pressing the tips of his slender fingers on the black tabletop. "I'll take this as being excused from the conversation."

"Stop." Foltr stretched a long, gnarled claw at L'zar.

"Say what you have to say, Grandfather, but make it quick."

The wizened raug pushed himself to his feet with a grunt and peered into L'zar's drunken eyes. Faster than his gnarled body seemed capable of moving, Foltr swung his walking stick back in both hands and cracked the hard knob against the side of L'zar Verdys' head.

The deafening sound drowned out the noises of dozens of other conversations around the bunker as every magical turned to see what had happened. L'zar stumbled sideways, his white hair flying around his face beneath the force of the blow. When he finally caught his balance and straightened, he smoothed his hair back with both hands and took a deep breath through his nose.

Foltr thumped his cane on the floor. "Now you are excused."

L'zar whirled and stalked across the chamber toward one of the dozen archways leading into branching tunnels. He waved a hand behind him and shouted, "Don't even think about stopping now, you ingrates. I'm just takin' a piss!"

Someone raised their drink in the air and cheered as L'zar opened the door with a motion of his hand and stumbled through.

Foltr groaned as he lowered himself into his chair and grabbed his drink. "He's a fell-damn ingrate."

Corian burst out laughing, that crazed, animalistic grin sharpening his features. Jara'ak, Elarit, and Maleshi joined him. The booming voice of the flickering dark magical rose above it all. Then he whisked away in a burst of black specks and materialized in front of the Bloodshine keg to refill his drink.

Cheyenne and Ember stared at each other. "That went well."

Ember snorted. "You gotta admit neither of us has any idea of what a fucked-up family really is."

"Can't argue with you there, Em." The halfling raised her goblet to her lips and took a small sip. "I'll take Bianca Summerlin over this any day of the week."

"Yeah, me too."

Catching Corian's gaze across the table, Cheyenne tilted her head. "He doesn't hate this whole world, does he?"

The nightstalker kept laughing. "You mean, you can't tell?"

"It's not like he gives anyone or anything special treatment."

Foltr laughed, propping his hands on his cane and shaking his head.

"L'zar had less to do with the way things turned out in our world than you might think. Sure, he hasn't done much to improve the situation."

"No, he went in the opposite direction." Elarit stared at the arch where L'zar had disappeared.

Corian glanced at the troll woman. "Until you, Cheyenne."

"I haven't improved anything, either."

"You have. More than you know. And things will continue to improve."

Cheyenne shrugged and stared at her drink. "Only after the Crown steps down in two weeks."

The nightstalker wrinkled his nose. "*If* she steps down."

"What?" The halfling's glowing golden gaze cut toward him again. "Nobody told me there was a loophole to our loophole."

"In two weeks, you'll bring her your terms. Once we've hashed out the details, of course. But she has the option not to accept them."

"You've gotta be kidding me." Cheyenne turned to Maleshi, not having to lean forward since Ember sat stiffly back in her chair in disbelief. "What happens if she doesn't accept?"

With her elbow propped on the table, Maleshi lifted a finger from around the silver skull and extended one slicing, glinting four-inch claw from the tip. "You get to fight again. Alone."

"I have to fight her again," Cheyenne said. "Great."

"To the death," Jara'ak added with a sneer.

"Oh, even better."

"Which is why we'll be focusing on arranging the terms in a way Ba'rael Verdys can't possibly refuse." Corian stared at Maleshi's extended claw until she retracted it with a sharp sound. "A fight for the Crown isn't an option any of us are willing to entertain, but know that it exists."

"And you'd win," Maleshi added before burying her face in the silver skull and chugging noisily.

Ember snorted. "Sounds like someone's entertaining the option."

"After the Crown steps down," Corian continued, "we'll turn our resources to washing out all the O'gúl filth lining Hangivol's streets. Things *will* change around here, but now that I've seen what's going on, it'll probably take us as long to clean up Ba'rael's mess as it took her to shit all over everything. Or longer."

"Wonderful visual. Thanks." Cheyenne raised her eyebrows and stared at the table. *I haven't had nearly as much to drink as the rest of these warmongers. Why am I so dizzy?* She felt Ember's gaze on the side of her face but couldn't bring herself to look at anyone.

"Okay, if Cheyenne's not gonna ask it, I will." The fae girl took another long drink of her Bloodshine. "Say we go back in, the Crown accepts the terms and steps down, and Cheyenne doesn't want to take her place?"

The halfling grimaced but didn't stop her friend.

Corian took a deep breath. "Then someone else will take it."

Cheyenne looked at him. "Someone like L'zar?"

The table burst into raucous laughter again. Maleshi pounded the metal surface so hard her fellwine sloshed all over her other hand, the edge of the table, and her lap. "No fucking way, kid. The last thing that drow thief wants is to sit on a dead O'gúl throne."

"Right." The halfling let herself grin as the howling laughter grew around her. "Because he could've taken it if he wanted to." *So why the hell did he need me for any of this?*

Foltr leaned toward her and cleared his throat. "If you do not want the rule the of new Cycle for your own, *Aranél*, there is a way to hand it off to someone else."

"What? You mean I can give someone the throne and say 'Here, have fun?'"

"There is a bit more involved, but yes."

"Of course there is." Cheyenne ran a hand through her hair and sat back in her chair. "Does it have to be a drow?"

Maleshi shrugged and stared thoughtfully at the tabletop. "Nothing in the old laws says a thing about *who* the Crown should be."

Corian laughed. "But show me a drow who doesn't want all the power and control for themselves, eh? You can't." When he turned his silver eyes on Cheyenne, Ember pointed at the drow halfling and cocked her head. "Oh. Your circumstances are a little different, kid."

"Why? Because I'm not full drow?"

"Probably."

Cheyenne tossed a hand toward him. "Fine. What about you then, Corian? Why don't *you* be the nightstalker to defy ages of drow rule and sit on that throne your own damn self?"

"Hmm. Tempting. Also, no."

She rolled her eyes. "Of course not."

"I go where L'zar goes, Cheyenne. You understand that a lot better now with your own *Nós Aní* sitting beside you."

Ember raised both hands in front of her and shook her head. "I didn't tell her to give *you* the throne."

"Trust me, that wouldn't have made a difference." He fixed the fae girl with a tight-lipped smile and drank from his tankard.

"Then who the hell am I supposed to shuck this whole Crown thing onto, huh? Seriously." Cheyenne leaned over the table and raised her voice. "Who here wants to sit on the throne of Ambar'ogúl as the Crown of the new Cycle? Anyone? Speak up now. I'm making a list!"

"To the *Aranél*!" Sakrit bellowed.

"The *Aranél*!" The other rebels took up the cry, swinging

toward the table with sloshing tankards and cheering Cheyenne, daughter of L'zar Verdys.

Beside her, Foltr snorted into his tankard.

Cheyenne slumped back in her chair again and shook her head. "I don't want it. This is ridiculous."

"For now, this is what you have to work with, kid." Corian shrugged. "Besides, even if you promised to abdicate right now, it doesn't mean shit until we sit down with Ba'rael and turn the new Cycle officially. The old laws don't include promises made at a drinking party underground."

"Ha!" Jara'ak pounded the table. "Maybe they should!"

"Feel free to rewrite them to suit your needs, orc." Foltr narrowed his eyes at the orc with the black bands around his tusks. "You wouldn't make it past the first two words."

"Bah." Jara'ak guzzled his drink noisily and reached for the nearly empty bottle of fellwine before emptying the rest of it into his tankard.

CHAPTER SEVEN

Cheyenne frowned at the few empty seats left at the table, then turned to scan the drunken magicals around them. *Two of them didn't make it. Why didn't I put this together sooner?* "Where's Nu'ek?"

Corian blinked heavily and leaned far back in his chair, scanning the chamber. "I know she was with us."

The halfling caught Maleshi's gaze, and the general shook her head. "Wasn't the Golra, kid. You can relax."

Corian asked, "How the hell do we lose one of our own *that* size? She was right."

A furious bellow burst into the chamber, followed by a laughing L'zar being thrown across the room through one of the open arches. Thunderous footsteps followed as the drow scrambled to his feet and smoothed back his hair. Nu'ek's broad shoulders tufted with red fur squeezed through the archway, followed by her massive head and the two horns protruding from her long red hair. She snorted and stomped toward L'zar, fists clenched at her sides. The bat-like wings that looked so strange on a creature her size stretched to their full span, sending a buffeting wind across the bunker's main room that spilled as many drinks as the rebels had been tossing all over themselves.

"I'm just playing, you overgrown bat." Grinning, L'zar stuck his hands in his pockets and shrugged. "I'd tell you to work on your anger issues, but you've already made considerable improvement."

"You *are* my anger issue, drow." Nu'ek loomed over him and stabbed a huge, claw-tipped finger into his chest. "My quarters are off-limits, and I don't care if I'm lying dead in them. Got it?"

"Well, *now* I do." Laughing, L'zar turned back toward the table, his mischievous air back in full swing. "Touchy."

"What the hell is that?" Ember muttered, staring at Nu'ek's hulking form as the Golra brushed dirt, plaster, metal parts, and dried blood off the front of her leather vest.

Cheyenne grinned and pushed herself up from the table. "Come on. I like this Golra, and I'm pretty sure she likes me. I'll introduce you."

"Pretty sure?" Ember floated out of her chair and moved hesitantly behind the halfling.

"Yeah. I mean, hey. Compared to L'zar, I'm like the tame drow everybody appreciates."

Ember snorted. "Wonderful."

Nu'ek saw them approaching and jerked her chin at Cheyenne. Folding her wings behind her back, she gazed across the chamber and scowled. "Sakrit! You said you were prepared."

"I am!" The ogre laughed and headed for his secret pantry of O'gúl alcohol. "You take so damn long doing whatever it is you do after a fight. I never know when you're ready to show up."

"The only thing you need to know is that I'm here and need a drink." Nu'ek glared at the ogre until he shot her a rude gesture. Then she laughed and turned her attention to

Cheyenne. "Well done, halfling. You returned to do the impossible."

"I didn't do it all by myself." Cheyenne smiled up at the huge Golra and stuck a thumb out toward Ember. "This is Ember."

"A pleasure. Not many fae come down into these tunnels."

Ember's eyes widened, and she chuckled in disbelief. "Yeah, I'm not sure many fae become a drow's *Nós Aní* and suddenly have the magic they thought they were born without, so it's a day of firsts for everyone."

Nu'ek laughed deeply and nodded. "A good day. Excuse me. I think Sakrit needs a good reminder of how easy it would be for me to rip his head off his shoulders if he doesn't hurry up with my refreshments." The Golra stomped toward the ogre, pretending to ignore the cheers from the other rebels she passed.

"That is one seriously gigantic magical," Ember whispered.

"Not even the biggest I've seen on this side, Em, but yeah. She's pretty big."

L'zar stepped up behind his daughter and the fae girl and bent toward the space between them to mutter, "And a thousand times more reliable than the scurrying little bastards you can't keep tabs on no matter how hard you try."

Cheyenne stepped away from him and shot him a deadpan stare. "Were you planning on telling me I might have to fight your sister if she refuses our so-called terms?"

"Oh. Not necessarily."

"Come on, L'zar. Can we cut through all this bullshit of what not to tell Cheyenne unless she calls everyone out on it?" His daughter frowned at him.

He laughed and shrugged, his hands still in his pockets. "There are so many other immediate things to think about right now, it honestly slipped my mind."

"Oh, yeah? It slipped your mind that I might have to fight

her to the death, and if I end up losing, the rest of you are screwed?"

"That won't happen." L'zar grinned and set a hand on her shoulder, squeezing tightly. "My daughter slapped her coin down on that altar without lifting a finger. She's got a hell of a lot more up her sleeve."

"She also thinks it's stupid to talk about her in the third person."

Chuckling, he let go of her shoulder and gestured around. "Just in case anyone else was listening."

"I doubt it. Me almost getting my ass handed to me in that courtyard is hardly as exciting as all the drinking going on."

L'zar's smile faded. "The forces that met you when you threw yourself over the edge of that balcony into the Heart did not belong to Ba'rael. Not her magic. That was everyone she's been feeding off of for centuries. *If* you end up having to fight, it'll be your power against hers. Only hers. You could take her with one hand tied behind your back."

"And you can't?"

"That's not how this works, Cheyenne. My time has passed. I'm freely handing it all over to you, and I will find that perfect combination of offer and pressure to make my sister step down off her decomposing pedestal. She can't do anything for two weeks. That's more than enough time to find her weak spot."

"You say that like you know she has one."

"Everyone does. Even you." L'zar spread his arms and shot her a mocking wink as he turned away to join the raucous party again. "Even me."

"It better not take longer than two weeks."

"You might not believe it, but I work best under pressure." He snatched his empty tankard from the head of the table and walked casually across the bunker, raising his cup at every toast thrown his way until he reached the new bottles of alcohol.

Ember leaned toward Cheyenne and muttered, "That kinda sounded like he was challenging you to find *his* weak spot."

"Yep. I'm sure if he had to pick one, he'd say it's me." The halfling shook her head and watched her father celebrating with the others like all their hard work was over and none of them had anything to worry about anymore. "I doubt he even knows what it is."

Ember glanced down at her tankard and shrugged. "I'm outta booze."

"Go for it, Em. Drink the night away with these weirdos. Who knows? Maybe all your magic will help you keep up."

"I am *not* trying to drink anyone under the table." Ember pointed at her friend as she floated toward the new keg spouting sparkling gold Bloodshine into empty cups. "Especially not Nu'ek."

The Golra held another keg in both gigantic hands, laughing at some crude joke before she upended the spigot into her mouth and drank right from the metal barrel.

Cheyenne snorted and shook her head, content to watch everyone else celebrate their first victory. Then her gaze fell on Elarit again, still sitting at the table and occasionally rolling her eyes at something Jara'ak said to the magical made of swarming black specks. Corian was now on the other side of the chamber, shaking his head as L'zar pointed at him and continued his story.

Probably an account of all the horrible things they did together in the name of chaos. Laughing, Cheyenne headed toward Corian's empty seat and sat down beside Elarit. "Hey."

The troll woman lifted her goblet to her lips. "Cheyenne."

"Thanks again for the activator."

"Oh, sure." Elarit chuckled. "Didn't take you long to learn to use it. That last message today was from you, right?"

"Yeah. Kinda came as second-nature, I guess." Cheyenne

leaned back in the chair and watched the other revelers. "What the hell are they doing?"

The troll woman stared at the small ring of magicals gathered at the far end of the chamber. Lumil stepped into the center with a fist held in front of her, leering at an orc, who quickly drank the rest of his fellwine before crouching in a ready stance. "Looks like a fight."

"We just got done fighting."

"This is for fun. I know that goblin woman would say that about every battle, but this is what happens when O'gúl warriors open their bottles and get down to serious business."

"You mean, a staged fight in front of their friends is the O'gúleesh version of a drinking game?"

Elarit cocked her head and set her drink on the table. "Sure. It's evolved a little. Used to be the loser had to cut off a finger or a toe and hand it over as the victor's prize."

"You're screwing with me."

"As fun as that would be, Cheyenne, I'm not."

Not sure whether to grimace or laugh, Cheyenne watched Lumil and the orc circle each other in the ring, calling out ridiculous insults to the howling of laughter as the other magicals pushed them toward each other.

Jara'ak and the swarming magical rose from their seats to watch the games, and Cheyenne took her chance. "You know, Persh'al *wanted* to be here."

Elarit turned slowly toward the halfling and raised her eyebrows. "I'm curious why you think now is the right time to bring up Persh'al. He's safe and warm in his Earthside tech cubby, isn't he?"

Okay, so she's a little bitter. I could've read that better.

"Yeah. He's still at the warehouse."

"Then I wouldn't waste time at *this* celebration worrying about what he's doing over there by himself."

"I'm not worried about anyone. I just thought you'd like to

know he wanted to be here, and he *didn't* come with us because of you."

The troll woman's eyes narrowed. "Because of me."

"You know, so L'zar wouldn't find some reason to kick you out or whatever." *This isn't going the way I wanted.*

"Why would he do that?"

"I mean, with Persh'al here, and everyone else all crammed together celebrating this."

Elarit pushed herself up from the table, and Cheyenne found herself staring at the long bloody gash in the side of the troll woman's tunic instead of her face. "I'm glad you enjoy the activator, Cheyenne. Don't mention Persh'al Tenishi around me again."

"I was trying to help."

"Stick to revolutions and saving this world from itself." Elarit snatched her drink off the table and stared across the chamber as she pushed in the chair with a metallic clink. "That's what you're good at."

Cheyenne stared after the troll woman as she stalked across the bunker. Elarit stopped once to refill her cup, then headed through one of the arched doors lining the room and disappeared. *That went well. Jesus, the magicals over here are all insane.*

The table jolted beneath her hand when Maleshi stomped onto the opposite end of it, stepping precariously over the newly opened bottles and waving her silver skull. A round of cheers and bellowing laughter rose from the onlookers. "You all wanted to see General Maleshi Hi'et's return, didn't you?"

"The Hand of the Night and Circle!"

Maleshi spun around on the table and snarled. "The Hand of the Night and Circle can eat the deathflame torch, for all I care! But Blade of the Untouched Eye? The Blade is alive and well!"

The rebels roared again, stomping their feet on the stone floor and pounding whatever metal they could find. The most readily available of that down here beneath the city was the table. Cheyenne pulled her hands away from the shuddering tabletop and caught Foltr picking up his tankard with a snarl of disgust before drinking for a long time.

Maleshi let out a wild howl, her head thrown back as she staggered across the surface. Then she drank deeply from the silver skull and snarled, "I marched through the fires of Azercól and drank from deathflame bowls!"

Cheyenne stared at the nightstalker woman stomping on the table in rhythm with her words, and the other rebels quickly took up the butchered tune. *No way. She's singing war songs on the table. At least she's not slitting anyone's throat.*

Barking a laugh, the halfling took a long pull from her goblet of Bloodshine and scrunched her nose at the bubbles that hadn't calmed since she'd poured her one and only drink.

Maleshi howled the ridiculously violent, bloodthirsty O'gúleesh song and thrust her fist at Corian when he walked alongside the table toward Cheyenne. Chuckling, he shook his head and waved the general's antics off before taking the empty seat beside the halfling.

"A part of me should've expected things to turn out like this tonight." He practically tossed his half-empty drink onto the table and slumped in his chair. "And I'm still surprised."

Cheyenne snorted. "Because Maleshi isn't usually the 'get up and dance on the table' type? Or because she is?"

"Who knows?" When Corian turned to look at the halfling, his body moved with his head, swaying in his chair. "We might not have another chance to talk like this after tonight, depending on how things go in the next few days."

"Oh, good. So get your deep, philosophical time in now while you still can."

"No philosophy tonight, kid," The nightstalker said, "I aim to drink myself into the depths of the abyss and fell-damn the rest."

"I can see that."

He chuckled and picked up his tankard again, pausing with it halfway to his lips. "I wanted to tell you I'm proud of you, Cheyenne. You did everything that was asked of you. Sure, you complained a little, but who wouldn't?"

She laughed. "You can stop the compliments right there, man. I get it."

"I'm serious. I'd stand behind a halfling who complains sometimes but follows through with everything she has any day. I do, and I will for as long as I can. It's a hell of a lot better than trying to back someone who talks themselves up too much and can't pull their own weight. Not saying you ever did that, by the way."

"I know. I'm not a big talker."

Corian hissed and bowed his head. "Am I crashing your private party over here?"

Cheyenne sat back in her chair, watching Maleshi's riotous, drunken march across the other end of the table as the rebels sang with her. "Nah, you're good. For a wasted nightstalker."

"Tonight, that's exactly what I am."

"Let me ask you something, though."

Corian lifted his head and shot her a crooked grin. "You picked a good time for it, kid. I'm an open book."

"Okay." Chuckling, Cheyenne nodded across the chamber at L'zar, who'd propped himself up with a hand on the wall and was pumping his tankard to the rhythm of the song, grinning the whole time. "That promise you made to L'zar..."

The nightstalker stuck a finger in the air. "The promise I *kept*."

"Right. The promise and the secret were the same thing, weren't they?"

Corian swiveled his head toward her and raised his eyebrows. "You'll have to be a little more specific, halfling. That list stretches to eternity and back again."

"Of course it does." Cheyenne grabbed the tankard from him and took a small sip of fellwine, squeezing her eyes shut as the green liquor burned down her throat and instantly into her veins. "Your promise to L'zar not to tell me who I really am. The daughter of an O'gúl prince. The Crown's niece and heir to the throne. That was why you wouldn't answer half my questions, wasn't it?"

Corian slowly took his drink back from her and managed to look sober enough to hold her gaze. "He didn't want you to know because he didn't want it to go to your head."

She leaned away from him with a dubious look. "Why would it?"

"Ah." The nightstalker lifted his tankard in L'zar's general direction and hissed out a laugh. "Because he let it go to *his* head. And because the asshole loves surprises."

"Yeah, no kidding." They chuckled, and Cheyenne folded her arms. "That's the most straightforward, honest answer you've given me since we met."

"In this world, kid, the truth isn't the great equalizer all you humans seem to think it is. Well, not *you*. You're obviously not human."

"I get it."

He hissed out another laugh and set his cup in his lap. "The truth in Ambar'ogúl has to be earned. We all have a right to it, but not everyone deserves it. If anyone in this room deserves the truth tonight, it's you."

"Damn straight it is."

Corian laughed and shook his head. "You earned it, plain and simple. It won't set you free, either. Shit's gonna get a lot more complicated after this."

"I can handle complicated." The halfling cracked a smile as Maleshi thrust her silver skull in the air with a roar, raining fizzy green fellwine down on everything around her. The rebels started chanting something Cheyenne couldn't understand and the general leaped off the table, caught by the outstretched arms of L'zar's followers thumping her on the back and toasting General Hi'et's return to Ambar'ogúl.

Just as long as I don't have to turn against what I believe in. Still not sure that isn't part of the deal.

CHAPTER EIGHT

Cheyenne had no way to tell how long she sat at that table watching L'zar's rebels drink themselves into a stupor, but by the time she started feeling tired, it couldn't really be called a party anymore. Some of the magicals, like Nu'ek and Foltr, had removed themselves some time ago to turn in. Most of them, though, had drunk until they couldn't drink anymore and sprawled on the table, the chairs, the floor, and in heaps on top of each other.

L'zar filled his tankard one more time from the dregs of the last metal keg on the table, whistling to himself. He took a drink and raised his eyebrows, then walked down the table toward his daughter. Someone snorted and rolled over when he nudged them out of the way with the toe of his shoe. "Come on. I have no idea what time it is, not that it matters, but if you sit there any longer, you'll end up just another passed-out magical who couldn't pull it together long enough to find a bed."

Cheyenne rolled her shoulders and grimaced at the ache in her neck. "I think I fell asleep at some point already."

"It happens. The beds are better, I promise. Even all the way down here." Chuckling, he stepped around a pair of legs sticking out from beneath the table and waved the halfling toward one of the archways in the wall.

"Hey, Em."

"Yeah." Ember looked up from her conversation with the magical made of swarming black specks and smiled tiredly.

"I guess we get beds."

"That's all you needed to say." Ember excused herself from the conversation and floated across the chamber as Cheyenne pushed to her feet.

"We're following His Royal Highness." The halfling gestured toward L'zar and let out a huge yawn as she went to collect her backpack. Somehow, it had lasted all night without being disturbed.

The drow chuckled as he passed a hand over the door. It slid aside to reveal a passageway beyond. "Not as satisfying to crack jokes about my lineage now that you know how far it extends, is it?"

"Oh, no, it's still perfectly satisfying. We all know I'm not talking about myself."

He entered the dark passage and walked slowly enough for the tired halfling and the floating fae to keep up. "The best thing to do now is sleep it off. Which I'm hoping those other idiots can manage relatively well."

"I'm not drunk, L'zar."

His golden eyes flashed in the semi-darkness when he looked over his shoulder at her. "Not on fellwine and Blood-shine, maybe. Victory is just as intoxicating, in my experience."

"Uh-huh." Cheyenne and Ember exchanged dubious glances, then the fae girl snorted and choked back a laugh.

"Tomorrow's a big day too. Different but big. We'll take a walk around the city, huh?" L'zar pointed at each door they passed in the hall, counting them silently in his head. "You'll get the grand tour of the grandest dump this world has to offer.

What you and Persh'al saw the last time was like pulling up a picture of Greece on Google Images and trying to convince yourself you've been there."

Cheyenne snorted. "Not the comparison I would've picked, but okay."

"If my comparisons annoy you, I promise that's at the bottom of my list of things to work on in the future. I want to show you the *real* Hangivol, Cheyenne. Give you a taste of what the capital and the O'gúleesh here are like when everyone's not too chickenshit to be themselves, scared of being sucked up by the walls and spat out into a bowl of the Crown's magic-sludge soup."

Cheyenne grinned at L'zar's back and stuck her hands deep in the pockets of her black trenchcoat. *Wasted L'zar sounds slightly more lucid than sober L'zar, and then he pulls out something like that.*

"And by 'be themselves,' I mean taking this city into their own hands again."

Ember's eyes widened. "You mean, like riots?"

"Of course. That's expected of every coup, isn't it?" He stopped at a door on the left, his finger frozen and pointing at it. "Let me tell you, there's nothing like an O'gúl riot. Beauty in one of its purest forms. Here we are."

The door crackled with blue light before sliding aside into the stone wall. A soft glow illuminated the room beyond, mostly hidden by L'zar standing in the doorway and grinning at the two young magicals, his golden eyes half-concealed by heavy lids. "I hope neither of you has a problem with sharing quarters for the night."

"We already share an apartment." Ember floated past Cheyenne into the room when L'zar stepped aside, her curiosity too great to ignore.

"Then that's settled." L'zar nodded firmly and turned toward his daughter. "Enjoy the rest of your night. Oh. And just so I don't spring it on you tomorrow, when we find the right time, I want to take you somewhere special. Just the two of us."

Cheyenne folded her arms and raised an eyebrow. "If you say 'father-daughter date,' I'll punch you again."

"You only *tried* to punch me last time." He clasped his hands behind his back and scanned the walls of the hall before chuckling. "Though I wouldn't be surprised if you managed it on a second attempt. I want you to go into tomorrow with an open mind. We'll go cheer and fight the power with the citizens for a while, and then you and I will take a little detour. If I'm never coming back after this, I plan to make the most of my final hurrah in this world."

She stepped toward the open door and squinted at him. "Why do you need me for that?"

"Because you'll love it. Goodnight, Cheyenne." With a small bow that looked oddly genuine, L'zar spun on his heel and marched farther down the hallway. His lilting whistle echoed behind him until the halfling advanced into the chamber and the door slid closed behind her.

"Because I'll love it." She laughed and shook her head. "Probably not."

"Okay, maybe you can help me with this one." Ember floated in the middle of the room, pointing at the massive bed along the far wall. It was draped in satin and finely embroidered velvet, and a mound of shimmering pillows covered half the bed from the center to the headboard. "What the hell size bed is that?"

"Whoa."

"Yeah. It's like two California Kings smooshed together, but it's not. It's all one fucking mattress." Ember drifted across the stone floor toward the bed and launched herself onto the pile of pillows. "Oh, my God."

Cheyenne laughed and slipped off her backpack before

shrugging out of her trenchcoat. "You know what? I bet they call this an O'gúl Prince."

The fae girl snorted and sat up. "You're stuck on this whole royalty thing, aren't you?"

"I'm pretty sure I'm handling it fairly well."

"True." Ember shrugged and flopped back onto the pillows, propping herself up with cushions beneath both arms. When Cheyenne dove onto the bed from the side, her outstretched arms didn't even make it to the halfway mark. "Jesus, this bed is gigantic."

"Might as well have our own separate rooms." Kicking off her black Vans, Cheyenne rolled onto the bed and sank into the pillows too. "I can't believe we did this, Em."

"I know. This whole day!" The fae cracked up. "And you! You're a drow princess! What the hell is happening?"

The halfling closed her eyes and sank even deeper into the pillows until they formed puffy, embroidered walls around her head. "Right now, we're lying on a giant bed in a medieval-looking bunker for techless magicals talking about my not-so-imminent rule as the next O'gúl Crown." This time, saying the words aloud did make her shudder. "That's not anything close to what I wanted."

"I know."

"I wanted to stop that psycho on the throne from making things worse everywhere and bringing her screwed-up war to Earth."

"Yep." Ember took a sharp breath and yawned, throwing her forearm over her eyes.

"So many things make sense now. I mean, I thought this was L'zar's attempt to overthrow a ruler and take everything for himself, but it's... Shit, I don't even know. It *is* about me, and I walked right into the middle of it, thinking I could drop a coin in a fucking bowl, go back home, and call it good. Ugh." Cheyenne snatched the closest pillow and pressed it onto her face. She waited in the muffled darkness for Ember to make a remark that would pull the halfling out of her own head, as usual. It didn't come. "Em?"

Slowly pushing herself up, Cheyenne thumped the pillow down by her friend's hand. Ember's mouth popped open, and she let out a loud, rumbling snore.

"Right. Apparently, I'm the only one who cares so much about what's happening that it's keeping me awake. Or I'm the only one who didn't get shitfaced."

She had to crawl almost four feet toward the foot of the bed to grab the extra velvet blanket folded on top of the heavy quilt beneath them. She dragged it back with her and tossed half the blanket over Ember, then fell back into the mountain of pillows and closed her eyes.

I'm the next drow heir. So what? It won't change a thing about me as long as I make the right choice, whatever the hell that is.

The next morning, Ember and Cheyenne woke to the sound of hurried footsteps, shouted commands, laughter, and the smell of food cooking. The halfling sat up in the huge bed, ran a hand through her mussed hair, and quickly changed into fresh clothes before gathering everything up again and slinging her backpack over her shoulder.

"Smells like breakfast, Em."

"Right. And I realized we didn't eat a single thing yesterday after breakfast."

"Huh." Pulling a hair tie from the pocket of her jacket, Cheyenne twisted her hair back into a loose bun and shrugged. "All the better to get wasted with, I guess."

"Very funny. I will eat anything right now if it doesn't run away."

"You sure?" Cheyenne studied the closed door to their guest

quarters as Ember quickly changed and collected her things too. "I told you about the last time I ate on this side, right?"

"Oh." Ember straightened, her green backpack dangling from her fingers. "You mean that Jell-O shit with the eyes?"

"Yep. And that was the fancy food."

The fae swallowed thickly and grimaced. "I take that back. I'll eat anything that doesn't watch me as I stick a fork into it. Wait, do they use forks here?"

"Kinda. Hey, did you see what L'zar did to get this door open last night?" Cheyenne pulled the activator out of her pocket and stuck it behind her ear, but the ensuing pinch and sync with her magic didn't come. *Of course not. We're in a bunker of magic only, no tech.* She dropped the silver coil back into her pocket and waved a hand over the door.

"What are you doing?"

"Trying to open the damn door." Cheyenne passed her hand over it again, then waved faster and finally dropped her hand on her thigh. "Why are you laughing at me?"

"Because you're waving at a door."

"You know, I could blast a hole in this thing right now, and we wouldn't have to have this conversation."

"Relax, Princess."

Cheyenne snorted and folded her arms. "Don't ever call me that."

"Just testing it out to see if it sticks. I know it won't." Ember stopped beside the halfling with a grin and passed her hand in front of the door. It lit up with blue lines and slid into the wall. "You might be L'zar's daughter, but you couldn't pass as a thief in any world."

"What are you talking about?"

"Sleight of hand, Cheyenne." Ember looked down at her left hand, her wrist pressed against her thigh as her fingers moved in a quick spellcasting gesture while she waved her hand in front of the door again.

It started to slide closed, and the halfling leaped forward. "Okay, I get it. You guys master spells easily." She grabbed the edge of the sliding door with both hands and shoved it back into the wall with an echoing boom. A shower of stone chips and dust rained down around the doorway, and Cheyenne turned to her friend. "We all have different skills."

Laughing, Ember rolled her eyes and followed Cheyenne down the semi-dark tunnel toward the bunker's main room.

When they stepped through the arch into the huge chamber, Cheyenne's mouth popped open. "They're all awake. *Working.*"

Ember adjusted the straps of her backpack and stared at the dozens of magicals bustling around the chamber, stacking crates, passing plates piled high with food, packing, and unpacking who-knew-what. "How great would it be if hangovers didn't exist in this world?"

Cheyenne chuckled when her gaze fell on the keg at the end of the black table, much larger than any from the night before. "Sorry to burst your bubble, Em. Smells like straight-up grog this morning."

"Oh." The fae's shoulders sagged. "I *knew* it was too good to be true."

"Did you drink too much last night too?"

"Definitely not. I was thinking about the future."

Maleshi approached them from the other end of the table, her face buried in her upturned tankard as she gulped down the entire thing. She stopped in front of the young magicals, wiped her mouth with the back of her hand, and grinned. "Nothing like this O'gúl piss to get you moving again in the morning. You want some?"

Ember leaned away from the general. "O'gúl what?"

"Nah, it's just grog. The real kind, not the shit I've heard about them serving in Peridosh." Maleshi turned and slammed the tankard on the table. "Does the job right. I heard you, by

80

the way. We still get hangovers on this side, but the hangover cures are hard to beat."

Cheyenne eyed the nightstalker woman. "Yeah, you're looking peppy."

"Thank you very much." Maleshi gave her a goofy little bow. "You two enjoy yourselves last night?"

"In weird ways, yeah."

Ember pointed at the general and cocked her head. "You definitely had fun."

Maleshi picked her teeth with an extended claw and shrugged. "I guess it was a long time coming. I'd like to say I got it out of my system. I'm back, which I never thought would happen. Just making the most of a weirdly nostalgic situation. There's breakfast over there if you want any."

"Does it have eyes?"

The general snorted. "Not that I know of."

"Perfect."

Ember elbowed Cheyenne in the side and muttered through clenched teeth, "Ask her."

"What?"

"Ask her about the thing."

Maleshi turned her wide, glowing silver eyes on the fae girl and grinned. "I'm standing right here, Ember."

Ember glared at the halfling until Cheyenne stepped back and gestured at the general with both hands. The fae girl asked, "Okay, fine. Is that thing real?"

Maleshi glanced over her shoulder and chuckled. "I don't follow."

Ember pressed her lips together and rolled her eyes when Cheyenne didn't step in to help her. "The fancy skull cup. That was, like, a symbol or something, right?"

"Oh." The general threw her head back and laughed. "No, that's a very real skull from a very dead magical."

Cheyenne stuck her hands in her pockets and nodded. "Let

me guess. His name was Dahal. Don't look *that* surprised. You said it like five times last night."

"Caught me." Maleshi gave them an exaggerated grin. "He was my mentor once upon a time. One of the fiercest warriors I've ever met, and he taught me almost everything I know. The rest of it I taught myself, and that's why he's dead. Any other questions?"

Ember swallowed. "Nope. That about sums it up for me."

"Great. Get some food while you can. When we head out of here, we're going in style."

"That's right!" Byrd straightened from where he crouched over a plate of food and slurped something noodle-like into his mouth before pumping a fist. "General Hi'et's finally getting her warlord's procession!"

"Shut up." Lumil shoved the goblin man in the back and Byrd stumbled forward, his arms outstretched to keep his breakfast on his plate.

Maleshi raised an eyebrow. "That's not what we're doing."

"Sure it is." Corian lugged a crate toward the other side of the bunker and grinned at them as he passed. "The O'gúleesh in Hangivol need to see their hero return."

"Uh, no. If anyone's the hero, it's Cheyenne."

The halfling pointed at her and shook her head. "Don't put that shit on me."

Maleshi laughed. "No procession for this warlord. I had my fun yesterday."

Jara'ak dusted off his hands after moving another crate and leered at the general from the other side of the bunker. "Should've known so many centuries on Earth would make you soft, Maleshi. You won't even take your moment, huh? It's gotta be shoved down your throat instead."

The general scowled at him. "Okay, fine."

"The Blade of the Unseen Eye returns to raze the streets of Hangivol!" The rebel who'd raised the cry ducked behind a group of magicals gathered around the breakfast spread, but they all echoed the cheer with grins and pumped fists.

Maleshi rolled her eyes. "I'm done listening to these idiots. Eat. Then we're getting the hell out of this place."

"Not a fan of long periods underground, huh?" Corian chuckled as he headed back toward them.

"Says the nightstalker who could've set himself anywhere in the world and chose an unfinished basement apartment with concrete walls." The general put her hands on her hips and stared after him with a raised eyebrow when he walked past. "That's right. It didn't take me long to find your not-so-secret lair, *vae shra'ni.*"

Corian laughed but didn't continue the banter.

"I need more grog." Maleshi snatched up her tankard and spun toward the far end of the table, wagging her finger between Cheyenne and Ember. "I'm serious. Eat something. You're gonna need it."

Cheyenne cocked her head. "She almost sounds like how I imagine most people's moms talk to their kids. I'll know there's something wrong when she starts telling us to wash our hands and not to play with fire or knives." Snorting at her joke, she turned toward Ember. "What's wrong with you?"

"She killed her own mentor." Ember grimaced. "And she drinks out of his skull."

"Nightstalkers, right?" Shrugging, Cheyenne headed toward the other side of the bunker and the strong scents of something at the very least edible rising from a table against the wall. "Still a good idea to eat, though."

"Is it? Is it really? 'Cause now I'm expecting to be handed a fork made from the bones of their enemies."

The halfling grinned. "That would be cool as hell."

CHAPTER NINE

Half an hour later, the surviving rebels of the Four-Pointed Star surged through the huge iron double doors out of the bunker and headed toward the upper levels of the capital. The stone halls echoed with their shouts and rowdy laughter, jests flying through the air as the magicals speculated on what they'd find when they reached the surface. Cheyenne found herself caught up in the excitement, not caring where they were headed first as the cheering, shouting rebels swept her along in the center of the procession.

They made their way through the underground tunnels beneath the city, passing the occasional pocket of O'gúleesh citizens meeting privately where others were least likely to look for them. Some groups cheered and launched spells through the tunnels in celebration, making everyone duck and call out jests about fighting each other after the Crown came crashing down. Some of the wayward groups even joined the procession, squeezing in on the sides and filling the passages even tighter with bodies crammed against magical bodies.

Everywhere, the whispers traveled through the halls, both toward the boisterous procession and away from it.

"It's Maleshi."

"General Hi'et. She's back."

"Endaru smiles on the Blade of the Unseen Eye."

Cheyenne's drow hearing picked up the fading echoes of surprise and awe the other magicals thought they were keeping hidden from the unwieldy parade. *They love their bloodthirsty nightstalker warlord, don't they? Good to keep in mind.*

Whether L'zar opened the blocked tunnels to them or someone else at the front of the line guided their procession, she couldn't tell. It didn't matter by the time the swelling river of sweaty, shouting, enlivened magicals burst through the final opening into the open air of one of Hangivol's outer circular levels.

Cheyenne paused beneath the pale gray glow of light muted by the dome around the city. Howling, roaring, cackling magicals streamed around her out of the tunnel, shouting and pumping their fists and sending magical bursts into the air as they followed the procession.

The lower levels of the capital were filled with chaos.

L'zar wasn't kidding about O'gúl riots.

Hangivol's citizens streamed through the open, crowded, dirty square, drinking and fighting each other, dancing and racing through the streets and in and out of buildings. From the rooftops of high-rise metal buildings around them came the clanging of at least a dozen magicals pounding on some kind of metal drums. Spells flew through the air like fireworks, most of them without aim or purpose.

A crackling ball of blue flames soared over the crowd from an upper level of one of the tall buildings and headed straight for Cheyenne. She stepped quickly aside and spun to watch the flames bash into a storefront on the street level right next to where they'd emerged from the tunnels. A second blue fireball careened into a metallic window two levels above, and the halfling whirled again to face the attacker. "Hey!"

"Relax, kid." Lumil's green hand came down on Cheyenne's shoulder and the goblin woman laughed, tossing her hair out of her yellow eyes. "Take a little time to check things out. I promise no one's getting hurt in all this. Not unless they want to. Ha!" With an exaggerated wink, Lumil removed her hand and went marching after the rest of the procession. She took off at a run when she saw two other magicals starting to fight each other, wanting to get in on the action.

"Check things out?" Cheyenne walked hesitantly after the procession and looked over her shoulder at the first storefront hit by the blue flames. Nothing was on fire, no windows or doorways destroyed, and the orange flash of protective wards reinforced by O'gúl technology faded into nothing. "Oh."

Ember floated up behind her with a wide grin. "You look *way* too interested in a shop. Fine, I can't read the symbols on that sign, but whatever it is, it can't be nearly as awesome as whatever's happening right now."

"They warded all the shops," Cheyenne muttered.

"Okay. Come on."

The halfling picked up the pace beside Ember and got a better look at the other unintended targets of wayward spells as the procession grew with every block they passed. "Em, when you hear 'riots,' what do you think of?"

"I don't know. Burning buildings and people breaking stuff and going insane. Maybe cops."

"Yeah. That's not happening here."

"You didn't expect the police to show up on this side when you challenged the Crown, did you?" Ember snorted and wiped the smile off her face when she caught her friend's exasperated glance. "Come on, it's funny."

"L'zar said there would be riots. I think this is it."

"Huh. Doesn't look very riot-y to me."

Cheyenne grinned. "I know. They're not rioting against the

city, just everything it stands for. You see any metal balls flying around?"

"Like the kind you fought at the binding ceremony?"

"Yep. That kind."

Ember looked at the high-rises and laughed at a group of magicals dancing on the rooftops. "Not one."

"The whole city shut down to keep itself running while the O'gúleesh flood the streets and party."

"I feel like that would be forever ago."

"Probably."

They quickly caught up with the main body of the procession, where the rebels had taken up some other battle song and were shouting it at the tops of their lungs. Citizens of every race flooded the main avenue from within shops and homes and dark alleys between buildings, all to get a glance at Maleshi Hi'et.

"Look where they're going!" An orc standing in the doorway of a darkened building grinned at his neighbor and pointed farther up the square.

"To Vedrosha!"

"Maleshi Hi'et's heading for Vedrosha!"

The metallic drumbeats grew faster and louder as the procession picked up the pace. Cheyenne grunted when a wide-eyed, snarling troll knocked into her on his way up the parade. Ember floated sideways to avoid the halfling barreling into her too. "Persh'al didn't happen to show you this Vedrosha by any chance, did he?"

"Didn't even mention it." Cheyenne tried to peer over the heads of the magicals in front of her but couldn't see a thing. "We're about to find out."

It was impossible to tell from inside the lower-level ring that the buildings stopped as suddenly as they did about a mile inside the outer wall rising around the city. Cheyenne's eyes widened when she stepped from beneath the looming shadows of the buildings into the only wide-open space she'd seen in Hangivol.

"So we found out." Ember folded her arms and frowned at the celebrating magicals leaping and running about. The rest of the procession headed to the left across the bare ground, with nothing between them and the curving shield dome signifying the outer line of the capital. "It looks like a giant parking lot."

"No, the parking garage is outside the wall and underground."

Ember laughed. "Wait, are you serious?"

"Yep. The walls ate our ride and everything."

"This place keeps throwing punches left and right."

Cheyenne smiled and nodded toward the crowd gathering around one section of the open ground. "Come on. I gotta see what they're pulling out next. There's nothing here."

"Okay. I'm gonna call it." Ember floated along beside her friend, unable to keep her smile from widening at the sight of so many O'gúleesh dancing and whooping in the open space, clinking tankards together and jostling each other in excitement. Somewhere behind them, the drummers had come down from the rooftops and now approached. "They're gonna build a giant bonfire and burn everything that makes them think of the Crown."

"Right. That would pretty much be the entire city, and it's made of metal."

Ember shrugged. "Fine. Debunked. Do *you* have a better guess?"

"Nope."

The drumming grew louder and closer behind them, but Cheyenne couldn't see the magicals approaching through the crowd, which had doubled in size in the last two minutes. She did, however, get an open view of Maleshi standing on a large square of metal that was much lighter and cleaner-looking than the ground around it.

The general spread her arms and lifted her chin. "We're here to take back what has always been ours!"

A cheer rose from the crowd, magicals roaring and cramming closer together to get a better look.

"Come on." Cheyenne grabbed Ember's wrist and practically pulled her through the crowd. It surprised her to find a path opening up in front of her when the O'gúleesh saw the drow girl in the black trenchcoat, followed by the fae girl hovering an inch off the ground. *Do they know who I am already? Not the halfling part. That would make this a whole different kind of crowd.*

They stopped at the edge of the crowd gathered around the fifteen-foot-square metal square on which General Hi'et stood. Maleshi's silver eyes flashed in the muted gray light when she met Cheyenne's gaze. Her lips parted in a feral grin, and she stepped off the brighter square. "Blood and glory, brothers. Rip this fell-damn thing apart!"

Two ogres stepped through the crowd from different directions, each carrying what looked like a pickaxe over their hulking shoulders. Cheyenne squinted at the tools-turned-weapons. "What are they supposed to do with those?"

A troll woman with thick bands of tattoos racing up both bare arms nodded at Cheyenne and leaned toward her. "They're breaking the seal."

Ember snorted. "How nice."

"On what?" Cheyenne asked.

"Come on. We're done pretending we've forgotten. For now, at least. It's in our blood."

"Right." *And if I keep asking, someone's gonna notice I'm not from around here.*

The ogres grunted and swung the deadly-looking pickaxes at the square of metal. The weapons hit the ground with a grating shriek and a burst of sparks. Maleshi shot a bolt of silver lightning at the metal square, and in five seconds flat, the entire panel blew away like ash on the wind to reveal a ten-foot pit in the middle of so much nothing.

A crazed, emboldened roar exploded from the crowd. Magicals jumped up and down, shoved each other forward, snarled and hissed, with the occasional word of O'gúleesh thrown in for good measure. Cheyenne removed the activator from her pocket and stuck it as covertly as she could behind her ear. After the sharp pinch of syncing tech subsided, she flicked her finger beside her thigh and managed to turn down the noise before she got a migraine.

They opened a giant pit outside the city, and there's hardly any tech out here.

Lines of code scrolled across her vision here and there, difficult to see through so many bodies and spread out far more than she'd seen with the activator feeding her information in Hangivol.

Maleshi howled and drew a thin, glinting silver dagger from a sheath at her hip before thrusting it over her head. "We let that bitch pin us down for far too long, but we know the old ways. The Crown wouldn't last two seconds in here, but I know every one of you bastards can hold their own in the ring that binds us all!" Grinning, she grabbed the blade with her other hand and sliced a deep cut into her palm, hissing at the pain. Then she raised her clenched fist over the ten-foot drop and let her blood patter onto the sand below for everyone to see.

The crowd erupted in wild, animalistic grunts, hisses, roars, and bellows. Cheyenne stared at Maleshi's blood, sinking into the white sand at the bottom of the square hole. *I thought we were done with sacrifices. And it sounds like a damn zoo out here.*

She recognized Jara'ak's bellowing laughter and stepped past two other jeering magicals to get to him. "What is this?"

Jara'ak brought his heavy hand down on her shoulder and gave her a quick shake in his excitement. His hand disappeared again before she had a chance to warn him about losing it. "The true heart of Ambar'ogúl, Cheyenne. The O'gúl fighting pits are officially open again, eh?"

"The fighting pits."

"By the blood of Op'paro, I've been counting the days." The orc slammed a huge fist into his opposite palm and chuckled darkly, glaring across the open pit at anyone who met his gaze and sucking in the drool pooling around his tusks.

"Jesus." Cheyenne stepped back toward Ember and shook her head. "Fighting pits."

"Seriously?"

"Yeah. Apparently, they're a real hit."

Ember grinned. "Awesome."

"All right, bloodletters, listen up!" With her dagger sheathed again, Maleshi ignored her bleeding hand and shrugged out of her military jacket before tossing it into the magicals gathered behind her. A troll man caught it, shook it in the air, then balled it up and dropped it at his feet. "We're celebrating a new turn today."

"And General Hi'et's return to the Glinting Eye!" someone shouted from the back.

The nightstalker woman pointed in the direction of the cry. "So I've been told."

Laughter cut through the snarls and roaring cheers.

"Who's gonna kick this off with me, huh?" Maleshi spread her arms and turned in a slow circle, her silver eyes glinting as she grinned like a lunatic. "Who's stupid enough to take me on in the first open fighting pit since K'laht the Everbright fell?"

Magicals shoved each other into volunteering, laughing and stomping on the metal floor beneath them.

Corian stepped forward, rolling up his shirtsleeves to reveal the tawny fur covering both arms. The general straightened and lowered her arms when she saw him, her eyes wide with amusement. Corian pressed a hand to his chest and dipped his head. "By your leave, General."

"Shit." Cheyenne stared at them, waiting for Maleshi to unleash her pent-up wrath at the other nightstalker, given the jaded history between them.

"What do you think?" Maleshi called to the crowd. "Is Corian Vedi'im a worthy sacrifice today?"

The crowd roared with laughter and approval, stomping and howling even louder now.

"Get the nightstalkers in the fucking pit!" someone shouted.

"Yes." Maleshi held Corian's gaze and nodded toward the gaping hole beside them. "Into the pit, *vae shra'ni.*"

Corian bowed and spun to head for the opposite side of the square while Maleshi did the same. He caught Cheyenne's gaze at the last moment and winked.

Ember leaned toward the halfling, her mouth open in surprise. "What's happening?"

"They're gonna fight each other." Cheyenne couldn't help a sharp laugh of disbelief. "Like I said. Nightstalkers."

CHAPTER TEN

By the time Maleshi Hi'et and Corian Vedi'im dropped into the fighting pit, the crowd of Hangivol's lower-level citizens had quadrupled. Magicals spilled across Vedrosha, the flat, open area at least the size of a football field. Many climbed onto the surrounding rooftops for a better view. Those who could fly or levitate did so, and the others got creative with stacking crates or unleashing their tech into the air to view the fight for them.

Cheyenne scanned the crowd, her activator highlighting the different tech pieces worn and operated by the O'gúleesh of Hangivol. Most of them were basic models compared to hers. *Makes sense. Elarit said she modified this one herself.*

A swarm of floating metal orbs headed toward Vedrosha from the inner circles of the city. Cheyenne watched them carefully, but the other magicals either didn't notice or weren't that concerned. When the halfling's activator picked up the data stream from the flying orbs, though, it made sense.

These aren't tech-dark like the Crown's police spheres.

With a quick flick of her finger to select the activator's offered command, Cheyenne's sight magnified the data streams flowing through the orbs as the blinking blue and yellow lights in the metal spheres rotated in multiple directions, capturing everything down here outside the O'gúl fighting pits.

So the fancy magicals in Upper Tech want to be part of this without leaving their shining upper-class streets. Might be as united as these guys are gonna get today.

The self-appointed drummers scattered throughout the crowd and produced deep, booming echoes from every direction around the open pit. Cheyenne stared down into the drop as Maleshi and Corian circled each other, grinning, and the gathered magicals erupted in a crazed chant punctured by snarls and bellows, feet stomping in rhythm with the drums.

The general spread her arms and extended glinting silver four-inch claws from all ten fingers. "I'm glad it's you, *vae shra'ni.*"

Corian crouched and extended his own claws, his silver eyes burning into hers. "I've been waiting a very long time for this."

"To get your ass kicked and finally settle everything between us? Oh, yeah. I know."

Cheyenne shoved her hands into her pockets to hide her clenched fists, despite the thousands of spectators who were coming undone in their excitement in much more obvious ways than clenched fists.

"Hey, you okay?" Ember leaned toward the halfling with a concerned frown.

"Not really." Cheyenne couldn't take her eyes off the nightstalkers circling each other in the pit. "You've seen a nightstalker fight before, right?"

"Briefly, yeah. I mean, I was a little busy trying not to get killed." Ember's chuckle stopped short when she realized how tense Cheyenne was. "From what I've seen, this'll be good."

Cheyenne gritted her teeth. "They're gonna kill each other."

"No way. This is all just for fun." Ember glanced at the hissing, growling, stomping spectators and cocked her head. "I think."

The pounding drumbeats had become such a part of the background out here in Vedrosha that when the drummers stopped all at once, it was startlingly silent.

The nightstalkers took their cue and began the fight. Silver flashes erupted from within the pit as Maleshi and Corian slipped into enhanced speed and raced toward each other, to the crowd's rising cries of approval. Cheyenne couldn't help herself. She slipped into drow speed to watch the nightstalkers fight so she could follow it.

Maleshi's swiping claws came down toward Corian's face, and he raised his own to block her attack, resulting in a shower of sparks when their natural weapons collided. Grinning, the general disengaged and sent a swift kick with the sole of her boot into Corian's chest. He flew backward across the pit and out of enhanced speed, his back slamming against the metal wall as sprays of sand burst on either side of him and hung suspended in the air. Then Maleshi dropped into regular speed, and Cheyenne was the only one watching a fight that hadn't yet continued.

This is ridiculous.

She fell into regular time again, and the roar of the crowd crashed back in. Corian finished thudding against the far wall as the sand fell back to the bottom of the pit and the flash of silver nightstalker light faded. He dropped into a crouch, the tips of his blade-like claws pressing gently into the sand as he stared up at Maleshi and chuckled.

The general spread her arms and gazed at the crowd with battle fire raging behind her silver eyes. The O'gúleesh magicals roared with primal excitement. Two separate fights broke out in the crowd away from the pit, but they were quickly dispelled so the spectators could focus their attention on the nightstalkers in the pit.

"Blade of the Unseen Eye! Blade of the Unseen Eye!" The chant grew louder and Maleshi snarled in appreciation, soaking it all in.

Corian sped toward her again in a brilliant silver flash, preceded by a burst of lightning crackling across the sand. In that split second, Cheyenne forced herself not to slip into drow speed again. *I can't keep up with this anyway.*

The nightstalkers' streaks converged, then Maleshi stopped on the other side of Corian, one arm wrapped around his middle with her claws pressed against his belly, the other hand holding the tips of her deadly blades against his exposed throat. She hissed in his ear and pushed him away.

The crowd went wild.

Corian spun and leaped toward her again, sending blinding streaks of silver lightning at her as he charged. Maleshi deflected each attack with a swipe of her claws, her eyes widening as a crazed laugh escaped her open-mouthed grin. Then Corian was on her again, slashing and swiping too quickly to follow without going into enhanced speed. The general blocked every attack, sparks flying up second after second as the air filled with the shriek and clang of nightstalker claws meeting, scraping against each other, and freeing themselves.

He ducked her next swing, blocked a second with his forearm, then brought his left hand slicing down toward her face and leaped away.

A lock of black hair separated from those hanging over her shoulders and drifted to the ground, scattering into individual hairs across the sand. Maleshi looked down at the hair he'd sliced from her head and grinned. "That's a first."

"First time for everything, *ma gairín*." Corian crouched again in a ready stance and jerked his chin at her.

With a dark chuckle, Maleshi advanced again, and this time, she didn't hold back.

The general's silver streaks of light flashed in strobing brilliance as she slipped in and out of enhanced speed too quickly for Corian to follow. Five seconds later, he was meeting her nightstalker speed as nothing more than a defensive tactic, but General Hi'et was too quick. Unbelievably quick.

She darted around him again and again, pausing in regular time for half a second to give the spectators the show they wanted. A spray of blood erupted from Corian's back, and he staggered forward, roaring. The next second, Maleshi's dark fist cracked against the side of his face. Corian toppled sideways, and she reappeared on his right to slash his thigh and spray more blood across the sand before shoving him in the opposite direction.

Corian limped in a circle, blinking in and out of his brilliant silver speed to catch her. But he couldn't.

Over and over again, Maleshi darted around her opponent, claws glinting in the muted light one second, more blood spraying from a new wound somewhere else on Corian's body the next.

She is gonna kill him.

Cheyenne found L'zar standing at the edge of the pit, arms folded and a satisfied smirk on his face as he watched General Hi'et demolish his *Nós Ainí* in the ring.

He's loving this. Of course he is. He doesn't give a shit about anyone else.

The halfling looked urgently back down into the pit in time to see Corian drop to his knees in the sand, snarling, his chest heaving as he raised his arm to feebly block Maleshi's next downward swing. She darted in a bright flash to his other side and sliced her claws across his ribs. Corian roared and lurched away, but Maleshi appeared in front of him again in the blink of an eye, claws retracted, and sent a vicious uppercut into the underside of Corian's chin. His eyes rolled back as he skidded on his back across the sand.

The crowd cheered and bellowed their approval, stomping and screaming the general's name. Maleshi ignored them all and tossed her hair out of her eyes, laughing through panting breaths as she stalked toward a prone Corian on the pit floor.

No way. Cheyenne's jaw ached from how hard she'd clenched it. *No way he is going to keep going after that.*

The general set one foot on either side of Corian's body, then dropped to her knees and straddled his chest. He coughed through a trickle of blood spilling from the corner of his mouth. Maleshi's claws extended again, and she pressed their tips into the side of his neck at the jugular. "Do you yield, *vae shra'ni?*"

Corian let out a gurgling laugh that turned into a cough. He lifted one hand to her thigh beside his chest and gave it a little squeeze before picking his head up off the sand as far as he could. "Are you kidding? Finish it."

His head thumped back into the sand with another wet, dangerously choking laugh. Maleshi's lips twitched as she grinned down at him with battle-crazed eyes.

"Maleshi!" Cheyenne shouted.

Whether the general heard the cry above the roar of the spectators didn't matter. Maleshi drew her claws across Corian's throat, the crowd lost it, and Cheyenne roared in fury and horror.

Instantly, General Hi'et leaped to her feet as Corian's blood spilled into the sand and went quickly to the closest wall of the pit. She pounded it with her fist, and a tall drawer slid out of the wall toward her. From it, she withdrew a thick torch of black metal that flared to life with green fire the second it left the drawer. Laughing, Maleshi thrust the torch in the air and screamed, "The O'gúl deathflame, brothers and sisters. For blood and glory!"

Then she swiped the eerily flickering flames of green and black across Corian's body and stepped back. His body erupted in flames, consuming him until the center of the pit was filled with green and black, turning the fallen nightstalker into a pillar of flame shooting four feet above the walls of the pit.

"What the fuck!" Cheyenne pushed magicals aside as she raced toward L'zar. "How can you just stand there? Do something!"

L'zar slowly removed his gaze from the flames, shot her a brief glance, and lifted a hand for her to wait.

"Fuck you." Cheyenne spun toward the edge of the pit, meaning to leap down into it.

Her father's cold, slender fingers clamped around her wrist and jerked her back.

"Let go of me!"

"Just wait." L'zar's golden eyes were filled with a calm but fierce warning. "Watch, Cheyenne. This is important for you to see."

"To watch him die?" She jerked her wrist from his grasp and turned to face the blazing pit again. L'zar's hand settled on her shoulder instead, maybe as a warning, maybe to hold her in place. Cheyenne didn't try to shrug it off this time because she saw movement in the flames.

The green and black fire spewed higher into the air, illuminating the faces around the pit with an eerie green glow. A warm wave of heat and magical energy passed through the crowd and funneled deep underground, spreading around everyone and beyond the city limits. The spectators chanted and stomped their feet in rhythm again, tossing their heads back to howl at the sky as they watched the green blaze intently.

The deathflame shrank, flickering slowly until it died and winked out. In its place stood Corian, palms turned outward and slightly raised beside his thighs, his eyes closed. A hush fell over the crowd when they saw him standing unscathed in the center of the pit.

Then the nightstalker's eyes flew open and settled on Maleshi. "Blood and glory."

She threw her head back and laughed before jumping up the wall out onto the flat ground, surrounded by cheering O'gúleesh. Then she spun and reached back down to help Corian up and out. Hands clapped his shoulders and back as the nightstalkers clasped forearms and grinned at each other.

"Think you got it out of your system?" he asked.

"Maybe. Maybe not." Maleshi squeezed his hand even tighter and cocked her head. "The pits are open now, *vae shra'ni*. We'll just have to let things play out."

Laughing, Corian released her and headed around the open pit toward L'zar and Cheyenne. The halfling stared at him in disbelief, a chill racing down her spine even as her eyes told her he was fine.

She slit his throat. She killed him. And the fire?

L'zar and Corian clasped forearms and shared a brief, sturdy hug, slapping each other on the back. The drow chuckled. "Looks like you needed that."

"Maybe I did." Corian turned toward Cheyenne and raised his eyebrows. "You're looking a little pale even for a drow, kid."

Cheyenne looked him up and down. "You're okay."

"Better than okay. I know you felt it. The deathflame."

"I don't know what the hell I felt." She lurched toward him and grabbed his arms, staring at the spot on his neck Maleshi had sliced open minutes before. A hard lump formed in her throat, and she forced it away as she stared at the nightstalker. "I thought you were dead."

"I could have been. If I'd yielded." Corian tapped the underside of her arms and cocked his head. "I'm pretty sure this is the closest you get to giving hugs, but you're digging into my arms."

"Shit. Sorry." She released him immediately and ignored L'zar's laughter. All around them, the liberated magicals got back to their celebration. The drums kicked up again, and the sound of metal slicing through metal ripped through the air as the metal covers over the other five fighting pits in Vedrosha were ripped off and destroyed. Cheyenne ignored it all. "Will someone please tell me what the hell happened? I can't wrap my head around this."

Smiling, Corian stood beside her and looked down into the fighting pit. "That was the deathflame, kid. One version of it, at least. You might say it's a kind of lifeforce running through this world. Keeping us sane. Whole."

She snorted. "You didn't look whole when you were bleeding out in the sand."

"That's part of the tribute." Corian tugged his rolled-up shirtsleeves back down over his arms. "The fighting pits have been fueling the lifeforce magic of Ambar'ogúl since the beginning. We fight. We spill each other's blood in the pits. Those of us willing to walk through the deathflame heal the land, which heals us in turn."

"Wait." Cheyenne scanned the sandy bottom of the pit, from which Corian's dark blood was gone without a trace. "Fighting. That's what keeps this entire world running?"

"Something like that, yeah. In the pits, at least. We all get an extra boost when a fighter refuses to yield and chooses the deathflame instead."

"And you have to almost *die* for that to happen?"

"It varies." Corian chuckled. "Maleshi doesn't end any battle without giving the people a good show."

"Jesus." Cheyenne rubbed her mouth and stared at the perfectly white sand.

Laughing and cheering with the other citizens around them, Maleshi joined Cheyenne and Corian and thumped a hand down on the nightstalker man's shoulder. "What a way to kick off these two weeks, huh?"

"It's relatively satisfying, sure."

Maleshi grinned at Cheyenne. "What do you think?"

"I think you're all insane."

"Ha! Probably. But we stay true to who we are, and that might make us saner than anyone else. That bitch should never have sealed these up."

Cheyenne frowned and glanced at the magicals dancing past them, whooping and roaring in excitement as they headed toward the other open pits to watch more fights. "That added to the mess the Crown made of this place, didn't it?"

"Oh, you told her?" Maleshi shot Corian a sidelong glance, and he dipped his head in humble acknowledgment. "I bet he didn't mention who came out of that fight with another victory under his belt, huh?"

"*Corian* won the fight?" Cheyenne's eyes widened as she glanced at them.

"I would have if he'd yielded. He never does." Maleshi tossed her dark hair out of her face and folded her arms. "Takes a lot of balls to get your ass whooped by an opponent and then *again* by the deathflame. The victory's his. I'd say he earned it."

"How does that even work?"

Corian cocked his head and grinned at the halfling. "Imagine the darktongue salve spread all over your body, kid."

"Yeah, I remember when that happened pretty clearly, thanks."

"And *inside* your body. Swimming through your veins and up into your head. If you're willing to choose that for the benefit of Ambar'ogúl."

Cheyenne nodded slowly and glanced into the pit again. "Of course you get the victory."

"Cheyenne."

She looked at Maleshi, who was smiling at her. "What?"

"You look a little pale."

Cheyenne rolled her eyes. "That's what happens when nobody tells me not to worry about my friends trying to kill each other. Hey, leave it up to the green flames turning Corian into a bonfire. No big deal."

"Okay." Corian chuckled. "Admittedly, we could have prepared you for that. Can't blame us too much for getting caught up in the moment."

"That's what you call it, huh?" Cheyenne snorted. "I almost lost it."

"I appreciate the sentiment, kid, however unnecessary."

"Obviously."

Maleshi lifted her chin and studied Cheyenne. "I'm more interested that she called us friends."

The halfling brushed away locks of white hair that had fallen out of her bun and folded her arms. "Yeah, don't let it go to your head. You're already swimming in deathflame insanity."

The nightstalkers burst out laughing.

"Come on. The whole day's a celebration, Cheyenne. Might as well make the most of it." Corian turned and nodded in the direction of the crowd swarming toward the other newly opened fighting pits. "Maybe you'll appreciate our O'gúl brand of beauty if you're not worried about two friends killing each other in the ring."

"That's a hell of a maybe." With a final glance into the pit beside them, Cheyenne followed the nightstalkers toward the other pits to join the celebration. *This world is ass-backward sometimes, but those two are looking especially chummy right now.*

"Cheyenne!" Ember floated through the streaming magicals, grinning and shaking her hands beside her head in excitement. "Did you *see* that?"

"Corian getting his throat slit? Totally."

"Oh, my God. That was amazing!" Ember laughed when Cheyenne scowled at her. "Not that Corian got this throat slit. That part sucks. I mean the fight. The fire. All of it. *That's* the fucking deathflame!"

"Apparently, yeah." Despite her shock, Cheyenne couldn't

help but laugh at her friend's passionate reaction. "*You* look like you're enjoying yourself."

"Of course I am! Come on, don't tell me you don't feel all this. I don't even know what to call it." The fae pointed at her friend and chuckled. "Happiness isn't the right word, but holy shit."

"They're free, Em."

"Yeah. I think I was going for 'connected,' but free works too. This whole thing is a lot bigger than I thought. What you did yesterday. Ah!" Ember pumped a fist and bobbed over the heads of the crowd before settling back down into her hovering position an inch above the metal floor.

"Was that a jump?"

Ember rolled her eyes. "I'm still working on that part. Doesn't quite feel the same as doing it with my own leg muscles, but I can't complain."

Laughing, Cheyenne moved through the crowd with her friend, leaning away when Ember let out a shout of excitement with everyone else. *Guess battle rage is contagious on this side. Can't be all that bad as long as nobody takes it too far.*

CHAPTER ELEVEN

A goblin and what looked like a giant hamster with bat wings and fangs got the first fight in the closest re-opened pit. The crowd of celebrating magicals had split among the six fighting pits in Vedrosha to watch the show. Others left the excitement to take to the streets of the lower levels again, dancing and drinking and celebrating in their own way now that they'd been satisfied by watching the first pit fight in centuries.

Cheyenne grimaced at the flying hamster thing darting around the goblin. "Any idea what *that* is?"

Ember grinned at her and shrugged. "Who cares? They're about to start!"

The fae girl pumped her fists, surprisingly into the fight and the raucous energy spilling through Hangivol. Cheyenne shoved her hands in her pockets and found herself studying the magicals around her fulfilling some primal O'gúleesh instinct. *Instinct for madness. That was the legacy I claimed yesterday with that damn coin.*

A hand settled lightly on her shoulder, and she turned to see L'zar behind her, gazing over her head at the crowd. "Perfect time for us to slip away, Cheyenne. They won't even notice we're gone. Come on."

"Yeah, okay." *Pretty much anything sounds better than being caught up in this right now.* Cheyenne nudged Ember's arm. "Em."

"Yeah." The fae girl turned her head but didn't look away from the fight.

"I'm stepping out with L'zar for a second."

"Yeah, sounds good. Have fun." Ember roared with everyone else when the magicals started fighting. "Get him!"

Cheyenne slipped away from her friend and followed L'zar's tall, erect figure as he practically floated through the spectators without a levitation spell. The magicals parted around them as they made their way out of Vedrosha and back into the main metropolis of the lower levels. *Like they know we're coming and step away without even seeing us. I bet he's got some kind of spell for that too.*

When they emerged from the crowd, L'zar paused to let her catch up. He rolled his shoulders, took a deep breath, and smoothed his hair away from his face before it fell around his shoulders again. "Gets loud out there, doesn't it?"

"I didn't think you'd have a problem with crowds."

He cast her a sidelong glance. "Only when they stop serving a purpose. This way."

They walked down the main avenue circling the lower level, where O'gúleesh freely brawled, drank, danced, and gathered in the street without fear of the Crown's ever-watchful gaze. A yellow-skinned gremlin leaped in front of them, cackling, and removed a ratty top hat from his head of frazzled gray hair. "A drow in Ritfarrin." The gremlin bowed low, leering up at L'zar and Cheyenne.

"And a gremlin." L'zar mocked the other magical's low bow, wiggling his head in lieu of removing a hat.

The gremlin cackled again and raced away from them, firing green sparks into the sky.

L'zar chuckled. "I like the ones who don't bother to remember who I am."

"Because they either love you or hate you, right?"

"Or they make fun of a drow in the lower levels and count themselves lucky to get away with it." L'zar clasped his hands behind his back and walked swiftly down the avenue. "Have you been to the Goldsmile dens?"

"I've seen them." Cheyenne stared at his profile and slowly shook her head. "If you're taking me to a drug den in the middle of an O'gúl riot, I'd rather jump into one of those fighting pits."

"Good. If you were anyone else, I might have given you the option of trying out one of Hangivol's finer vices. I hear the service has improved since the last time I was here."

"Yeah, because everyone's getting wasted on whatever they can to forget about how shitty things are."

"How shitty things *were*." L'zar raised an eyebrow when he glanced down at her. "You're changing all that now."

"I'm not doing anything."

"Really?" He swept his arm in a wide gesture toward the celebrating streets, every store empty or nearly empty as Hangivol's citizens forgot their everyday grind to revel in the turning of the new Cycle. "Does this look like nothing to you?"

"This looks like magicals taking a hard-won break from being ground into the dirt by the drow who are supposed to protect them."

"And *you* are changing all that." L'zar kept moving, dipping his head and smiling at the magicals who crossed their paths.

A hunched ogre wearing more scars than clothing stepped out a doorway in the shadows between the metal buildings and held out a sealed flask. He wiggled it so they'd hear the liquid sloshing and leered at them. "Two drow beyond the Heartland, eh? Either of you care for a little augur spice?"

"Ooh. Tempting." L'zar danced away from the ogre with a little bow, then peered into the darkened doorway behind the magical. "You open for business?"

"Making the most of this fortnight before we see how the Cycle turns." The ogre chuckled darkly. "You're welcome to come in and look around."

"Hmm." L'zar bit his lip, paused, then shook his head. "Another time, perhaps. I know where to find you."

"You always do." The ogre bowed at the waist and disappeared into the darkened doorway again.

Cheyenne watched until even his bright yellow eyes disappeared, then hurried to catch up with her father. "I'm gonna take a wild guess here and say he was hawking illegal stuff."

"That wasn't hawking, Cheyenne. That was astutely seizing a business opportunity." L'zar said, "He's a darkseller. Deals in stolen items."

"Oh, so you'd be a regular customer, then."

"Stolen *organic* items."

She snorted. "What, like nightstalker blood and gremlin toes? Maybe skaxen whiskers just for fun?"

"Don't be ridiculous. Skaxen whiskers are useless."

"You're serious."

They veered around three brawling trolls on the side of the street, and L'zar looked over his shoulder to watch them a little longer before facing forward again. "Of course I'm serious. You hit the other two right on the head, though."

Gross. Cheyenne grimaced and tried not to think about a jar of severed yellow toes being rattled around in the ogre's hand instead of the flask.

L'zar stopped abruptly, leaned back, and peered into another dark alley between buildings. "Here we are."

He didn't wait for her to realize he'd doubled back, and

Cheyenne spun to look for him before catching a fleeting glance of his white hair disappearing. Rolling her eyes, she hurried after him. "You gotta give me a heads up before you disappear into dark spaces."

"You won't need a heads up if you keep up." L'zar turned another corner, winding his way through the maze of dark alleys.

Gritting her teeth, Cheyenne jogged to catch up with him and had to keep jogging so she wouldn't lose him after every turn. *How can he be moving this fast and walking normally at the same time?*

Her activator pulled up fewer and fewer data streams from within the metal walls as they moved deeper into the lower levels. Then L'zar stopped beside a wall on their right and reached out to press his hand against it. Metal sections peeled away beneath his touch, clinking and folding together like a slinky made of square pieces before a doorway revealed another covered dark passage beyond.

Cheyenne looked at the thin lines of gray light filtering through the tops of the buildings around them. "We couldn't have walked here from the *outside?*"

"What, you don't enjoy navigating a maze?" L'zar gestured toward the opening. "You get points for a keen sense of direction, Cheyenne, but this does *not* lead back to the outer limits."

She eyed the dark passage and lifted her chin. "Where does it lead?"

"I'm about to show you, aren't I? Hurry up. The wall won't stay open much longer." He stepped into the passage, and the metal pieces started to unfold and close up the hole.

Cheyenne leaped forward and squeezed through the moving pieces with half a second to spare before the wall sealed once more. A ball of pale violet flames burst to life in L'zar's hand to light the way for them as they continued down another series of twisting, turning corridors. Shadows danced across the walls, and Cheyenne slid her hand along them when she realized the activator wasn't picking up anything here. *Feels like stone.*

"No tech in the walls down here, huh?"

"No magicals, either." L'zar lifted his hand to illuminate the walls, peering closely at one before continuing. "No one wants to go where we're going."

"Oh, wonderful."

He chuckled. "Why waste technology on a place you know no one's going to visit? Of course, there's not much on the outside stopping others from getting *in*."

Cheyenne rolled her eyes. "Right. Just what's on the inside that makes them wanna stay *out*. Care to enlighten me about that?"

"Not really."

The tunnel headed slightly downward but nowhere near as far as the tunnels leading into the Four-Pointed Star's secret bunker. Then L'zar snuffed out the purple flames in his hand and exited the tunnel, stepping aside to let Cheyenne through.

"Whoa."

They stood in a small courtyard made entirely of black stone. It looked much like the courtyard in the heart of the Crown's fortress, but this one was the size of a small house. Two twisted, gnarled trees grew from the cracked stone floors, their branches coiling in every direction. From the branches hung potted plants, tendrils, and leaves overflowing from the tops in shriveled black threads. Bottles of dark-colored glass dotted the courtyard, filled with shimmering liquids and lights of every color, though they were all muted and tinged with a darkness that made Cheyenne's skin crawl.

"Looks like someone failed at their gardening attempts."

"Not at all." L'zar clasped his hands behind his back again and walked slowly across the courtyard, reaching up with one extended finger toward the closest potted plant hanging from a tree branch. The shriveled black vine pulsed with sickly green light like an electrical current and lifted away from the pot toward L'zar's finger. He smiled thinly and removed his hand before the plant could make contact. "This is how they're supposed to be. The magical responsible for flora in here is very good at what she does."

"So." Cheyenne turned slowly around, eyeing the dark corners of the courtyard and the tattered, frayed black cloth draped over one wall. "Who is this magical, exactly?"

L'zar chuckled softly. "I wouldn't call her a friend, but if there's one magical in this fell-damn world my sister truly fears, it's Ur'syth."

"Ur'syth?"

"Say it three times, and she'll appear in front of us."

She snorted. "They let you watch *Beetlejuice* in Chateau D'rahl?"

L'zar merely smiled and turned to casually stroll across the courtyard.

Cheyenne followed him, ducking when the branches of the gnarled tree shivered and creaked, reaching out toward her. "What does she do?"

"All sorts of things, Cheyenne. Be quiet." L'zar peered into a dark corner of the courtyard, then straightened and turned slowly around again. "Ur'syth! Dark Mother. I can't say I expected to find you in the Heart, but I'm sure you didn't expect me to find you here either, did you? Come out and see what I've brought with me." He stuck his hands in his pockets and shot Cheyenne a playful wink.

She stepped away from the tree, scowling at it as the branches returned to their original positions. *This better be one of those quick in-and-out visits. I like creepy stuff, but this takes it to a whole new level.*

CHAPTER TWELVE

"Ur'syth?" There was laughter in L'zar's voice as he strolled across the courtyard. "I'll summon you if I have to, but we both know you and I are past that point. Don't keep me waiting too long."

The black cloth hanging over the wall whipped in a wind that didn't blow through the rest of the courtyard. L'zar's eyes widened when he saw the fabric move. He met Cheyenne's gaze and nodded toward the tattered black sheet before it billowed out into the courtyard as if the wind came from the wall itself.

"You're early." A grating voice like sandpaper came from behind L'zar, and he whirled, laughing when he saw the hunched, shriveled figure draped in black rags.

"So, you *were* expecting me."

A shrouded arm rose from the tattered folds, and a dark-gray finger poked from the end of the sleeve toward L'zar's face. The crone's features were invisible in the thick blackness within her hood. "I expected you at the end of days, Weaver, when the deathflame takes us all and Ambar'ogúl sails upon the tides of all its dead. Which basically means never. So yes, you're early."

The figure sidled forward and returned her hand to the folds of her tattered rags. "Show me what you've brought, then. Is it a gift?"

"Of sorts." L'zar stepped aside and turned to gesture toward his daughter. "Cheyenne, come meet Ur'syth."

Cheyenne straightened and stared at the shriveled figure. She raised an eyebrow. "I'm good."

The crone wheezed with laughter, batting L'zar aside with a flapping hand to approach Cheyenne. The drow stepped easily out of her path and watched her limp toward his daughter.

Cheyenne glanced at him and stuck her hands in her pockets. *I was seriously hoping to leave the creepy stuff behind today.*

"You." The crone lifted both hands to her hood and pulled it back in a puff of dust and black particles that danced behind her in the still air.

The halfling's stomach clenched when she saw Ur'syth's face—wrinkled lines in dark flesh, beady black eyes, black paint flaking on her face from forehead to chin, and sharp, pointed teeth within a mouth as red and glistening as freshly spilled blood. The face from her dreams. "*You.*"

The sharp teeth glinted at her when Ur'syth's lips twitched into a sneer. "I am always myself, *hinya*. You are something else half the time, are you not?" The crone raised a hand toward L'zar and waved him forward. "Who is this?"

"Cheyenne."

"You gave me her name already, you grinning idiot. Who *is* she?"

L'zar clasped his hands behind his back and straightened, that feral glint in his golden eyes giving him a disturbingly hungry look. "My heir. My daughter, Ur'syth. Why else did you think the new Cycle turned when you felt it like the rest of us? The Rahalma has already received her *marandúr*. It's done."

Ur'syth gazed at Cheyenne's face, or at least her fully black eyes glinted with movement. *No pupils. I can't tell what the hell she's looking at.*

The crone nodded at her, her blood-red tongue poking out between her lips. The spittle left behind on her lips and teeth looked a lot like blood too. "As it was foretold."

"No." L'zar stalked toward them, his smile widening into a twitching grin. "Your prophecy was shit, Oracle. Sure, it took me a thousand years or more to prove it, but I did. That's *my* daughter standing before you. The Crown's newest challenger."

"Yes, you said that too." Ur'syth turned to peer up at the drow, one shoulder hunched to the side. She cocked her head and sneered. "Did you bring her here to label me a heretic, or to prove to yourself that you've achieved whatever victory you sought?"

He stared calmly down at her and shrugged. "Both, most likely."

The crone narrowed her eyes at him, then burst into wheezing, gasping cackles.

L'zar's golden eyes flickered toward Cheyenne's. Her nostrils flared and she shook her head. *Proof for me too. No one in this world is sane.*

The drow thief pressed his lips together and stared down his nose at the Oracle hag cracking up in front of him. Ur'syth flapped a wrinkled, mottled gray hand in front of her face, the black rags fluttering around her bony wrist. One cloth-wrapped foot thumped softly on the stone floor, and the crone shook her head as quickly as her deteriorating body would allow.

"I'd love to share the jest with you," L'zar muttered, his smile thin and tight now in irritation.

"You would, wouldn't you?" Ur'syth fell into a fit of hacking coughs and spat out a nasty black ball of phlegm. It landed in one of the potted plants, and a black, shriveled O'gúleesh version of a Venus flytrap snapped its brittle mouth closed around the unexpected offering.

Cheyenne wanted to spit herself and clenched her jaw instead. *No wonder the Crown hates this creature.*

Ur'syth cleared her throat, her sharp, pointed teeth glinting in her red grin. She wagged a finger at L'zar. "It's all fun jests and playful mischief for the Dark Smiling Weaver until he realizes what a fool he's been. Until he discovers he made himself the center of a universal jest much larger than himself."

L'zar's nose twitched. "And what might that be?"

"My prophecies are always fully and completely true, you drow-headed buffoon."

He gestured at Cheyenne again. "Clearly."

"*Clearly*, you didn't take my interpretation of the threads at the full value with which I delivered them. *Clearly*, you came out of my circle that day already assuming I was wrong."

"You were."

"All this time, and you're still dumber than my plants. Ha!" Ur'syth moved around Cheyenne again and peered up at the halfling. "I told you every child of yours you pursued would perish before their time. This one only lived because you abandoned her from the start. Quite a blow to your overinflated ego, isn't it?"

L'zar snorted and eyed the crone up and down. "I suspected you already knew where the loophole was."

"Not the prophecy's loophole, *Cu'ón.* Mine." The crone hissed out another laugh, pricking her shiny red tongue with her sharpened teeth. "I merely failed to spell it out for you. Wouldn't be much of an Oracle if I had, eh?"

"Now you know I found it."

"Oh, sure. She knows too. Don't you, Cheyenne?"

Hearing her name on the crone's tongue, slightly accented at the end with growling O'gúleesh sounds, sent a chill down the halfling's spine. She forced herself not to back away from the beady eyes inching closer despite Ur'syth being at least two feet shorter.

"If he left you to suffer in our sister world, to grow into what you are now standing here before me, tell me how you came to my front door together."

Cheyenne stared at what she thought were the centers of the Oracle's all-black eyes. *Maybe the whole thing's one giant pupil.* "I followed him through the streets."

"Oh. You think you're as amusing as he thinks *he* is. I can't say I'm surprised." Ur'syth's tongue ran over her sharpened teeth. From within the folds of her tattered robes came the sound of nails scratching dry flesh. Cheyenne's nostrils flared. "Did you seek him out, then? Did you pine after your nonexistent father and search the threads for him like he searched for you? Eh? Did you blaze a trail of scorched earth and broken promises like he did?"

Cheyenne pursed her lips, fighting back the spitting snarl she wanted to shove in the old Oracle's face. *She's goading me. Don't get pissed and stupid, Cheyenne.* "No. I didn't seek him out."

"And yet here you are together, yes? Here you've returned, to Hangivol, the seat of the O'gúl Crown, to claim your birthright and turn the new Cycle toward you, a fully acknowledged drow in all her glory. Don't be obtuse, girl. I know you couldn't have done it without him."

The halfling took a deep breath. "I went after an orc who almost killed my friend. Then I found L'zar safe and snug in a half-assed Earthside prison, and he took it from there."

"Oh, is *that* all?"

"Long story short, yeah."

"Very simple. Very amusing." Ur'syth hissed out more laughter and tilted her head from side to side. A black-nailed finger stabbed toward Cheyenne's face. "And you didn't once go looking for the man who sired the magic running through your veins?"

"I stopped wondering who my father was when I was six, so no. It's more like he fell into my lap."

"Ah!" The crone shrieked with laughter, which cut off abruptly when another coughing fit wracked her.

Cheyenne closed her eyes and turned her head away. *Please don't spit again. Jesus, I can smell her breath.*

"L'zar Verdys does have that tendency, doesn't he? *Falling where everyone else least wants him to land.*" Ur'syth winked at Cheyenne and looked her up and down again. "And here you are now. The youngest of how many dead, L'zar?"

"That doesn't matter."

Cheyenne looked at him sharply and bit her lip, glaring at him. *All his dead kids, and he says they don't* matter?

"Perhaps not to you, Weaver. Perhaps not to the rest of us. But they mattered." Ur'syth nodded slowly. "Oh, yes. But not as much as this one." In a blur, the Oracle's hands lashed out from under her robes. Clammy, ice-cold hands clamped around Cheyenne's wrist while the crone jerked up the sleeve of the halfling's jacket.

Cheyenne immediately yanked her hand away in disgust and rubbed her wrist on the side of her jacket.

Ur'syth cackled. "Oh! Did I startle you?"

"I don't like being touched."

"Of course not. That's the easiest way to see the truth, isn't it?" The Oracle pointed at the thick silver band around Cheyenne's wrist. "Especially when someone went through such pains to hide it from the rest of us. Born Earthside to a human mother, I see."

"My mother has nothing to do with this," Cheyenne snarled, her composure snapping as her drow magic burned up her spine. Purple light flared behind her golden eyes.

Ur'syth grinned. "Not yet." She pointed at the metal cuff and turned toward L'zar. "I should have known *your* hand was the one to snatch up that little trinket."

The drow thief smiled back at her with a shrug of fake humility. "I've got a reputation to uphold, Ur'syth, and we both know you wouldn't have given it to me."

"It's been put to an acceptable use." The Oracle stepped away from Cheyenne, giving her another once-over with those glistening black eyes. "L'zar's halfling heir, eh? It *shouldn't* make a difference in the matter of a new Crown turning her own Cycle. But it might. Or it might not."

Cheyenne gave the old magical a bitter smile. "It hasn't stopped me so far."

"Indeed."

"Ur'syth." L'zar lifted his chin when the Oracle turned to face him again. "Read the weave for my daughter."

"What do you bring as an offering?"

He removed his hand from behind his back and held out a small vial filled with a dark liquid that looked like muddy water. Wiggling the vial at her, L'zar raised his eyebrows. "Right off a darkseller."

"Ah. Come then." Ur'syth waved her hand for L'zar to approach, and he set the vial gently in her wrinkled gray palm. Her hand and the vial disappeared into her tattered robes, and she sneered up at the thief.

"Make it a good one, Oracle."

"That's for *her* to decide." The crone sidled past Cheyenne toward the base of the gnarled tree on the right and grunted as she lowered herself to the stone floor.

L'zar headed toward his daughter and dipped his head. "This will be fun."

"What?" Cheyenne glanced at the haggard gray face emerging from the pile of tattered black rags on the ground and shook her head. "No. No one said anything about more prophecies. I don't need any more of that kind of crazy in my life."

"Too bad, Cheyenne. It's already been paid for." He leaned

toward her and lowered his voice. "You don't change your mind once the offering's been accepted. Not in Ur'syth's house." L'zar nodded, then stepped past his daughter and calmly sat in front of the crone, crossing his legs beneath him.

Cheyenne let out a deep, frustrated sigh and swallowed. *I already know this is gonna be bad.*

CHAPTER THIRTEEN

Ur'syth reached out for the closest potted plant on the ground beside her. The courtyard echoed with the grating crunch of small stones scraping across the ground beneath the metal pot. The dead-looking plant inside it shrieked when the crone's hand plunged into the pot and ripped out a large, blue-pulsing root. The thing squirmed in her tight grip, mewling like a baby animal. Ur'syth scooted the pot aside and raised the root to her mouth. Her pointy teeth tore into its flesh, and it let out a piercing scream as glowing bright blue sludge squirted from its center. Most of it dribbled down the Oracle's open mouth as she laughed, but a handful of wayward specks splattered the hem of Cheyenne's trenchcoat where she sat beside her father.

"Ugh." She leaned away from the crone, her drow sense of smell picking up the thick decaying odors mixed with the scent of copper and the stench of rancid fish.

Beside her, L'zar chuckled.

"Shut up, both of you." Ur'syth thoughtfully chewed the piece of root in her mouth and used the other half of it like a paintbrush, drawing the blue sludge down the line of paint on her face from forehead to chin. Grinning, she tossed the other root away and spat a purple-blue wad into her gnarled hands. Once she'd rubbed that into her palms like skin lotion, she set the backs of both hands on her knees and closed her eyes.

Cheyenne shot L'zar a sidelong glance. He gestured for her to keep watching. *Maleshi was right about Oracles. I'm done with them.*

A low, crackling moan came from Ur'syth's slightly parted lips. When her eyes fluttered open, they were white, rolling around in her head. Her voice rose in volume, not in thousands of tones like the raug Oracle's voice but just hers, grating and gravelly.

"The Cycle turns."

The crone was silent for so long, Cheyenne snorted. "Is that it?"

L'zar raised a finger to his smiling lips and stared at the Oracle.

"Crowns rise and fall. Tides of power raise all bloodlines into the Everweave. The bright is no more, and the darkness abides. The sword will pierce the heart. Shackles unbinding. Shackles pinned to pillars of hidden dreaming. A Crown is not a Crown without the blood of all. The blood of one will consume the Crown. The blood of one will lift the tides. The blood of one will sway the doorways into endless flux, and the gates will fall to ruin. To tear, to grieve, to unite the rift between what has always been and what will never be. But only here."

Ur'syth swayed where she sat, her voice lowered again into mumbled words Cheyenne couldn't make out. Then she sucked in a deep breath, her eyes rolling back in her head, and slumped against the tree. When she opened her eyes again, they'd returned to their unnatural all-black shade.

"Really?" L'zar stroked his chin and frowned at the crone, who was struggling to push herself away from the rough bark at her back. The tree shuddered and groaned in protest. "I said, make it a good one."

"And *I* said it was up to the *Aranél* to decide whether or not it's *a good one.*" Ur'syth coughed and pointed weakly at the halfling. "You are the only one who can make the decision, Cheyenne. Choose wisely."

Cheyenne blinked. "I have no idea how to tell if a prophecy is good."

The old crone wheezed with laughter again and shook her head. "Not *that* decision, *hinya*. The blood of one will do many things, yes? You must choose the one."

"I have no idea what you're talking about."

Ur'syth cocked her head abnormally far toward her shoulder and grinned. "Ask your father to help you with that one, eh? He's had thousands of years to practice the art."

A thunderous, bellowing explosion rose from the center of the city. All three of them saw a shimmering mushroom cloud of strobing colors peeking above the highest wall of the court-yard. "What was that?"

L'zar slowly lowered his hand to the stone floor to push himself to his feet. "I don't know."

The ground bucked beneath them without warning, making the trees creak even louder and the hanging plants swing violently from their ropes.

The muted gray sky beneath Hangivol's domed shield flashed with brilliant colors one right after the next, and another explosion wracked the center of the city. Ur'syth's glass vials and jars toppled over onto the stone and rolled in every direction. The ground shook so violently that the second tree ripped half its roots from the ground and lurched forward, suspended sideways when the rest of its root system held fast however many feet below the surface.

Ur'syth shrieked at the sky. Cheyenne looked again and only saw colors. *What's making her freak out?*

The old Oracle convulsed where she sat, her pointed teeth chattering and her wrinkled hands flapping away from her lap over and over as if she tried to shoo away a cat. Streaks of black light pulsed from her fingers.

Cheyenne and L'zar leaped to their feet to avoid being blasted by the Oracle's magical fit. "Seriously, L'zar, what's going on?"

"I said, I don't know. Can't tell you any more than that."

"What's wrong with her?"

Ur'syth trembled on the stone floor, her arms jerking in awkward directions. A thick choking sound burst from her mouth.

"We can at least do something to help her!"

"If you want to get close to whatever magic she's letting off right now, Cheyenne, be my guest." L'zar staggered sideways across the trembling stone floor and caught himself with a hand on the sideways-leaning tree. Roots snapped with an earsplitting crunch, and the tree fell the rest of the way to the ground.

"Ur'syth?" Cheyenne shouted over the next round of rumbling explosions from the city center. "Can you hear me?"

The ancient Oracle shrieked again, whipped both hands out to either side in a moment of lucidity, and disappeared.

"What?"

"Come on." L'zar snatched her wrist and dragged her across the courtyard, ducking beneath the rocking potted plants and the dangling vines now lashing out toward the fleeing drow.

"You guys get a lot of earthquakes on this side?" Cheyenne shouted.

He pulled her into the stone passage leading to Ur'syth's courtyard and finally released her wrist as she hurried after him. "Not really."

"How about new portals opening up when and where you least expect them?"

L'zar snorted. "This isn't a new portal, Cheyenne. This is the city."

"Really? 'Cause I've been around *twice* when those things opened up Earthside, and it looks and feels exactly like this."

"Those new portals are overflow. The real problem's right here. Stop talking and move faster."

Gritting her teeth, Cheyenne stumbled when the tunnel bucked and shifted. She and L'zar caught themselves against opposite walls and pushed into a run. A minute later, L'zar passed his hand over an indiscriminate metal wall, which vanished instantly and led them right into the main avenue of Hangivol's lowest level.

The halfling gazed at the open area and glanced back once before the wall shimmered into place again. *Did he take a shortcut?*

L'zar stopped in the center of the avenue, his golden eyes wide as he craned his neck to take in the bursting, churning magic spilling into the sky from the center of the city. He ran a hand over his mouth and took a deep breath.

"So, who's blowing up the Heart?" Cheyenne stopped beside him. Screams echoed down the avenue from far away, growing louder as the magicals on the outskirts of the city realized what was happening.

"Who do you think?"

"The Crown wouldn't blow up her own—"

"Not on purpose, Cheyenne. That doesn't make her any less of a fell-damn idiot. Let's go." He reached for her arm again, but she leaped out of the way.

"We have to do something."

"There's nothing to be done!" he snarled and pointed at the dome. "This place is about to rip itself apart."

A splintering crack rent the air, followed by another massive tremble in the ground beneath them. Then a bright line of multicolored light raced down the center of the outer level's main avenue, zigzagging in a jagged fissure and spewing magical light into the air.

Cheyenne's activator was working overtime to analyze everything that was happening within and below the city. It responded to each of her thoughts as if she were processing it all, and she pointed at one of many cracks splintering outward across the ground from the Heart of Hangivol. "We can fix this."

"Don't be an idiot."

"Fine. I'll do it myself." She took off down the avenue, darting away from the magical blasts shooting up from the crack in the ground and trying to keep her balance as the entire city shuddered in an endless quake.

"Cheyenne!" L'zar roared. "Get back here!"

She flipped him the bird without stopping and disappeared around the bend in the street.

With a snarl, L'zar whirled toward the outer edge of the city. A mile away, the shouts and screams of the O'gúleesh at the fighting pits rose above the constant rumble beneath the streets. *We could've been out of here by now and left this whole thing behind us.*

Hissing, he turned back and took off after his daughter. *You're gonna get us both killed, Cheyenne. And you won't be able to climb out from under that debt to be paid.*

CHAPTER FOURTEEN

Cheyenne leaped away from a branching crack splitting off from the main fissure. Her activator pulled up a huge, blinking yellow arrow. *Right around the corner. That's where we can put it back.*

A shrill scream came from her right, and she skidded to a stop to see a group of magicals running out of an alley toward her, their eyes wide with terror. One of the buildings behind them started to sink, crumbling in on itself as the ground buckled beneath it. Cheyenne scanned the stats the activator gave her and nodded. *I can make it.*

"Stop!" L'zar grabbed her wrist again and jerked her back.

Cheyenne whirled and slammed her fist into his face, powering it with a sphere of crackling black energy balled in her hand. L'zar grunted and staggered backward, blinking against the daze as she shook out her hand. "Either help me or get the fuck out of here, but don't try to stop me again."

"Wait!"

She darted toward the slowly collapsing alley where the screaming magicals still spilled out of the space between buildings. "Over here!" She waved them toward her, and the frightened O'gúleesh headed her way without a second thought. "How many more are in there?"

"I don't know." The troll she asked barreled past her as he answered, looking over his shoulder.

The buildings crashed against another, spewing sparks and shrieks as metal ripped into metal. Cheyenne ran toward the collapsing alley and threw up a shield of dark, shimmering drow light. The force of the top half of the building toppling onto her shield made her cry out in an effort to keep it up. Marching closer, she raised her hands above her head and sank to her knees when more of the building toppled onto her broad shield. *A little heavier than that construction site. No problem.*

O'gúleesh raced past her, dragging each other along. A wide-eyed goblin dropped his tankard on the ground, and Cheyenne snarled at him when he stopped to pick it up. "Go!"

He jumped and scurried around her. With a deep breath, Cheyenne slipped into drow speed and released the shield. As soon as she got to her feet, L'zar barreled into her, and they both went flying away from the collapsing building and the spray of unleashed magic spewing through the closing alley faster than either drow could move.

Grunting, Cheyenne rolled across the cracked metal and pushed herself to her feet.

"Are you okay?" L'zar scanned her as he approached.

"So you decided to help. I'm fine."

"We need to go."

"Not yet." She spun and scanned the avenue for the source of the bright yellow arrow in her vision. "I can turn all this off. Probably temporarily, but it's something."

"Cheyenne, I can't risk it."

"You don't get to decide for me!" She stalked toward the yellow arrow blinking in her vision, ignoring his growl of disapproval.

"You're making this incredibly difficult."

"No, that would be you."

The ground bucked beneath them again, but she managed to keep her balance this time. When she finally reached the blinking yellow arrow, the activator displayed brand new lines of code and overlapping diagrams along the wall of a short, squat building another block off the main avenue. She studied the data and pressed her hand to the wall.

"We don't have time for you to play around with this shit," L'zar snarled. Right on cue, another explosion came from the center of the city.

"Shut up." Cheyenne selected the best of the activator's next presented options, and with a swipe of her finger against the wall, the O'gúl version of a breaker box opened in a recessed square in the wall. She bent over and reached inside as far as she could, feeling for the lever the wall should have created on its own under her command.

"What are you doing?" L'zar ran his hand over his head and looked between her and the mushrooming cloud of volatile magic spewing toward the top of the dome-shaped shield.

She ignored him and finally found the lever, giving it a quick jerk as she poked the illuminated symbols on the wall. A loud, pressurized hiss filled the avenue. When she looked up, she saw the muted gray dome above Hangivol shimmer, flicker, and disappear. The released magical cloud caught inside burst from the top of the city and rose straight into the sky like a beacon.

Metal and earth groaned around them, and Cheyenne removed her hand from the hole in the wall before it sealed itself.

L'zar's mouth popped open as he stared at the clear sky above them. "Did you just do that?"

"That and other things, yeah."

"How? You know what, never mind. Let's go."

"Wait." Cheyenne glared at him as she stalked down the

block again and entered the main avenue. The spewing magical light dimmed beneath the giant crack in the ground, then tiny metal squares folded and unfolded themselves along the fissure, drawing the floor slowly back together and sealing the crevasse in less than a minute.

The ground stopped trembling, and a deep groan rose from beneath the city before everything was still and quiet again, except for the column of magic still spewing from the center of Hangivol into the sky.

Cheyenne gestured toward the mended ground. "Told you."

"Incredible." L'zar chuckled, slowly shaking his head. "You instinctively knew how to do whatever that was?"

"This activator is no joke." With a flick of her finger, she dimmed the scrolling data feeds on every metal surface so they wouldn't distract her. *Better keep it on just in case, though.* "What idiot thought keeping a magical shield around a city filled with brewing magic was a good idea?"

He spread his arms. "Again, nearly every bad choice in this place can be traced back to Ba'rael. That shield was one of the first things to go up when she started making changes."

"It was part of the damn problem. Those fellfire pits outside the city. No one would be working those today, right?"

"Not a chance. No one's working."

"Good, 'cause I just let off a whole bunch of magical pressure through them. That's what this was, right?"

L'zar blinked at the magic shooting from the city center as his daughter stormed past him and back down the avenue. "If you're talking about all the magic my moronic sister was storing in her torture chambers, I'm inclined to agree with you. Yes."

"Good thing the moron gene ended with me."

The drow thief spun and followed her, laughing. "And I had nothing to do with that, huh?"

"No, I don't think you did." Cheyenne stopped and whirled

on him, shoving a finger in his face. "The Crown isn't the only one around here I can blame for making stupid choices. What the hell *was* that back there?"

He tilted his head. "Which part?"

"The part where you kept running away like a coward to save yourself. The part where you tried to drag me with you when I clearly knew what I was doing and could save this city and the people *you* told me I'm here to protect!" She shoved his chest with both hands, and L'zar staggered backward.

His smile disappeared. "I don't want to lose you too, Cheyenne."

"This isn't about me, this is about your self-righteous power games. You're willing to let everyone else fend for themselves, even if they end up dead, because they aren't part of your master plan."

"Cheyenne!"

"Shut up!" She launched a crackling sphere of black energy at his face, and he ducked but didn't step back. "If you want me to do any of this, giving the Crown her terms, taking the throne or not taking the throne, helping to put this screwed-up world back together, don't even think about telling me I'm wrong or that I don't understand. I get how you work, L'zar. It's great that you wanna protect me, but it's too late to think I'll start listening to you now over what *I* know I can do."

He pressed his lips together. "I did get you out of the way of all that magic shooting through the alley."

"Please." Cheyenne rolled her eyes and turned away from him to stalk down the avenue again. "I wasn't even close to being in real danger."

With a deep breath, L'zar took one more look at the pillar of dazzling, churning magic spilling into the sky and hurried after his daughter. *She's not exactly like me, not in this.* When he caught up with her, he stuck his hands in his pockets and easily matched her agitated stride. "You know, you would make an *excellent* Crown if you decided to stay. I'm inclined to think your human blood is responsible for that."

She snorted. "You're not a selfish asshole because you're *not* human, L'zar. Me being half-human doesn't make my decisions for me either."

"Maybe. Maybe not." The drow thief chuckled and didn't say another word.

Cheyenne snuck a quick glance at him and found him staring at the blue sky as they walked down the avenue. *Looks like I got my point across. Maybe you* can *teach an old drow new tricks.*

CHAPTER FIFTEEN

They met up with the others at the fighting pits in Vedrosha. Most of the magicals had scattered and returned to their homes and stores on the lower levels. Some O'gúleesh remained to help with the cleanup, which mostly amounted to getting the magicals lying on the ground back on their feet and inspected for serious injuries.

Cheyenne found Ember surrounded by magicals holding bleeding faces and arms, clutching whatever hurt and waiting their turn. The fae girl reached toward the next injured magical in line, her palms glowing with a slightly brighter violet light than her other spells before fading again.

The healed magicals stared at their mended wounds and bowed to the fae girl, muttering their thanks before heading out of Vedrosha to regroup somewhere else. Cheyenne waited for Ember to tend to the last of them, then approached.

"So you're whipping up healing spells now after magical disasters, huh?"

Ember grinned when she saw the halfling and raised her pink-tinged hands. "I don't even *need* spells. It just happens."

"You know, I've heard things about the fae's innate healing."

Cheyenne snorted. "The only things that come out of my hands are magical bombs and whips."

"Everybody's got a calling, right?" Ember's smile faded as she glanced at the column of magic at the city's center. "What happened?"

Cheyenne looked over her shoulder at L'zar, who had joined Corian, Maleshi, and some of the other rebel magicals to explain his version of events. *Probably downplaying his panic to get the hell out, too.* "Remember that room we fought our way through yesterday? With the pool of black whatever and the bubble of light in the ceiling?"

The fae girl frowned. "Yeah. They were stealing magic in there."

"That magic had to go somewhere, right? I'm pretty sure the Crown sucked up too much of it and overloaded the city somehow. I fixed it for now. I think."

"That was you, huh?" Maleshi's strained smile made her look incredibly tired when she approached them. "You just happened to find the O'gúl breaker box to turn off the dome shield and let off the extra pressure."

"No, I found *one* place where I could access all those things. I'm sure there are more on different levels."

Maleshi briefly set a hand on Cheyenne's shoulder and nodded. "Whatever you did, it seems to have worked. We can't be sure how long it will last, though."

"I know. That's a problem."

Corian joined them with a concerned frown. "And it could quickly turn into a large, very dangerous problem. You made the right call, kid. Honestly, I'm glad this happened. Now we know what else we have to deal with when your two weeks are up."

"You mean, getting all that extra magic back under control, so it doesn't rip up the city?"

"Forget ripping it up." Corian scratched behind his tufted

ear and grimaced at the pillar of shimmering light. "Hangivol could be blown off the map entirely, and millions of citizens with it."

"What about dampening wards like Maleshi cast on the portals?"

Maleshi shook her head. "Those new portals were apparently just overflow."

Cheyenne cast a scathing glance at L'zar, who conveniently chose that moment to turn away from the group and study the escaping magic. "So I heard."

"Dampening wards or binding spells are only a temporary patch, anyway. I'm not sure they'd be any more effective than what you did. Obviously, we can't keep trying to hold this magic *in*. The Crown's attempt at that already failed."

Ember rubbed her arm and shrugged. "What about evacuating the city? Get everyone out of here, and then if something happens…"

"I like where your mind's headed, Ember." Maleshi shook her head. "But that would make things even worse. It's a small part of the bigger picture, but the last Nimlothar tree still stands at the center of the Heart. At least, I hope it does after this, and it won't do any good for this world if the capital disappears off the face of it. The Crown and the Heart will both be gone. That leaves a massive power vacuum around here, and Ambar'ogúl will become the biggest battleground any of us have ever seen. Bigger than anything in the world's history, I'd bet. Hangivol isn't just a city. It has a power of its own."

"Like, it's alive?" Ember watched the nightstalkers.

"In its own way." Corian dipped his head, clasping his hands behind his back. "The kind of explosion that could very well take out this entire city won't be contained. Imagine someone nuking Washington DC and taking out the entire eastern half of the US with it. Not something we can afford to let happen."

Cheyenne folded her arms. "So, what do we do?"

"That's what we need to figure out." Corian glanced at L'zar's back as the drow thief watched the magical pillar and listened in on the conversation at the same time. "And quickly. We can't afford a long deliberation about this."

L'zar's rebels gathered around one of the open fighting pits, everyone sitting down at the edges and dangling their feet, claws, or hooves over the white sand below as they discussed their options.

Cheyenne fought back a smile as she gazed around the square of deliberating rebels. *Not as sophisticated as sitting around a table, but I guess it works.*

"So, a hold's out of the question, then?"

"Of course it is. It would take all of us combined to hold back a fraction of what's seeping out of the Heart as we speak."

"I don't suppose Ba'rael's alchemists came up with a way to distribute magic to more than one individual."

L'zar snorted. "She must be furious right now."

Corian shot him an exasperated glance. "I'm normally fond of your ability to find amusement in every situation. Now's not one of those times."

"Just an observation, *vae shra'ni*." The drow shrugged and set his hands behind him on the metal floor to lean back and look up at the clear blue sky.

"Do we know any conjurers?"

"Not closer than three days from here, and you know they won't accept a journey by portal. Impossible to pinpoint them anyway."

"What about our alchemists?"

"We don't *have* any alchemists, Jara'ak. She took them all."

A dozen more options were offered, and the conversation

grew into a shouting match as the Four-Pointed Star realized they were wasting time and still couldn't come to a satisfying conclusion. L'zar raised his eyebrows at Cheyenne and leaped away from the edge of the pit, shoving his hands in his pockets and pacing across the open metal ground.

"All right, stop. Stop!" Maleshi raised both hands, and when the magicals around her kept arguing, she sent two bolts of silver lightning into the opposite wall of the pit. They stopped immediately and looked at her.

"Well?"

"I'm not sure yet. I can't think when you're all squabbling like these two." Maleshi tossed a hand toward Lumil and Byrd, who were sitting along the adjacent wall of the pit. Lumil elbowed Byrd in the side, and she bumped her into her other neighbor with a grunt.

Corian lifted his head. "We could take a request to the *Sorren Gán*."

L'zar spun toward the pit and shook his head. "Absolutely not. Keep thinking."

"None of us wanted to say it, brother, but it's the most obvious solution."

"There's always a way around the obvious solution, Corian. Cheyenne's proof of that." L'zar nodded at his daughter and picked up his pacing again. This time, it was tense and aggravated.

"L'zar." Foltr smacked his stick against the pit wall beside his dangling legs. "You know how that could help us. Follow that knowledge and set your cowardice aside, will you?"

The drow thief whirled on the elderly raug and snarled, "I'm *not* going. That's my final word, and if I have to order each and every one of you not to mention it again, I will."

Foltr laughed deeply and swung his cane up to point at Cheyenne. "You gave up the right to give us orders when you handed over your blood right to your daughter. Unless *she* orders me to be silent, I'll sing about the *Sorren Gán* all night if I have to."

L'zar's eyes widened, and he sneered at the shriveled raug. Foltr raised his thick brows, and the drow snarled before spinning away into more pacing.

"I think that's our best option at this point." Corian nodded and pushed himself up. "Does anyone disagree with me?"

The rebels exchanged wary glances but didn't offer any protest.

"Then we'll send out a party. I'm happy to make the journey again."

"I'm not," L'zar spat. Corian ignored him.

"There's a first time for everything." With a wry chuckle, Maleshi stood and dusted off her pants. "I wouldn't miss this trip for the world. Hell, for both of them."

"Anyone else who wants to be part of this is welcome." Corian nodded at the rebels slowly rising from their makeshift seats. "L'zar's coming, of course. Ember, you're free to stay here with the others if you like, though I'm sure you won't because Cheyenne, we need you with us."

"Okay." Cheyenne accepted Ember's hand for a boost to her feet when the fae girl floated instantly off the edge of the pit. "What do I have to do?"

"Whatever you do, don't look forward to it." L'zar snorted and headed away from the pit.

"All right. Whoever's with us, get ready to move out. We're leaving now." Corian shot Cheyenne a wary glance, then nodded and headed after L'zar.

"What's a *Sorren Gán?*" Ember muttered.

"I'm the last person to ask about that, Em."

"Sakrit." Maleshi approached the orc and clasped his forearm. "On General Hi'et's orders, get these pits closed up for the time being. It hurts to say it as much as it hurts to hear, but we can't risk overloading the city with power until we've cleared out the worst of it."

"They'll understand. We had a good few hours with the pits for the first time in centuries. They can wait a little longer if it means they can use them the way they were meant to be used. I'll take care of it."

"I know." Maleshi clapped a hand on his shoulder and nodded before joining the rest of their party following L'zar.

Cheyenne hurried after her father and Corian. "Hey, wait a minute."

Corian looked over his shoulder at her and Ember, who was floating closely behind. L'zar showed no sign that he'd heard her.

"We talked about the whole 'no more secrets' thing, so who's gonna tell me where we're going and what the hell a *Sorren Gán* is?"

L'zar snarled. "I'm so *sick* of hearing that name!"

"At least tell me why I have to go. I mean, not that I wouldn't, but nobody even *asked* me."

Corian slowed to fall in beside her. "You and L'zar are the only ones it will listen to."

"Why? Because we're *royalty*?"

In front of them, L'zar snorted. "No. Not even close." He stepped aside and let them pass, fuming at the ground and refusing to meet his daughter's gaze.

Corian put a hand on Cheyenne's back and urged her to keep moving.

"What the hell's wrong with him?"

"We might have a chance to talk about it on the way there, kid. Just leave it alone for now. When L'zar's ready to stop throwing a fit about it, he'll fill you in."

The group of rebels made their way underground to the Four-Pointed Star's hidden bunker. The place had suffered a little damage from the magical earthquake, but it wasn't enough to make it dangerous. Cheyenne grabbed her pack from where she'd left it beside the wall that morning and stared at the fallen chunks of stone scattered across the huge metal table. "One more downside to not having any integrated tech down here, huh? Can't just patch the holes in the wall with a bunch of smart metal."

Maleshi moved her fingers in a quick spell. The stone chunks on the table and scattered around the main chamber illuminated with silver light and whisked toward the opposite side of the room, where they fell in a neat heap against the wall. "It's an easy enough fix."

Ember grabbed her own backpack and slung it over her shoulders. "I would've said you could use your fancy earth magic and stick it all back up where it goes."

Cheyenne shot her friend a brief smile and shook her head. "I can rip the ground apart and shove it back together again, Em. Not sure it's refined enough for filling holes in the ceiling."

Maleshi, Corian, L'zar, Byrd, and Lumil quickly packed and got ready to head out. A handful of the other rebels darted between them, dispersing prewrapped packages and small metal boxes. A grinning goblin handed these to Cheyenne and Ember too. Cheyenne frowned at the box. "What's this?"

"Drow eat like everyone else, don't they?" Chuckling, the goblin hurried away to take care of some other preparation.

When the journeying party had gotten everything together, Corian pointed at a large arch on the far right side of the chamber. "We'll take the transport shuttle out to Ki'uali. That's the farthest point."

"No objection to that." Maleshi hefted a pack onto her shoulders and nodded at Cheyenne. "Let's move out."

Foltr cracked his cane against the floor, the sound amplified by a spell to get everyone's attention, which it did. L'zar turned to shoot the old raug an irritated glance. "What?"

"I'm coming with you."

"Foltr," Corian started, "this isn't—"

"We're heading a lot closer to the dens than most parties ever go, and I've been where we're going."

L'zar snarled. "We both have, Grandfather. At least *you* get to stand there and watch." The drow spun back toward the arch and disappeared into the corridor beyond.

Foltr smacked his wrinkled lips and hobbled after him, his cane clicking on the stone. "Don't let this place fall to ruin while we're gone."

"Depends on your definition of ruin, old one!" a rebel shouted. A handful of others laughed, and the aged raug waved them away before joining the rest of their party and entering the tunnel.

Ember leaned toward Cheyenne in the semi-dark tunnel echoing with over half a dozen pairs of footsteps. "So, we're taking a tunnel?"

"To a transport station, I guess. Like a subway."

"Oh." Ember frowned. "You'd think they would've come up with a more sophisticated way to get places on this side, right?"

"I said, *like* a subway. Trust me, it's sophisticated enough."

"L'zar," Corian called after the pissed-off drow leading the way.

"Say another word, and I'll bring this tunnel down on top of us."

Corian cleared his throat before muttering, "And we press on."

Cheyenne watched the nightstalker shake his head, and those in the tunnel fell into a tense silence, punctured only by their quickening footsteps. *They're all putting up with massive drow mood swings 'cause that's what they've been doing forever anyway. Guess L'zar's got more to teach me than I thought, like how not to be that drow throwing tantrums.*

Ember chuckled softly and whispered, "Little tense in here."

The halfling snorted. "Yeah. This is what it's like to be around me when I'm pissed all the time, isn't it?"

Ember shrugged. "At least we know who you get it from."

"Fair enough. I'm working on it." Cheyenne raised her voice enough for everyone in the tunnel to hear, including L'zar. "Someone told me meditating has a lot of great benefits."

In front of her, Corian snorted and shook his head.

CHAPTER SIXTEEN

The high-speed shuttle waiting for them in Hangivol's lowest level, Halter's Deck, was a lot more modern than the one Cheyenne had ridden with Persh'al. The doors opened seamlessly without anyone having to poke and prod the commands, and they filed into the compartment.

"Wow. Somebody sprang for the luxury seats in this one, huh?"

Corian went to the control panel at the front of the compartment. "The transports that get used the most are the ones that need the most updates. Honestly, if I were the one in charge of updating these things, I'd get rid of the one-track-per-shuttle system. It's a complete waste."

While everyone else flopped down on the roomy seats covered in soft, cool fabric and arranged like a lounge in the back half of the cabin, Cheyenne set her backpack down on the closest seat and joined Corian in the front. "It is a little weird that something with this much juice only goes one way."

"Juice." The nightstalker laughed dryly and scanned the blank panel in front of him.

Cheyenne watched his indecision and leaned forward to catch his gaze. "Having trouble figuring out where to start?"

"I spent all this time getting ready to bring you here for one reason. Didn't expect to be heading out of Hangivol with an alternate purpose, and I seem to have forgotten the need for an activator of my own."

"I'd offer to lend you mine, but…"

"No, thank you," Corian said to her. "You sure you know how to drive this thing?"

"It does go in a straight line."

"Very funny."

"I got this." Cheyenne nodded toward the seats in the back, and the nightstalker turned swiftly to take one for himself, scratching the back of his head. "Everyone good to go?"

"No." L'zar slumped in his seat at the very back, both legs stretched out in front of him with his ankles crossed and arms folded, and glared at the slick metal floor. "It's not too late to open those doors again."

Cheyenne slid her finger along the starter sequence the activator neatly lit up for her on the control panel. A low whine filled the shuttle, quickly rising to a high pitch that faded into silence again. Lights blinked on, the device powering the cabin with a mix of magic and tech thrummed to life, and the doors let out a soft hiss as they sealed from the inside. "Whoops."

L'zar looked at her and narrowed his eyes. "Don't pretend to make mistakes, Cheyenne."

"Why not? Does it insult you?" She turned back to the control panel and activated the rest of the powering sequences.

"No, it makes you look like you're trying too hard. Insulting me is a lofty goal, though."

Cheyenne chuckled and braced her feet before swiping the panel one last time. The shuttle hummed louder and tore out of the transport station at top speed.

"Whoa." Ember slid against Maleshi, gave her an apologetic

smile, and shifted back into her own seat. The general grinned at her before sharing a glance with Corian across the compartment.

"Way smoother than the last one." Cheyenne's eyes widened as the activator pulled up the hundreds of extra commands her first transport shuttle hadn't offered. She played around with it, swiping up on the display and changing the walls from shiny silver to black, then white, then a panoramic view of a forest wrapping around the shuttle.

"Hey!" Byrd cringed in his seat and stared at the trees around them.

Lumil burst out laughing and pointed at the goblin. "You thought this shit was *real*?"

He chuckled nervously. "Some updates. Damn, it *looks* real, though."

"I'm pretty sure no one would build one of these things through a forest," Cheyenne called from the front, now fiddling with the ambient lighting. "Or if they did, the forest wouldn't exist after a shuttle's first trip through. Anybody know how fast we're going?"

"Do enlighten us." Maleshi leaned forward and propped her forearms on her thighs, grinning at the halfling who was enjoying herself so much up front.

"No problem." Cheyenne wiggled her fingers over the control panel and shrugged. "I mean, seeing is believing, right?"

She selected the shuttle's invisible walls, and almost everyone in the party let out shouts of surprise when the floors, walls, and ceiling disappeared around them. Even L'zar sat up straight in his seat, drawing his feet back toward himself to peer beneath the shuttle at what looked like nothing but dirt and dry grass whizzing past beneath them.

"This is so cool," Ember muttered, her luminous violet eyes locked on the wall behind Corian's head. He turned slightly to see what she found interesting, then clenched his eyes shut and shook his head.

Cheyenne turned, and her smile faded when she saw the massive pillar of magic bursting out of Hangivol far behind them. "Wow. That looks bad even from here."

"The decision's been made, Cheyenne." L'zar waved his hand, feigning indifference and failing to pull it off. "No use in looking behind us if we're not headed that way."

"Uh-huh." She turned back to the console and managed to return the opacity to the back wall alone while the rest of the shuttle remained transparent.

Foltr chuckled, both gnarled hands resting on the top of his cane. "Your daughter's skills rival your own, L'zar."

Cheyenne stuck her hands in her pockets and stepped slowly toward the back of the cabin to take the empty seat beside Ember. "Old-world magic versus the new generation of tech advancement, huh?"

"The two aren't comparable." L'zar stared at her, but the corner of his mouth twitched in a tiny smile.

"I don't know." Maleshi sat back against the cushion and crossed one leg over the other. "I never saw *you* pull up anything quite like this, and we've taken plenty of shuttles."

"Just the two of you?" Corian looked sharply at Maleshi and raised an eyebrow. "When?"

She shook her head and waved him off.

L'zar's smile widened as he stared at his daughter. "When Cheyenne's abilities rival my own, I'll be the first to bend the knee. I don't need to stick a piece of metal behind my ear to manipulate the threads *I* see."

Corian snorted. "No. You have to hole yourself up in a vacuum and meditate for four hours minimum. I agree, it's much more convenient."

Byrd and Lumil sniggered and stared at the drow thief, who was slowly being pulled out of his brooding. L'zar interlaced his fingers and set them on his lap. With a final smile at Cheyenne, he dropped his head back against the cushion of his seat and closed his eyes.

Corian pointed at him. "See?"

They rode the transport shuttle long enough to get hungry and pull out the so-called lunches packed in metal boxes. Cheyenne lifted the square of dark-green chewy-looking something and narrowed her eyes.

"Don't eat that all at once." Corian pointed at it and popped a bright-red nut into his mouth. "That's better left for when we run out of everything else."

"Yeah, I'm pretty sure I know what this is." Cheyenne sniffed the square and dropped it back into the box. "Energy bar, huh?"

"Something like that."

"Yeah, the FRoE has something like it on the other side." She opted for what looked like a strawberry except for being a deep, shiny purple with heart-shaped leaves. *Doesn't taste like a strawberry either, but it's way better than that bar.* "How do those people over there have the same recipe for a brick of stinky magical fuel?"

Maleshi and Corian exchanged knowing glances. The general shrugged and picked at the food in her rebel lunchbox. "Those friends of yours."

"They're not my friends." Cheyenne shook her head and dropped the berry leaves into the box. "Associates, maybe. That's it."

"Whatever the case, when they see something they like when the refugees cross over, they put their own spin on it. Let me guess—their version is mass-produced and comes in a plastic wrapper."

"Huh." Cheyenne closed the metal box and stuck it back in her pack. "You know a lot more about them than they know about you."

Corian chucked. "That's the way we like it."

Despite the shuttle's high speed, they traveled for at least another three hours before Cheyenne's activator sent her an alert that they'd be slowing down soon. "Looks like we're almost there."

Byrd scanned the empty open land around them and frowned. "What part of the nothingness gave you that impression?"

She stood and went to the control panel, bringing the walls, ceiling, and floor back to their usual shining metal. Then she pulled up a map on the front wall for everyone to see. "Wow. We're way out in the middle of nowhere."

"Oh, yeah. Look at that." Byrd snorted. "Could've said you saw it on a map."

Shortly after that, the shuttle applied its braking system and decelerated to a smooth, efficient stop. The doors hissed and slid open on their own, and the traveling band of magicals pushed themselves out of their seats, groaning and stretching as they filed out of the shuttle.

Ember gave a mocking grimace as she floated out of the shuttle. "What area of town are we in again?"

"Ki'uali," Lumil muttered behind her. "Not a town. More of a waystation." The goblin woman's eyes widened when they stepped around the front of the train. "Ghost town, I guess."

The shuttle doors closed again, and the bullet-shaped O'gúl train powered up to head toward the capital with zero passengers. Cheyenne didn't turn to watch it leave. "What happened here?"

"Looks like the same thing that's been happening every-where else." Corian readjusted his pack and nodded for everyone to follow him. "Persh'al painted a clear enough picture of what you saw the last time."

Foltr scowled at the abandoned village surrounding the transport station, the end of his cane digging into the dirt at his feet. "Four hundred years."

"What?" Maleshi looked at him over her shoulder and stopped when she saw the old raug's trembling lips curl into a grimace.

"I was last here four hundred years ago, and the Ki'uali station was an active village. Full of trade. Pups scurrying around underfoot."

"A lot happens in four hundred years, right?" Ember gazed at the rotting buildings falling apart.

"Not here." Maleshi approached the raug and clapped a hand on his shoulder. "Come on, Grandfather. We need to keep moving."

Foltr snarled but didn't protest, thumping his cane with unnecessary force into the ground as he fell in line.

"Watch out over here." Corian pointed toward the closest slanted building on their way up the wide dirt path that led into the mountains behind the village.

"Yeah, that looks like what Persh'al and I saw." Cheyenne leaned toward the building to peer at the dark lines of black sludge climbing the walls of the building like snaking vines. *Shiny vines that pulse like worms.* Wrinkling her nose at the mixed scent of decay and old urine, she kept moving after the others.

Lumil's boot squished into a puddle of thick sludge off the path, sending out black ooze in rivulets like a scurrying swarm of maggots before she lifted her foot again. Beside her, Ember scowled and floated away from the mess. "Ew."

"Oh, yeah. It's not always the case, but right now, I'd say 'ew' and the death of the land go hand in hand."

"Wait." Cheyenne stopped and sniffed at the air. *Definitely urine. How did I let that one go?* "Anyone else smell something?"

"Yes." L'zar spun and eyed the abandoned buildings. "We're not alone."

Byrd snorted. "Really? I know half of us here can smell fae, but I doubt we'll find any here."

"Not fae." L'zar stepped back down the path, his eyes darting from one rotting building to the next. "But the smell of piss doesn't hang around for four hundred years."

A howling shriek split through the air, and a dark shape darted between the buildings. Grunting and sharp, warning hisses followed, then more dark blurs moved across the village.

Corian pressed his lips together. "If we keep walking, we're not a threat."

Lumil snorted. "Yeah, great idea. Let's turn our backs on those. What the hell are they?"

The closest building on their right shifted and collapsed the rest of the way, then a snarling, rabid skaxen leaped from behind the next building over and charged at Byrd.

Byrd unleashed two balls of green fire at the skaxen, hitting it in the chest and stomach. The other magical staggered backward and looked down at its chest. Loose rags hung from the skaxen's skin, and beneath them, the same black sludge oozed from its pores, giving it an eerie sheen as if the magical had slathered itself in black oil. The skaxen thumped its chest, sending a spray of sludge in all directions, then attacked again.

"Seriously, what the hell?" Byrd sent out more green fire, stopping his attacker long enough to step away from the snarling, flailing creature.

"What happened to him?" Cheyenne asked.

"Anyone wanna help first and ask questions later?" Byrd shouted as the skaxen just kept coming.

Lumil conjured the spinning disks of blazing-red runes around her fists. "I gotcha."

A mottled black-orange skaxen leaped from the ruined village and landed on Lumil's back. The goblin woman roared and flung her attacker away, then stalked after that one instead. "Come back here!"

A dozen more skaxen wearing rags and covered in oozing black sludge swarmed from the wreckage toward the traveling party. Black sludge dripped from their fangs and ran beneath their orange skin in thick lines like veins. Cheyenne took a step back. "Jesus, look at their eyes."

"They might look the same, Cheyenne, but those are not the eyes of Oracles." L'zar hissed at the oncoming swarm of rotting skaxen while Byrd and Lumil finally managed to put down the first two.

"They're gone." Corian's blade-like claws extended in a glint of silver. "We're fighting animals now."

If I couldn't smell them dying, I'd say he was wrong. Cheyenne summoned two sparking black orbs and nodded. "This sucks."

When Lumil's fist came up into her attacker's face and sent the skaxen-thing flying back into a rotting building, the rest of the crazed pack turned to look at the damage. Then they charged.

Cheyenne sent blast after blast into the oncoming horde, knocking them back into each other. Orange-black bodies flew, spraying black sludge in every direction, but they kept coming.

Maleshi and Corian darted around the attackers in flashes of silver light, going as close as they dared to the sludge-soaked grass and the rotting village. Their claws glinted in the light as they came down on any mottled body part in their way. The skaxen screamed and clutched bleeding stumps. One kept crawling toward Maleshi's foot with one hand as it clutched its eviscerated stomach with the other.

She put it down with another swipe of her claws and kept moving.

Foltr raised his staff and swung it at the creatures, making contact every time with thick smacks and blasting them back with red light from his gnarled, outstretched hand.

Ember froze behind the line of fighting, staring at the bleeding, burned, or disemboweled skaxen clawing across the ground to get at the magicals standing against them. "Holy shit. We're fighting magical zombies."

Cheyenne flung black tendrils from her fingertips, which coiled around the neck of a skaxen leaping right toward Ember and jerked the creature backward. It let out a strangled choking sound and Cheyenne stepped aside, releasing her tendrils to send two black energy spheres into the thing's throat. "Can't really say *we* if you're just standing there, Em."

"Right." The fae girl blinked and stepped forward, shoving outward with both hands. A wall of brilliant violet light shot away from her and spread across the scrambling, snarling lines of rotting skaxen. The force of her attack threw them back like bowling pins, and the lost creatures convulsed on the ground before lying still.

"Whoa." Cheyenne spun around toward her friend. "That one new?"

Ember shrugged. "I think so."

L'zar dodged a skaxen's swiping claws, stepping around the thing with his hands clasped behind his back and watching it move.

Cheyenne turned with the others to watch the drow not fight the creature. "What is he doing?"

As if to answer her, L'zar flicked his hand toward the creature. A concentrated burst of white light hit the skaxen in mid-air as it leaped toward him and blew the blighted magical to smithereens. Thick, sludge-covered chunks of skaxen rained down around the drow, who'd raised a shield around himself and held it until the revolting deluge subsided.

Byrd and Lumil guffawed in surprise, pointing at the mess and shaking their heads.

Ember doubled over and turned away, dry-heaving at the side of the path.

Grunting, Foltr watched the path beneath him as he trudged onward, thumping his staff into the dirt. "A waste. Pure waste is what it is."

Corian headed toward L'zar, frowning at the bodies littering the ground between them and the not-so-abandoned village. "That was a little excessive."

"In the end, perhaps." L'zar's fingers moved quickly to lower his shield, then he stepped toward the closest intact body and bent over it for a closer look. "I wanted to see how this worked."

"What, you mean, how an entire village of skaxen mutated with the blight over four hundred years?" Cheyenne stopped beside Ember and set a hand briefly on her friend's back. "You okay?"

"Yep." Ember straightened and swiped her violet-streaked hair away from her face. "I can't believe I didn't puke. I'm good."

"This wasn't a generational mutation." L'zar straightened again and stepped back to study the black-oozing bodies. "No skaxen village would have a new population in only four hundred years, if it's even been that long since these were tainted."

Corian said, "So, they were infected."

"That's one way to look at it. Touched, perhaps." L'zar strode up the path and scanned the foothills ahead. "The wildlife Persh'al mentioned were mutations. I would've said these skaxen contracted this from the water or a tainted food supply, but I can't, can I?"

Maleshi shook a glistening black chunk off the toe of her boot and joined the rest of the party. "The rot found them in their homes. It's still the Outers, but at a different point of the O'gúl compass. This shouldn't be possible."

"No, it shouldn't." L'zar stared straight ahead and picked up the pace. "We're running out of time a lot more quickly than I expected."

CHAPTER SEVENTEEN

After fighting off the tainted skaxen, the group's mood was considerably dampened. Even Lumil and Byrd agreed to an unvoiced truce and didn't nag each other as they moved up into the mountains. The path rose steadily, and the mood only worsened.

L'zar eventually led them off the path and through the mountains in a direction only he knew. They passed a small pond in a clearing, but it was filled with the same oozing black sludge, every tree and bush and blade of grass around it shriveled into blackened husks. Farther on, a flock of strangely squawking birds dove toward them from the sky, intent on attacking despite hardly being able to fly straight. Their bloated bodies smacked into tree trunks and overhanging branches, throwing some of them off course or to the ground. Most of the birds exploded on impact, raining bird parts and chunks of sludge. Those on the ground flapped around miserably, croaking in denial of their circumstances before Cheyenne put them out of their misery.

"That's probably the only good way to handle it," Ember

muttered, staring at bird carcasses oozing black sludge. "Don't beat yourself up."

"I'm not." Cheyenne trudged after the others, gritting her teeth. "I want to figure out how to stop this while we still can."

The next time the group came upon a village, they were cautious of approaching too close. The magicals living up here in huts in the mountains weren't blighted like the skaxens at the transport station, though it took longer than it should have to discern that the dark smudges on their faces and bodies were from dirt instead of the cursed ooze eating away at Ambar'ogúl.

"If we're moving farther away from Hangivol into the Outers," Cheyenne muttered as they passed the village, "how did those magicals skip out on getting infected?"

Corian shook his head, warily eyeing the troll youngsters staring at him from where they sat on the ground in front of the village's adults. "Doesn't seem to be any rhyme or reason for this, and we can't afford to assume there is one."

A troll elder hobbled toward the strangers, squinting so harshly her scarlet eyes practically disappeared within the folds of her wrinkled violet skin. She thrust a finger toward L'zar and moved it between him and Cheyenne. "Black spirit you bringin' out to us, nah. Keep movin'. Keep out them no-light *wadeen*."

With a hiss, the old troll waved the travelers away, shouting after them in a combination of the Outers dialect and old O'gúleesh Cheyenne didn't try to understand. She stepped toward Corian and looked over her shoulder at the entire troll village staring after them. "I'm guessing there's some story about drow being evil spirits."

"Nope." He shook his head. "Just O'gúleesh so far removed from civilization, they've forgotten what a drow is."

"For real?"

"You saw the inner city, kid. All the drow holed up close to the Crown and the Heart. Drow aren't freely roaming around in the Outers anymore. Not like they ever did in large numbers, but it's obviously been a lot longer for this tribe."

Maleshi fell behind the party and stopped, facing the old troll head-on and spreading her arms in supplication. "Do you know me, Grandmother?"

The troll elder scoffed, her long, washed-out scarlet braids swinging over her shoulders. "Ha! Nightstalkers lookin' like all the same, dem, yeh. I know one pushed mine out far back in these hills. Now we pushin' yours, yeh. Run quick. These pups want nothin' with claws and hush-hush lyin'. Shoo!"

The general swept her gaze over the three dozen trolls staring silently at her, many with fearful curiosity in their eyes but most of them with pure hatred. Pressing a hand to her heart, Maleshi gave the old troll woman a small bow, then hurried to catch up with the others.

Cheyenne didn't notice Maleshi had fallen behind until the nightstalker stepped in line beside her as the party followed L'zar up the next rise into the mountains. "Why'd you stop?"

"Just to talk." The general grimaced and clenched her fists. "I've seen that old troll before."

"What?"

"Long time ago, kid. Not long enough for me to forget the tattoos on her arms. Apparently long enough for her to forget *my* face."

"Who is she?"

"A hell of a fighter, that's for sure." Maleshi cleared her throat and took one last look at the edge of the village through the trees behind them. "I don't know her name. I should, though, shouldn't I? I'm the reason her tribe's all the way out here."

Ember floated along quickly behind them. "I know General Hi'et comes with a long line of titles and honors, but I'm sure your leaving this world for Earth doesn't make you responsible for what's happening on this side."

The nightstalker smiled bitterly. "I am well aware of that, Ember, and I appreciate the sentiment, but I am responsible for this specifically."

Cheyenne stared at Maleshi's profile and waited for the general to keep going. *She'll say more. She wouldn't have brought it up if she didn't want to talk about it.*

"I can feel you staring at me, kid."

"I can feel you about to explode, General."

Maleshi snorted. "Maybe. After Ba'rael turned the new Cycle, she didn't waste any time putting all her grand plans into action. I served the Crown back then. Got my orders and carried them out unquestioningly, not thinking about what kind of Crown would give those kinds of orders."

Up ahead, Corian cleared his throat without turning around to look at them. "We all had our parts to play."

"Oh, sure. And I played mine very well. That's not an excuse."

"Whatever it was," Ember said, "it can't have been that bad. The magicals in the capital went crazy when they saw you this morning."

"The magicals in the capital only saw a fraction of what I did in the name of the Crown." The general looked into the upper branches of the stunted trees dotting the mountainside as they climbed after L'zar. "I led more war parties than I can count into the Outers right after Ba'rael took the throne. We cleared out the valleys and farmland first. Took the livestock, then the forests, then the mines. Everywhere we went, everywhere she sent us, O'gúleesh had been living their lives relatively peacefully for ages. We all knew that, and we moved them out without a second thought."

Foltr grunted and thwacked his staff against a tree trunk. "It's all in the past, *hinya*."

"Sure, until the past looked me right in the eyes five minutes ago and had no idea who I am." Maleshi shook her head. "That troll was one of the few who fought back. Very few did, and she was one of even fewer I didn't cut down for standing up to the Crown to protect what was theirs."

Cheyenne swallowed. "Shit."

A bitter laugh escaped the general. "Yeah. That tribe is all the way out here because of me. Who knows, maybe they've been here the whole time, but probably not. If this blight is moving as quickly as we think, I'm sure they've relocated more than once."

"Ambar'ogúl will heal itself," Corian muttered. "We'll make sure of it."

"After how many lives are taken, *vae shra'ni*? Huh?" Maleshi hissed. "I should've stopped her when I realized what she was doing. I could've taken her back then before she started stealing more magic than even she can handle."

At the head of the line, L'zar stopped short and spun to face them, propping one foot on a boulder set into the hillside. "Then you would have started this war way before its time. Maleshi Hi'et would have fallen from her high horse as our greatest warlord, the factions would have turned against each other *and* you, and nothing would have changed. What would have happened then, hmm? *I* would've had to stand up and take a throne I never wanted, and I'm not even sure L'zar Verdys as the Crown of Ambar'ogúl would have been any better than Ba'rael the Spider. Feeling sorry for yourself doesn't suit you, General. Keep moving."

Without waiting for a reply, he spun back and trudged farther up the hillside.

Maleshi stared after him for a long moment before shaking her head and moving on.

"I hate to say it," Cheyenne muttered, "but he might be right."

The general laughed bitterly. "Don't let him hear you say that."

"I've heard enough to know that when you left, it gave everyone here the hope they needed. That it was possible to escape from all this. That at the very least, you weren't dead, and in the best-case scenario, you might come back."

"Best-case scenario. Ha. That turned out to be me branding myself as a traitor to the Crown and taking up arms against her at *his* side." Maleshi nodded toward L'zar. "And it took *this* ragtag group shoving their way through my front door to get me moving again."

Foltr grunted. "Don't include me in the band of misfits, Blade of the Unseen Eye."

"Of course not." Maleshi glanced at him over her shoulder and smiled thinly.

"Sometimes, we have to live through the worst-case scenario to pull ourselves out of complacency. It's ugly and effective, isn't it?" The raug chuckled as he thumped his staff into the leaf-strewn mountainside. "I heard you made a comfortable bed of lies for yourself in our sister world."

"Yes, thank you." Shaking her head, Maleshi scoffed. "I was quite comfortable. Maybe someday I'll return to it."

Foltr's sharp laugh echoed through the trees. "But not today."

"No. Today, I'm following a mad drow into the jaws of the *Sorren Gán*."

Ember gulped. "Jaws?"

"A figure of speech. Mostly."

CHAPTER EIGHTEEN

"So, I have a question." Ember swiped her hair out of her eyes, floating easily over the increasingly difficult terrain. The rest of the party was breathing heavily as they finished the last of their climb over a fallen mound of boulders L'zar had refused to take them around.

Cheyenne wiped sweat from her forehead and readjusted the straps of her backpack. "Might as well go for it, Em."

"I'm thinking. It was, what, mid-morning when we left the city? We had that ridiculously long train ride or whatever it was, and now it feels like we've been hiking through these mountains for just as long."

Maleshi let out a winded laugh. "None of those are questions."

"No, I know. But it makes me wonder how long the days are here."

"Still not a question."

Cheyenne snorted. "Don't tell me General Hi'et can't infer the question anyway."

"Oh, I can infer plenty. For one, this fae over here has the time and energy to contemplate elongated daylight in

Ambar'ogúl while the rest of us are focused on marching with our actual feet on the ground."

Ember scowled at the back of the nightstalker woman's head. "Hey, believe me, if I *could* march with you, I would in a heartbeat."

"I know." Maleshi shifted her pack on her shoulders and nodded. "I'm messing with you. The days are longer over here, and that's the best answer I can give. Not much of an issue coming into this world, but I tell you what. When I went Earthside, it took me months to get used to the days cut short by at least a third."

"A third?"

"At least. It might even be half."

"Stop." L'zar's order cut sharply through the woods around them, and the group instantly halted. He peered through the sparse trees as they gave way to more rocks and eventually cliffs in the distance.

Cheyenne looked around and waited for the explanation. "Something on your mind, L'zar?"

"You couldn't handle half of what's on my mind," he spat, turning around, not to look at her, but to scan the way they'd come and the mountainside below them.

"Right, because you have such a clear understanding of what I can handle."

"Shut up." The drow's gaze flickered past her as if he didn't even see his daughter standing in line with the others following him.

Cheyenne frowned. *He looks like he's losing it. If he goes all space-drow on us again, I'll lose it too.*

Lumil glanced at L'zar and tried to follow his gaze. "Anything in particular we're looking for?"

L'zar hissed and stepped away from the party, peering through the trees. A rustle in the short, scruffy bushes on his right made him turn, and he launched a blazing dart of white light at them.

An angry, frightened squeal erupted from the shrubbery, followed by a creature with mottled dark-brown skin and three horns protruding from an elongated snout. It scrambled across the loose earth, yellow eyes wide before L'zar's next attack caught it squarely in the side and dropped the creature on the spot. The animal snorted once, sending up a spray of leaves away from its snout, and lay still.

Ember stared at the thing. "Is that a pig?"

Corian raised an eyebrow at the dead creature. "Something like one, yeah." He looked at L'zar. "And apparently such a threat that L'zar had to deal with it for us."

L'zar grunted. "It was moving."

"Not a good excuse," Cheyenne muttered.

"It's mutated too." The drow tossed his hand toward the O'gúl version of a wild boar and kept moving. "Wouldn't want that thing attacking us and spreading the blight, would we?"

Corian stared after him and slowly shook his head before exchanging concerned glances with Maleshi.

Five minutes later, L'zar spun wildly and sent a wave of blinding white light at the tallest tree they'd seen in half an hour. The branches exploded, and startled gray birds shrieked as they fluttered down the mountainside. The furry dark-purple body that fell from the tree squeaked once and lay still on the ground.

Ember looked from the purple thing to the tree again and blinked. "I don't even know what that might be."

"Not a threat, L'zar," Corian warned.

"You don't know that," the drow hissed. "You don't know anything out here. *I* do."

"Jesus, you need to chill out." Cheyenne walked steadily across the shallow incline and tried to get L'zar to look at her.

"Pigs and birds and whatever the hell that purple thing is aren't our main concern right now."

L'zar whirled on her, his eyes wide and maddened with the first sign of fear she'd seen in him since he'd projected himself into her head, trying to make sure she wasn't dead. "You have no idea what we're about to face, Cheyenne. If I feel like losing my shit, there's a damn good reason for it. Enjoy your ignorance while it lasts. You'll understand soon enough."

Kicking up a spray of leaves, dry twigs, and fallen pine needles, the drow thief stalked toward the destination only he knew. The rest of the party exchanged silent, wary glances.

Corian said, "I think we're getting close."

Maleshi scoffed and gestured toward L'zar, who was storming off ahead of them. "Really? How could you tell?"

Cheyenne looked at Ember, who offered a clueless shrug. *He better pull himself together before we need him for something dangerous.*

Not long after that, L'zar led them down a steep ravine into a valley. Cheyenne noticed how quiet the valley was—no birds, no animal noises, not even the wind rustling through leaves. A cold tingle prickled down her spine. She finished sliding down the last of the loose shale behind Maleshi as the nightstalker offered Foltr a hand. He took it for a moment, then brushed her away from him before moving on with his staff.

The halfling looked at the sprawling valley in front of them and felt dark, grieving anger boiling up inside her. "What the hell?"

The valley was filled with the gnarled, twisted shapes of nearly a hundred trees towering into the sky. She could feel the power that used to be here and knew it had been stripped from the empty husks stretching in front of them. *Nimlothar trees. A whole forest, and they're all dead.*

"Keep moving," L'zar muttered with a grunt, passing the dead trunks as if he didn't notice them.

Like he's been here before. Cheyenne clenched her fists as they moved through the dead forest. The Nimlothar trees towered above them, every branch bare of leaves and devoid of life. A trace of the power that had once connected them to the drow race still hung thick in the air.

She stopped and reached out to touch the twisted black bark. A chunk fell away beneath her fingers and crumbled to dust that fluttered away in the low breeze. Her fingers stung with the residual pain in the ruined tree's memories, and she sucked in a sharp breath. *This is what losing an arm feels like. It has to be.*

"Cheyenne," Maleshi said her name softly, but there was a warning in it. "Keep moving."

Blinking back the tears welling in her eyes, the halfling gritted her teeth and pressed on. The weight of so much dead, stolen power in the forest pressed on her like a physical force. "What happened here?"

Corian looked at the branches with a pained frown. "I'm sure your first guess would be right on the mark."

"The Crown killed them." Cheyenne felt the truth in her bones and forced herself to keep her rage under control. *Hold it together, at least until we're out of here. This place doesn't deserve any more damage or pain.* "Just so she could have the last Nimlothar all to herself in the Heart."

L'zar scowled and kicked up the dry, dead soil like a spoiled child who didn't get the candy he wanted. "I mourned them too when I first saw this place. I don't like it any more than you do, but she honestly did our kind a favor when she wiped out this forest."

"*What?*" Cheyenne glared at her father. "How could this possibly be a good thing?"

"This place was a living snare, Cheyenne."

"A snare for what?"

L'zar briefly paused and turned as if to finally look her in the eye. His gaze drifted upward instead, and his lip curled in a sneer. "Drow."

"That doesn't even—" Cheyenne started to say when Corian put a hand on her shoulder and slowly shook his head.

"Not here. Later."

She swallowed thickly and stormed away from him, staring at the ground because she couldn't bear the sight of so many dead husks stripped of the power they didn't deserve to lose. *This place was sacred, not a snare. L'zar's still keeping his damn secrets. That'll end soon, even if I have to* make *it end.*

The dead, still silence was overwhelming as they moved through the Nimlothar forest. When they emerged on the other side, the ground dipped into a bowl-shaped clearing made entirely of stone. Flames flickered across the clearing like light dancing across water. Small plants, sparse bushes, and short trees with narrow trunks dotted the curving stone floor, but everything burned with continuous flames of green, red, and purple. Ash blew across the clearing amid the constant crackle and the occasional burst of sparks from the endlessly burning plants. Even the wind was silent.

Cheyenne studied the strange phenomena with a pit of hesitation in her stomach. "I don't get it. Stone doesn't burn."

L'zar shot her a quick sideways glance like he'd forgotten she was there and scowled. "It does here. Everything burns." He jumped down into the bowl-shaped clearing and stared at the massive cave on the opposite side. The stone mouth of the cave burned too, mostly with yellow and orange flames of natural fire, but with random bursts of white fire and purple sparks.

Cheyenne studied the cave but couldn't see anything past the raging fire that shouldn't have been able to burn without fuel. *It's magic. That's all the fuel anything needs on this world.*

L'zar headed toward the closest burning plant, a withered lily, casting a quick spell before reaching down and plucking the whole thing from the stone. Scowling, he moved to the next plant and the next, harvesting burning stems and leaves and flowers. Foltr grunted and handed his staff to Maleshi before heading into the center of the clearing to help L'zar with his task.

"What are they doing?"

Corian leaned toward Cheyenne and nervously licked his lips. "It's an old ritual, kid, to call out the *Sorren Gán* for a little chat, more or less. It guarantees a certain protection for us. Walking into that cave without it would end our journey right here."

She looked up at him and raised her eyebrows. "Seems a little strange that we'd have to protect ourselves if we're coming to this thing to ask for help."

The nightstalker grimaced. "This *thing* has a fondness for drow."

L'zar spun toward them, his eyes wild and his arms full of burning plants. "Don't downplay what we're facing, Corian. It likes the way we taste, plain and simple."

Cheyenne blinked and stared at the flaming mouth of the cave. "The *Sorren Gán* eats drow?"

Corian dipped his head. "When it can."

Ember swallowed. "Holy shit."

"We're here for a bargain," L'zar spat as he broke a flaming green branch off one of the trees with a sharp snap. "To come to an agreement so it'll stomp its fiery ass all the way to the capitol. We may be a delicacy for the *Sorren Gán*, but its main food is magic."

"Magic." Cheyenne folded her arms. "It eats drow and magic."

"I don't have time to listen to my damn echo, Cheyenne." L'zar trudged across the clearing, dropping his fiery armful in the very center before moving on to another plant.

"What's spilling out of Hangivol right now should be a decent feast for the *Sorren Gán*. One would think that in and of itself would be enough to entice it out, but these things don't leave their lairs if they can help it."

"So beyond dangling an exploding magical carrot in front of it, how do we get it to leave?"

"We make the trip worth its time. Placate it however we can, and in return, it should agree to make the journey and take care of the most immediate problem at the capital."

With a snort, Cheyenne shook her head and watched her father and Foltr gathering flaming tribute to the *Sorren Gán*. "'Should.' That means none of you is sure this will work."

"We don't have any other options, kid. We're asking the *Sorren Gán* for help as a last resort. No way to hide that from the creature either, because we only have this one card to play. It's always a gamble with them."

L'zar's bitter laughter came out as a snarl. "Gamble. We're just full of fell-damn euphemisms today, aren't we?"

Corian leaned closer to Cheyenne and lowered his voice. "This one is best known for a willingness to put its appetite aside and at least listen to offers. Countless drow have tried to make deals with this particular *Sorren Gán* if they get that far. Very few of them make it out alive to see the deal fulfilled, but L'zar did. Once."

"Shut the fuck up," L'zar hissed. "I need to concentrate, and you running your mouth about the past isn't helping."

Ignoring his touchy mood, Cheyenne widened her eyes at her father as he bustled around the stone clearing. "You've done this before?"

"No. The last time, I didn't have a bunch of idiots buzzing in my ears while I was trying to focus."

She turned toward the nightstalker. "Corian, what are we getting ourselves into here? Seriously. I need to know before I go barging in there like a clueless moron."

He blinked at her above a small, cautious smile. "Sounds

like you're finally coming to understand the importance of being prepared."

"I blame you for planting that seed." Cheyenne raised her eyebrows. "Tell me."

Corian took a deep breath, then turned his back on L'zar and the stone clearing as if that would keep the drow thief from overhearing the conversation. He leaned toward Cheyenne's ear and whispered, "I've only seen your father truly scared on two occasions. The first time was before he walked into that cave thousands of years ago."

As she studied the cave, Cheyenne muttered, "And the second time?"

"When he came back out. Honestly, Cheyenne, that one was worse. I think that's when he started to lose his mind."

When he leaned away from her, Cheyenne looked into his glowing silver eyes. He gave her a reassuring nod, but his concerned frown expressed what he really thought. The night-stalker turned away and jumped down into the stone clearing, standing with his feet spread wide and his arms folded to watch L'zar and Foltr preparing for their *Sorren Gán*-summoning ritual.

Shit. The drow prince who doesn't care about anything is about to take us to the one thing in two worlds that terrifies him. Won't this be fun?

Ember floated toward the halfling and gave her a weak smile. "Everything okay?"

"I have no idea, Em. After all this is over, I'll let you know, okay?"

"Yeah, sure. Anything I can do?"

"Cross your fingers, maybe?"

Ember raised both hands and crossed her fingers. They smiled at each other, but it didn't make either of them feel better.

L'zar returned to the pile of burning plants in the center of the clearing and knelt to rearrange them in a pattern for his ritual summoning. Foltr grunted and started to lower himself to his knees beside the drow, but L'zar grabbed the ancient raug's arm to stop him and shook his head. "You've done enough, Grandfather. This one's on me."

Foltr snorted. "It won't help *you*, but I'm relieved to hear you say it. For my sake."

L'zar chuckled humorlessly and went back to work arranging the burning twigs, branches, and long flowering stems. When he'd finished creating the O'gúleesh symbol with the flames, he stood and cast a summoning spell, his lips moving in a barely audible whisper. Then he spat on the symbol, and every patch of fire, flickering flames, and burning plant flared with renewed strength. The multicolored flames roared to three times their normal height, the burning cave most of all. The fires flickered in and out of different colors, favoring green and black, and a roar like howling wind and crumbling stone came from the mouth of the cave.

A low, rumbling laugh filled the clearing, and the fires settled back to their normal size. The voice coming from within the cave and echoing maddeningly within the bowl-shaped stone clearing was deeper and far more sinister than any voice had a right to be. "Come now, little drow. I told you two thousand years ago you and I would become good friends. It didn't take nearly as long as I thought."

L'zar grimaced at the mouth of the cave and lifted his chin. "I've come back with another proposition for you, *Sorren Gán*. Will you hear it?"

The *Sorren Gán*'s growling laughter made Cheyenne's eyes water, the sound vibrating in her head and chest. "I will always listen to *you*. I see you've brought another of the dark ones with you this time."

"Yes."

Cheyenne clenched her fists. *It's talking about me.*

"Only the two drow on my doorstep may enter today," the *Sorren Gán* rumbled. "I can't stand the smell of the rest of you."

The flames around the cave changed to dark light and shrank to reveal the unimpeded entrance. It was pitch-black inside.

Baring his teeth in a silent snarl, L'zar turned to the rest of the group and gestured toward Cheyenne without looking at her. "Let's go."

"I thought we were all supposed to go talk to this thing together?"

"Clearly the plan has changed." L'zar bowed his head, grimacing at the stone. He couldn't bring himself to look at any of them. "I'll drag you in there if I have to, but this will be a lot easier if you come willingly."

Right. Willingly into the private cave of a thing that eats drow. Perfect.

Clenching her jaw, Cheyenne glanced at Ember, nodded, and hopped down into the clearing. Behind her, Byrd swallowed and muttered, "Good luck."

What do I say to that? "Thanks."

She walked past Corian, who dipped his head in acknowledgment.

Even the nightstalker doesn't think we'll make it out of this one in one piece, and here I am, following L'zar into the fire.

When she reached her father, L'zar lowered his arm to his side again and turned to the cave entrance. The second they reached the mouth of the cave, the flames burst to life again, seemingly blocking their path. L'zar rolled his eyes. "It's fucking with us. Let's go."

"Uh-huh." Cheyenne stared at the flames licking inches from her face and let her father step through first. When he didn't scream or shrivel into a drow crisp, she rolled her shoulders and entered behind him.

CHAPTER NINETEEN

The multicolored flames were cool against Cheyenne's skin, but on the other side, the cold permeating the pitch-black cave made her pause. *If the cold's bothering me in here, it'd probably kill the others—that or the smell.*

As her eyes adjusted to the darkness, she realized the cave was much larger than it looked from the outside. It stretched endlessly in front of them, the stone walls rising into the side of the mountain until she couldn't see the top. Flames flickered across the walls, black smoke wafting in the frigid darkness. *Looks a lot like the in-between if you ask me.*

On the far side of the cave was a massive lake, the surface covered in endless purple flames. The crackle and hiss of unnaturally burning stone and the occasional spark tossed into the air punctured the silence. L'zar took three steps forward, Cheyenne at his side, then dropped to one knee without warning.

She frowned down at him. "What are you doing?"

He didn't lift his bowed head. "We're not here to fuck around. Kneel."

"Yes," the *Sorren Gán* roared in its overwhelmingly brutal

voice. "You learned that lesson the first time we met. Didn't you, L'zar?"

Cheyenne quickly scanned the dark cave and couldn't see a thing. *Where the hell is it?*

L'zar's cold fingers clamped around her wrist and he jerked her to her knees. She pulled her hand away and scowled at him.

"What's wrong with you?" she whispered.

His golden gaze burned into the black stone floor of the cave in front of them. "Right now? Everything."

From the back of the cave, a yellow-orange glow grew within the darkness. Cheyenne looked up and watched the massive creature made of fire and thick black smoke emerge from some hidden recess in the cave's walls. It was at least thirty feet tall and had tongues of fire dripping from its broad shoulders. Four arms extended at its sides, two of its hands splayed out, the fingers tipped in black claws that trailed thick lines of smoke behind them. The *Sorren Gán* might have had horns, but then again, they might have been smoke. Clawed feet stomped across the ground, making it tremble beneath them. The lake of fire shuddered, and two massive, fiery wings spread from the Sorren Gán's back with a fan of more black smoke before settling against its sides again.

L'zar kept his head bowed, clenching his jaw so tightly he thought his head would explode. *The first time was for me. This time, it is for Ambar'ogúl. Fuck taking the throne, but I won't let the place burn before I leave it forever.* His balled fists ached, and still he didn't look up at the *Sorren Gán* stalking toward them. He sure as hell could feel it.

The fiery beast let out another low, ominous chuckle. "I enjoy this sight very much. Now tell me why you're here."

"We need your help." L'zar swallowed. "*I* need your help."

"With the afterbirth of the foulness your sister spawned." The *Sorren Gán* stopped yards in front of them, casting burning light over the kneeling drow. The smoke wafting off its body was so thick, Cheyenne expected to choke on it at any minute. "Tell me why you wish to have this threat subdued, L'zar. We both know you do not seek the O'gúl Crown."

"No." L'zar bowed his head even lower and pressed his fists against the stone.

Cheyenne shot him a sideways glance and tried looking at the *Sorren Gán* but couldn't face the blazing light. *L'zar is bending the knee. Why?*

"I don't want to rule," the drow continued. "But I don't want to see Ambar'ogúl destroyed, either."

A flaming tail lashed out from behind the *Sorren Gán* and struck the stone floor with a burst of sparks. "Why?"

"Because I don't want to be remembered as the Weaver thief who brought an entire world to its knees. Not like this."

"Wrong." The beast stepped closer and snorted a thick plume of rancid black smoke into both drow's faces.

Cheyenne turned her head away from the worst of it and caught a glimpse of her father's fists and arms through the dispersing smoke. *Shit. He's shaking.*

"You've had time to practice your lies, little drow," the *Sorren Gán* rumbled. "But not nearly enough to make them convincing. Tell me why you want to save this world."

L'zar's lips trembled when he opened his mouth. He pressed his lips together and glared at the floor in humiliation. "It's my daughter's legacy. She deserves all of it. I owe her that much, at least."

Cheyenne's eyes widened despite the smoke stinging her eyes. *First time I've heard him own up to anything, even if it's under duress.*

"Hmm. Yes." The *Sorren Gán* chuckled again and stopped looming over the kneeling drow, taking a step back. Its wings shot out again, fanning more smoke through the cave, and its other two fists opened to stretch clawed fingers in anticipation. "Honesty is your weakness, isn't it, little drow? Your inability to humble yourself makes you weak. That is why you've come to me again. Someone has to make you face your trembling terror. We made you strong before, did we not?"

L'zar glared at the floor, his jaw clenching and unclenching.

The flames around and within the *Sorren Gán* erupted with a roar. "Did we *not*?"

"Yes!" L'zar breathed heavily now, pressing his fists into the stone floor so hard they bled.

Cheyenne wrinkled her nose at the smell. *What the hell happened between these two?*

"And now you return for more of the same." The *Sorren Gán* extended a hand toward L'zar as if it meant to rest the fiery paw on the drow's hand, but it didn't. "Why should I travel such a long way to Hangivol? It means nothing to me if the wealth of magic your sister pilfered destroys one city or a thousand. The magic will find me anyway."

L'zar's head lifted an inch, and he managed to settle his gaze on the creature's clawed, burning feet. "Name your price."

"You know I require something now."

"Yes."

Cheyenne flinched away from an unnaturally long tongue of flame licking toward her face.

"This daughter of yours is different," the *Sorren Gán* growled. "You knew I would want her."

L'zar straightened and turned toward Cheyenne. "That's not what I had in mind."

"Nor is it something you would refuse me, hmm?"

Cheyenne stared at her father. *He better say something.*

L'zar swallowed and opened his mouth, but nothing came out.

"L'zar." She raised her eyebrows.

His upper lip twitched as he stared into his daughter's eyes. "You'll be fine."

"Are you fucking kidding me?"

The *Sorren Gán* thundered with dark laughter. The sound echoed through the cave and made the floor tremble as much as the creature's footsteps. "Your loyalty pleases me very much, L'zar."

"You can't bring me in here and toss me to this thing as a quick snack!" Cheyenne leaped to her feet, blinking away the tears against the smoke spewing from the *Sorren Gán's* body. "I'm not doing this."

"You have to, Cheyenne."

"No, I don't. *You* have to grow a conscience and a goddamn spine. Look at you. You won't even get off your knees to give me up. I came in here willingly, but not as a fucking sacrifice."

"You don't have to be willing," the *Sorren Gán* growled. *"He* wasn't the first time."

"What?"

The fiery beast laughed again, shaking the cave around them.

"I'm done, L'zar. You can follow me out or stay here and die on your knees. I don't give a shit." She whirled toward the mouth of the cave and stormed off.

The flames around the entrance flared in blinding brilliance and a wave of smoke barreled toward her, pushing her back across the stone floor even as she dug her feet in. Coughing and gasping for breath, Cheyenne let her rage fuel the drow magic building inside her. *Think of the Nimlothar seed. And the dead forest.*

Cold pressure coiled around her leg and whipped it out from under her. She crashed to the stone and spun onto her back, glaring up at the *Sorren Gán* as a coil of black smoke extended to drag her toward it. Purple and black light burst from her body, glowing brighter from behind her golden eyes, and her magic burned through her veins with renewed force. *Yeah, that's more like it.*

She fired countless rounds of black energy spheres at the

Sorren Gán's flaming head. It only laughed harder, dragging her with it as it retreated from L'zar. Cheyenne lurched upward and grabbed the coil of black smoke before summoning two more energy spheres, and the smoke burst into black shards that caught fire as they flew through the air.

The *Sorren Gán* roared in fury, its barbed tail lashing the ground as it stepped toward her and reached out with one of its four hands. Cheyenne raised a shimmering black shield as a roaring column of fire shot toward her. The shield stopped it, but the freezing cold that enveloped her when she expected heat made her pause.

"You *will* give me what I seek," the *Sorren Gán* roared as the column of flames subsided.

Cheyenne lowered the shield, her fingers numb, and reached out with her connection to the earth to find that ledge of resistance. "Fuck you."

When she pulled with both hands, the stone floor erupted in front of the *Sorren Gán*. A massive slab of earth broke free and hurtled toward the flaming beast, knocking it back across the cave.

"Cheyenne."

"And fuck *you*. Trying to give me up like this." She stormed toward the cave entrance again, but before she took two steps, black smoke ballooned from every dark crevice of the cave and enveloped her. Cheyenne couldn't see a thing as she stumbled forward blindly, waving the smoke away and trying to catch a breath as it seared into her lungs and muddled her thoughts.

The next thing she knew, she was flying through the air, sailing out of the black smoke and high above both L'zar and the *Sorren Gán*, who was staring up at her with blazing eyes of smoke and fire. There was nothing to grab, nothing to wrap her black lashing tendrils around even when she released them and tried to find purchase. The last thing she saw before she plunged into the hissing, raging lake of fire on the other side of the cave was the *Sorren Gán*'s mouth splitting in a wide grin, spewing flames and smoke. Its laughter echoed through her head as she fell into the lake.

The unbearable cold coursed through her before her drow magic took over. Cheyenne's body erupted with black fire that rushed across her skin, blocking the cold as she sank into the bright, burning substance. *This shit is definitely not water.*

Something told her she could take a breath, and when she did, her lungs were free from the burning smoke. Black flames burst from her eyes as she gazed at the terrifying images coalescing around her in the fiery substance. Screaming faces contorted in terror and anguish. Humanoid shapes fighting each other, burning, destroying, wailing.

Cheyenne kicked out at the fire surrounding her, but it didn't get her anywhere. Finally, her feet touched the bottom of the lake, and she took a tentative step forward. Flames moved around her, propelled by the drow fire racing across her skin. Gritting her teeth and clenching her fists, she took step after slow step up the incline of the lakebed back toward the shore.

When I get up there, those bastards are in for it.

CHAPTER TWENTY

"The ultimate test, is it not?" The *Sorren Gán* loomed over L'zar, who sat cross-legged on the cave floor, his head hanging between his slumped shoulders. "Does L'zar Verdys truly hold within his insignificant hands the ability not to show restraint, but to relinquish everything?" Another thunderous laugh rose from the beast's chest. "You are a slow learner, little drow. Once I break her as I broke you, perhaps your daughter will be capable of withstanding what you cannot."

L'zar stared at the ground, clenching and unclenching his jaw. *If I'm right, she already does.*

He leaned away from a tendril of smoke the *Sorren Gán* extended to caress his face. "You're so emotional, L'zar, not a trait I envy in any of you. With time, I see that withering away with all your other weaknesses. You will see."

A burst of flame erupted from the lake on the other side of the cave, and the purple fire fell away as Cheyenne, covered in black drow fire, stormed out of the lake and headed for L'zar and his unlikely master. Purple flames fell like water behind her with each step and burned like scattered pools of ignited oil.

L'zar lifted his head and watched her, wide-eyed, with the ghost of a smile.

The *Sorren Gán* stepped back, stretching its wings wide again and roaring with laughter. "I seem to have been mistaken, L'zar. Between the two of you, her blood flows much stronger."

L'zar gazed up at the beast's face, constantly shifting in the flames, and grinned. "You gave me what I was missing, didn't you?"

"I gave you what you *needed*," the *Sorren Gán* hissed. "You came to *me*. *You* begged me for the cleansing, and I poured everything I had into your soft flesh. Surprise or not, little drow, do not be ungrateful."

"*I* am." Snarling, Cheyenne raised her hands toward the *Sorren Gán* and unleashed a column of her own flames, hissing and black as they crashed into the beast's chest.

The thing turned to face her and spread its four arms. "Here she is."

Cheyenne roared and fired again, blasting the *Sorren Gán* over and over with drow fire as the flames flared around her body and flashed behind her eyes. Every attack was swallowed by the beast's form, and it laughed again.

L'zar could barely see his daughter beneath the flames, but he leaped to his feet and hurried toward her. "Cheyenne."

"No!" She kept attacking as she stormed toward the thing that ate drow and had tossed her into the burning lake. "I told you I was done."

"Cheyenne, it won't do anything."

"No, *you* won't do anything."

"I can explain."

Shouting in rage, Cheyenne whirled on her father and sent a ball of black flames hurtling into his chest. It threw him toward the cave wall, and he pulled the same trick he'd used before. The black fire consumed his body and he spread his arms, slowing himself before hitting the wall and hovering over the cave floor before lowering himself to the ground. The flames curled inward and almost sank into his skin, then they were gone.

Cheyenne summoned a churning sphere of black energy and stormed after him. "Don't tell me you can explain."

"I can."

"You *sacrificed* me! Just like that." She launched the energy sphere at him, and he batted it aside with a flash of white light. "You didn't even try to find a better way. All you did was tell me I'd be fine!"

A chuckle escaped him and he shrugged. "And so you are."

"Stop laughing!" Cheyenne hurled two more attacks at him. L'zar deflected the first, but the second caught him in the shoulder and spun him off-balance.

Finally, she reached her father and took a black-flaming swing at his face. He ducked and tried to grab her wrist. Cheyenne brought her other elbow up toward his throat, but L'zar blocked it with a quickly raised forearm and stepped aside. "I'm serious, Cheyenne."

"You're never serious. That's the problem!"

"Stop." He parried another punch and tried to pull her against him. "Stop trying to fight me and listen."

"Stop pretending you give a shit about me!" Cheyenne snarled as she kept up the attack, launching punches that would send most magicals crashing through the walls. L'zar was too quick.

The *Sorren Gán* watched the squabbling drow for a moment before its fascination dwindled. It snorted another cloud of thick black smoke and flicked two of its hands toward the mouth of the cave.

Cheyenne and L'zar were ripped apart by the *Sorren Gán's* magic and went sailing through the wall of fire blocking the cave entrance and out into the stone courtyard beyond.

The halfling braced herself for the fall and tumbled across the stone, rolling as much as she could.

Lumil leaped up from where she'd been sitting in the clearing, eyes wide. The other magicals in their party got to their feet to watch L'zar sliding on his back into the center of the bowl-shaped clearing too. Both drow trailed thin wisps of smoke behind them. Cheyenne's black flames had been snuffed by the *Sorren Gán's* disposal of her and her father.

"Shit." Cheyenne slapped the real fire igniting the hem of her trenchcoat and two spots on her sleeves. *Dammit, I just bought this thing.*

L'zar scrambled to his feet and slapped at the fire singeing his pants and the front of his shirt. When he finally got it all out, he straightened his shirt and smoothed his long white hair away from his face with both hands.

"So." Maleshi folded her arms and blinked at the drow. "How did it go?"

L'zar lifted a hand and opened his mouth to answer. Words escaped him, so he gestured at Cheyenne.

The flames blocking the cave entrance flared brighter, and the *Sorren Gán's* voice boomed across the clearing again. "You have amused me, at the very least. This I will accept as payment. For now."

"Endaru's balls." Byrd smiled in relief. "I didn't think that would happen."

"In three days' time," the beast roared, hidden behind the flames guarding its cave, "I will make the journey to Hangivol, and I will feast on the product of Ba'rael Verdys' stupidity. Do not wait another thousand years to visit me, L'zar. I did miss you."

L'zar spun and shot the cave the middle finger as the *Sorren Gán's* terrifying laughter faded.

"Three days?" Corian rubbed his mouth. "I guess it's better than never."

Cheyenne whipped the back of her trenchcoat around, looking for any errant fire she might have missed. L'zar approached her and reached out toward her face. "Are you all right?"

She slapped his hand away. "Don't touch me."

"I want to make sure you're all right."

Another churning sphere of crackling black energy flew from her hand. He stepped quickly away to dodge the attack, and her magic cracked into the stone behind him, sending black and purple sparks everywhere.

"Whoa, whoa." Corian rushed toward them. "What happened?"

"Ask *him*." Cheyenne launched another energy sphere, but Corian threw off her aim when he pushed her arm down.

Then he grabbed her shoulders and turned her around to look at him. She tried to struggle out of his grasp, but he gave her a quick shake. "Cheyenne!"

"What?" she snarled.

"Cut it out."

Breathing heavily, she tried to look over her shoulder at L'zar, who merely straightened his shirtsleeves before clasping his hands behind his back and turning away from them.

"Don't look at him, kid. Look at me."

"You're not the one I want to kill, Corian, but if you don't let go of me, I'll fight you too. I already punched you once. Imagine what I can do *now*." Cheyenne jerked his hands off her shoulders and spun toward L'zar.

"What happened in there?" Maleshi asked, stopping hesitantly beside Corian.

Cheyenne jabbed a finger at L'zar. "That asshole sacrificed me to the *Sorren Gán*."

Maleshi unfolded her arms. "What?"

Corian bared his teeth in a snarl. "L'zar."

The drow thief slowly turned around and spread his arms. "I wouldn't say that's an accurate recounting."

"Bullshit! That's exactly what happened. You didn't even try to fight for me. You're a fucking coward, and I think ripping your head off your shoulders would do more good for all of us than any of your shitty plans."

"Cheyenne, I understand you're upset."

She roared and lunged at him. Corian and Maleshi went after her in twin flashes of silver light, and Cheyenne found herself struggling against both nightstalkers holding her back. She tried to slip past them, snarling, but they held her shoulders and yanked her back.

"You need to stop, kid," Maleshi growled. "This isn't the right way to handle it."

"Sure feels right." The halfling jerked against their hold, and they pulled her back even farther.

"We'll figure it out," Corian muttered, "but you have to let this go. Right now."

Cheyenne sneered and shoved her face up to his. "You weren't *there*. You have no idea what I saw!"

"Hey."

Cheyenne turned at the sound of Ember's voice and shot a quick glance at her friend before the fae's hand smacked the halfling's cheek. Cheyenne's head barely moved, but the shock of it took the fight out of her for two seconds.

"Oh, shit." Byrd sucked in a breath and pressed his knuckles against his teeth. Beside him, Lumil ran a hand through her mop of yellow hair and watched silently.

"Ember."

"Get it the fuck together already. What's wrong with you?"

"Hey, I'm not the one who tried to feed my daughter to a—"

"Shut up." Ember pointed at Corian and Maleshi. "Let go of her. She's not one of your prisoners."

Corian cleared his throat and slowly slid his hands off

Cheyenne. Maleshi released the halfling's other shoulder and raised her hands, backing away.

The halfling rolled her shoulders and lifted her chin. "What happened back there was—"

"Inexcusable. Horrifying. A massive betrayal. Yeah, I get it." Ember grabbed her friend's shoulders and squeezed. "We can talk about it later. Right now, you're starting to sound a lot like the drow you're so set on blowing to pieces. Got it?"

Cheyenne blinked. *Jesus, I probably do look like a raving lunatic.* She glanced at L'zar, who had his hands in his pockets and was staring at the ground.

Ember shook her gently. "Got it?"

"Yeah. Yeah, Em. I get it."

"Okay." Ember released her and asked, "So what now?"

"If it's all right with Cheyenne," L'zar muttered, slowly looking up at his daughter with a small frown, "I would very much like the chance to explain what happened."

"You can't leave it alone for five minutes, can you?"

"It's important."

Cheyenne spun and stormed past the nightstalkers. "Give me five minutes."

L'zar looked at Corian and gestured toward his daughter. The nightstalker pointed at him in warning. "Don't push it."

"Okay." The drow raised his hands in submission. "I'll wait."

Cheyenne walked across the bowl and slumped against the slope, her back curving with the shape of the smooth stone. Light tapping sounded on her right, and she snorted when she saw Foltr sitting on the lip of the stone bowl, swinging his staff over the edge and hitting the rock.

"Time heals many things, *Aranél.*"

"Yeah, well, I don't think five minutes is enough to patch up this mess." *Not even five lifetimes. I should never have trusted him.*

The old raug nodded slowly. "We shall see."

CHAPTER TWENTY-ONE

"Can I sit?"

Cheyenne glanced at L'zar's shoes beside her. "You were timing me, weren't you?"

"Only with an internal clock. It's pretty accurate after the first thousand years."

She snorted and didn't protest when he lowered himself to the stone beside her. The rest of their party had gathered on the other side of the clearing to give the drow space for a much-needed chat.

L'zar kicked out his legs in front of him and said, "I'm sure you've picked up on the fact that I was here once before."

"Yeah, two thousand years ago. And you found yourself a master. Sounds like some kind of messed-up drow BDSM without any of the benefits."

He slowly looked at her with a growing smile. "And those would be?"

"I don't know, it just came out. Say what you need to say."

"Ba'rael wasn't the only one looking for more power, Cheyenne." L'zar wrapped his arms around his bent knees and hooked his fingers together. "We shared the same brand of youthful stupidity back then. Honestly, I wonder sometimes if it's changed much."

She scoffed. "How observant of you."

"Most days, I like to think my stupidity is slightly less prevalent these days." L'zar shot her a sidelong glance and smiled. "My sister was too much of a coward to leave the safety of her precious city and risk everything she had to get what she wanted. I was too much of an idiot not to consider that coming here the first time would give me everything I wanted in all the worst ways. But I came. The Nimlothar forest was still thriving then. The rest of this place is unchanged."

"What's your point?"

"My point." The drow chuckled. "I came here wanting power from the *Sorren Gán*, and it showed me how to get what I wanted. I know exactly what it's like in that fell-damn lake, Cheyenne. I spent more time down there than I care to remember all at once, without coming up for air."

"You know you can breathe in there, right?"

"No. You could. I could not." L'zar turned his head toward her, then looked away. "I died in those flames. The part of me that makes me myself died, and when I did, I saw the threads right there in front of me, laid out in perfect order and with such clarity."

Cheyenne shifted her position and frowned across the clearing. "I have no idea what you're talking about when you bring up threads and weaving and whatever."

"Hmm. What you see with that activator, lines of code and data and the various outcomes of a single command, I see with magic. Those are the threads. The bonds tying us to every living thing in this world and Earth. To *ourselves*." He shrugged. "As I died, I found the threads to pull myself out of the flames. Maybe it was only a return from the brink of death and not real death. Who knows? L'zar Verdys, the O'gúl *Cu'ón*, fell into the fire, and L'zar Verdys the Smiling Weaver walked out of it, the same and not the same. Sometimes, I wonder how far from myself I've gotten since that day."

"Everyone says you were an annoying little shit from the beginning, so it can't be that far."

They both laughed, and L'zar nodded. "There is that. But we're talking about you."

"Right."

"When I walked out of that lake, Cheyenne, the *Sorren Gán* told me something I never expected to fully understand. I had the power I wanted, sure. I'd survived. I rewrote what would have been the end of my story and transformed it into something like the middle, or at least the end of the beginning. I had the *Sorren Gán*'s full approval and what it called 'my power,' but it told me I would not be the last one to use it."

"Meaning me." Cheyenne nodded. "I get it. I'm your kid, I got your drow powers. Sure."

"No. I'm sure you've noticed our abilities are not the same." L'zar chuckled. "And you can't read the Weave like I do."

"Well, you can't handle computers."

"That's a fair assessment. The day you told me you'd unlocked your final ability and used the black fire, though?" L'zar said, running a hand through his hair, "That was the moment I understood what the *Sorren Gán* meant."

Cheyenne waited for him to continue, but the pause felt far too long. *He's still stalling.* "I have a feeling there's something more to this. Otherwise, you lost me."

"You get your drow fire from me, Cheyenne. *And* from the *Sorren Gán*."

"Wait, what?"

"In plainer words, drow fire was not one of my abilities when I passed my trials. I'm fairly certain that came from my time spent in the lake, under the *Sorren Gán*'s control in its domain. To save myself, I took a piece of that beast's magic as my own and came out with a new fierce power I couldn't explain. No one would have listened anyway, except for you. You were born with it."

Cheyenne leaned away from him and frowned. "That's crazy. You're telling me I'm part-*Sorren Gán?*"

"Hardly. You just have its magic in your blood."

"Magically speaking, L'zar, I'm pretty sure that's the same thing."

He looked her in the eyes, a small frown flickering across his eyebrows. "It most certainly is not." With a grunt, he pushed to his feet and walked across the clearing toward the others. "And now I need a drink."

Cheyenne stared after him, trying to make all the pieces fit. *It sounds like total crap, but it makes sense. I could breathe in the lake, didn't lose my mind, and couldn't hurt the damn thing with my most powerful ability.*

She shook her head. "Later. I can think about that later."

She stood and headed after her father. Corian gave her a wary smile. "Everybody good?"

"'Good' is probably a little strong, but I don't want to kill him anymore."

L'zar smirked but didn't look at her.

"That's acceptable." Corian rubbed his hands together and gazed around the gathered circle. "Time to figure out what happens next."

"Don't we go back to the capital and wait for that thing to come and suck out all the extra magic?" Ember asked.

"We could."

L'zar lifted his chin. "I can't think about what happens next until we get out of here. And I'd prefer not to waste another day at the very least traveling the way we came so I can find a quiet place to put my head together."

"Right." Corian glanced at the cave entrance and cocked his head. "We have plenty of that to do still."

"And if possible, I would prefer to return to Hangivol with

much more of a plan than we have now when it comes to the terms of Ba'rael's secession and Cheyenne taking the O'gúl Crown. If she wants it."

Maleshi shrugged. "The plan we have now is nonexistent."

"What exactly do we have to sit down and think so hard about?" Cheyenne asked.

L'zar's smile widened. "Where my sister's weakest point is and how to exploit it."

She gestured toward the burning cave. "After everything that happened in there, you want to talk about exploiting weaknesses?"

The other magicals glanced around in confusion, but L'zar and his daughter stared only at each other.

"You make an excellent point." The drow nodded, and his smile bloomed into his trickster grin. "You can't tell me it's not extraordinarily effective."

She laughed. "No, I guess not."

"We can go to Hirúl Breach." Foltr lifted his staff and gestured farther into the mountains. "Another few hours through the next pass."

Lumil snorted. "Hirúl Breach? You know, I heard they call that place the Crown's Bastion."

The old raug grunted and stuck his stick into the ground. "The *last* Crown, yes. K'laht traveled there often, and Hirúl Breach welcomed him with open arms and everything they had to give. There is no love lost between them and Ba'rael."

L'zar narrowed his eyes. "No love lost, or they hate her?"

"They despise the Crown of this Cycle, L'zar. As they should."

The drow clapped his hands together and pointed in the direction Foltr had indicated. "Then by all means, that needs to be our next stop. A few hours is much better than an entire day. Lead on."

"I'm not leading us anywhere," Foltr blustered. "But I can get us inside."

L'zar leaned toward him and shook his head. "I don't know where it is."

"Of course you don't." The old raug thumped his staff against the drow's calf. "You never went farther into these mountains than *this* cursed stinkhole."

"We should go somewhere else." Maleshi folded her arms and squinted into the woods.

L'zar cocked his head. "Come again?"

She rolled her eyes and glared at him. "Do I have to spell it out for you, L'zar? Hirúl Breach is the closest hub to the den at Felagtrok."

"Ah, yes. And this is apparently an issue for you." L'zar tapped a long, slender finger on his lips. "Care to elaborate?"

"You know exactly what I'm talking about."

Foltr patted the general's arm and nodded. "If there were survivors, Maleshi, they would most likely be there. And yes, they might be uncomfortable with our presence."

"Uncomfortable?" The nightstalker woman closed her eyes. "You know that's not the way those raugs see it."

"They will see past what you have done as Hand of the Night and Circle, *hinya*." Foltr nodded and thumped his staff on the ground. "They will not forget, but they will understand."

Lumil snorted. "Yeah. Raugs understand with their fists."

"Just like you, eh?" Foltr pointed the end of his stick at her legs. "Don't make me use this."

"I've been to Hirúl Breach," Corian muttered, giving Maleshi an apologetic smile. "It's a good idea, and it'll help us, whether or not they enjoy a visit from General Hi'et."

Maleshi grimaced. "Fine. What's done is done, and everyone's made up their minds."

Corian nodded. "I'll open a portal."

Foltr looked at him. "You can port that far, eh?"

"I've connected two spaces a lot farther apart than that, Grandfather," Corian said, "Though I'd be a lot more comfortable with it if we got away from this cave first. The last thing I want is a *Sorren Gán* feeding on my trail."

"Excellent point. It would follow you and ask for more." L'zar chuckled and stepped out of the bowl-shaped clearing to trudge through the slowly thickening forest on the other side. "Things are already looking up. I can feel it."

Cheyenne nudged Maleshi with her elbow. "I don't need to know the details, but if I got sacrificed on purpose to make a point, I'm pretty sure you can handle a few raugs who recognize you and might hold a grudge."

The general scoffed. "You just keep broadening your horizons, don't you, kid? Here's hoping you're right." Maleshi stalked after the others, and Cheyenne sighed.

Ember leaned toward her. "Talk about mood swings."

"Right? I think I understand a little better where they're coming from now."

"Oh, yeah?"

"I mean, most of it's still 'cause he's losing his mind, but there's a reason for that too."

Ember folded her arms and eyed the halfling. "When we get more than a minute, you have a hell of a lot to tell me, don't you?"

"More than I can even think about right now, Em." Cheyenne stepped onto the lip of earth above the clearing and headed after the others. "I might need a little more time to sort it all out in my head."

"Sure. While you're doing that, how's your face?"

Cheyenne snorted. "You hit like a fae."

"Huh. I have no idea if that was a compliment, but thanks."

"It definitely was." The halfling cast her friend a sidelong glance. "Good thing I have you to slap some sense into me, right?"

"That's exactly why I'm here. Friends don't let friends kill their crazy-ass fathers."

"Ha. Hopefully it won't be a thing again, but you might have to remind me of that once or twice."

Ember raised her hand and shook it in a goofy wave. "I'll be ready."

CHAPTER TWENTY-TWO

After a half-hour hike through the mountains, Corian stopped to open a portal for them into Hirúl Breach. They stepped through the dark window of light and found themselves on a stone plateau at the edge of a mountainous canyon. Natural rock walls stretched high all around them, and in the center was Hirúl Breach.

"Well." Foltr frowned at the rising towers of stone and dark metal tech. "The place has certainly changed since I last came through."

Corian nodded slowly. "Tell me about it."

"For a tribe opposed to technological advancements, I'd say they're doing pretty well for themselves." L'zar bowed to Foltr and gestured toward the wide staircase carved into the stone of the plateau, which descended to the front gates of the city. "How about now, Grandfather?"

"If it gets you to stop making a mockery of yourself, Weaver, I'll lead the fell-damn way." Foltr thumped his cane with each step as he approached the staircase, and the party moved from their vantage point toward the raug city below.

"Not sure what he means by technological advancement,"

Cheyenne muttered. "There's tech here, but it's not like anything in Hangivol."

Corian looked at her over his shoulder. "For Hirúl Breach, it's a huge step forward. They're stonemasons, or at least they *were*. Looks like they've taken it upon themselves to add old-world tech to the mix. The buildings are a lot higher, and they *have* front gates this time, so it must be doing something for them."

Ember peered over Corian's head to look down at the whirring, rumbling machines of black metal rolling slowly across the open area in front of the gates. "Old-world tech as in war machines?"

"Same look, different purpose." Corian chuckled. "It's pretty ingenious of them. The Crown can't hack into their machines with her fancy new gadgets that won't sync up. They've made themselves as autonomous as anyone can get out here."

"They're protecting themselves." Cheyenne eyed the machine of black, glistening metal passing in front of them when they reached the bottom of the staircase. *That one looks way too much like those diggers.*

"That's what it looks like, doesn't it?" Maleshi gazed at the high metal gates in front of them. "And they built a city."

"A trade city, looks like," Corian said, "It wouldn't house nearly as many magicals, but if something *did* happen to Hangivol, we might be looking at the runner-up for a new capital."

L'zar scoffed. "Right. Everyone in Hangivol will throw out their activators and come swarming out here to live in the dark ages of O'gúl tech. Brilliant analysis." He thumped the back of his hand against Corian's chest and shook his head. "Hangivol will be fine."

"Sure."

"*Salut!*" The gruff shout came from atop one of the towers beside the gate. "*Qui êtes vous?*"

Foltr extended a hand toward the traveling party and nodded. "Let me speak to them first, eh? Just a few minutes, and I'll get us inside."

Cheyenne and the others waited halfway between the bottom of the stairs and Hirúl Breach's front gates.

"A word, brothers!" Foltr shouted at the towers.

A lot of banging and clanking came from within the gates, then a door opened at the base of the tower, and two raugs in matching gray uniforms marched out to meet with the old magical wielding his trusty staff.

Cheyenne cocked her head as she listened to the conversation. The only words she could pick out were *Aranél* and *Cu'ón*, but she recognized the language. She turned toward Maleshi and pointed at the raugs. "Are they speaking French?"

"*Oui.*" The general chuckled at Cheyenne's confusion. "Don't tell me you never wondered why a separate world full of magic and every race under the sun except the human race was full of magicals speaking English."

"Of course I wondered." Cheyenne folded her arms. "I guess I figured it was because of the portals or something. I don't know. You guys travel back and forth all the time, don't you?"

Corian snorted. "Only some of us, kid."

Maleshi shot him an exasperated glance but couldn't help a smile. "It has something to do with the portals, sure. Our worlds are connected. Nobody can argue that. Very few O'gúleesh magicals speak the old O'gúleesh tongue day-to-day, minus the few colorful words thrown in for fun."

"So, what? Everyone just speaks English and French instead?"

"Try *all* Earth languages." With his hands clasped behind his back, L'zar wiggled his eyebrows at his daughter and grinned. "Earthside portals exist all over the world. It wouldn't make sense if we only spoke English and French over here, now would it?"

Cheyenne shook her head in disbelief. "How long has this been a thing?"

Corian shrugged. "As long as the portals, I assume. It's anyone's guess."

"The only pure O'gúleesh language still intact is our alphabet." Maleshi chuckled and stared wistfully across the small courtyard in front of the gates. "Let me tell ya, kid, it took me a hell of a lot longer than I expected to nail down reading and writing after I made the crossing. Just one of those things you don't think much about when you're abandoning your post and a dying world to start over fresh."

Ember slid her hands down her cheeks and let out a surprised chuckle. "Raugs speaking French. Now I've seen it all. What else is there?"

Corian smiled at her. "The Golra have a fluent understanding of almost every Chinese dialect."

Cheyenne barked a laugh, then cleared her throat. "Nu'ek too?"

"Probably."

Foltr nodded at the raug guards and turned slowly toward the group, shambling back with his staff clicking on the stone.

L'zar dipped his head toward the ancient magical. "Well?"

"It's a start." Foltr looked at Ember and raised his thick brows over wrinkled eyelids. "They need your help."

"*My* help?" Ember glanced at the others. "You're not talking about just me."

"Yes. Just you." Foltr grumbled something unintelligible, then looked at Maleshi. "They don't want us here. Especially you, General."

"They recognized me, huh?"

"Yes. They also made it perfectly clear they have ended all ties with the capital and whatever fate befalls it." He lifted a crooked gray finger at Ember. "But they need you."

"To do what?"

"They need a fae. A healer. There's a dying raug inside those gates who stands to meet the final deathflame far before his time. If you can save him, these gates will open for all of us. They'll give us a warm raug welcome, and we can sit down with whomever we like to discuss how they can help us."

L'zar chuckled. "'Warm raug welcome?' There's a term you don't hear every day."

"If it didn't exist before, it will after this." Foltr waved Ember forward. "Let's get it done."

"For real?" Ember looked at Cheyenne. "Is he serious?"

"It's healing, Em. No spells. You just do it, right?"

The fae glanced at Foltr, who was shuffling away again. "I guess."

Cheyenne nodded. "You got this."

L'zar sat down outside the front gates, stretching his legs out in front of him and propping himself up with his hands. "We'll be waiting for you. Try to be quick about it."

"Oh, sure. I'll just rush the healing of a dying raug. No problem." Rolling her eyes, Ember floated after Foltr, clenching and unclenching her fists at her sides.

L'zar chuckled. "I like a fae who talks back to me."

Corian snorted. "You like anyone who talks to you at all."

"Not true, but nice try."

Cheyenne watched Ember and Foltr follow the guards through the door at the base of the massive gates. "So we wait."

Maleshi set a hand on the halfling's shoulder and dipped her head. "We're not storming into *this* stronghold, kid. I can tell you that much."

"As long as they let her back out."

"If she heals this raug, they will."

When the small door shut behind the raug guards, Cheyenne sat down on the ground too and crossed her legs. "There's no if. She'll get it done. That's what fae do, right?"

"It certainly seems that way."

CHAPTER TWENTY-THREE

Ember floated behind Foltr and their raug escorts into Hirúl Breach. She didn't get to see much of it after they passed through the gate, but it was enough to convince her she'd walked into one more giant city she knew nothing about. *And I'm here playing magical doctor. Okay. I can do this.*

The guards led them into a long, low building built against the wall of the canyon. They climbed three sets of narrow staircases and stopped in front of a heavy wooden door. One raug pressed his palm to the door and nodded at her. "Don't let him kick you out, fae. He does that."

"Okay."

He shoved the door open and gestured for her to walk in. She floated through the door, and the other guard held out his hand to block Foltr from entering as well. "Only the healer, old one."

Foltr grunted and lifted his staff, preparing to knock the guard's hand aside. "I'm old, brother. Not useless. I can help."

"Not if you catch what eats this one."

"Hmm." Foltr stepped back and called through the door, "I'll be outside, girl. Call if you need anything."

"Right." Before she could say anything else, the guards pulled the heavy door shut with a bang. Wrinkling her nose, she scanned the room. One wall was open to the outside air, pulling in a small breeze that made the lanterns sway on their hooks in the ceiling. *They could knock down all the walls, and it still wouldn't improve the smell.*

Grimacing, she floated toward the large bed on the other side of the room, where a mottled gray hand poked out from beneath layers and layers of thick blankets. "Hello?"

A wheezing cough greeted her.

That doesn't sound good. What am I doing? I'm not a raug doctor.

"I came here to help."

"Get out." The voice was raspy and dry, more like a croak. The red claws at the tips of the raug's nails flicked toward the door. "Let me be."

"See, that's not an option. You need help, and that's what I'm here to do." She floated slowly along the side of the bed, fighting not to wrinkle her nose.

The raug lying beneath all the blankets and furs didn't look old enough to be so sick or on the edge of death. *He's huge. Bigger than Gúrdu.* Ember stared at the bulging muscles of his arms and shoulders. Her eyes widened when she saw the black lines snaking up his arms beneath his gray flesh. *Just like the skaxen. How the hell am I supposed to fix this?*

His chest rose and fell with a constant wheeze, his large eyes closed over a grimace of pain and determination.

"What's your name?" she asked.

"If you don't know my name, you shouldn't be here." The raug slowly rolled his head toward her, and his eyes fluttered open. "No. Send the other healers, girl. I don't want a fae in here." He broke into a fit of hacking coughs. The bed groaned beneath him as his huge body lurched, and he thrust his hand toward the door. "I said, get out."

"You don't want a fae in here, huh?" Ember waited for the

coughing to subside, then reached for the edge of the blankets and cautiously peeled them away from his chin to expose his chest. "I don't wanna be in here either, so it looks like we both have to do something we don't like. Deal with it."

The raug growled at her, his glowing orange eyes narrowing. "Where are the other healers? *My* healers?"

"I don't know, and I don't care." Folding the blankets over his legs, she fought not to grimace at the thicker lines of black streaking across his chest and meeting in a dark stain over his heart. *Assuming raug hearts are in the same place as human hearts.* "Doesn't look like *your* healers had much luck. Just think of me as a last resort."

He sputtered and clenched his eyes shut, and for a minute, Ember thought he was choking. Then a grin split his lips, revealing sharp, pointed teeth and a black tongue behind them. She rolled her eyes.

"Last resort or last rites? The deathflame's calling my name, either way."

"Which you still haven't given me, by the way."

"Bah." He turned his head away from her and lay still, breathing quickly and shallowly. "Do your best, then."

"What happened?"

The raug grunted. "Apparently, I didn't think to have a fae on hand every damn place I go."

"Okay. I get it." *Big guy got tainted by the blight, and now he's punishing himself for it.* "Has it happened to anyone else?"

A low growl escaped him, and he kept his eyes closed. "No. I got this on a mining expedition, fae. Been in this room for three fell-damn days since I returned."

"Then let's hope I got here fast enough."

He started to chuckle and fell into a fit of coughing even worse than the first one. Ember glanced at the stone shelves cut into the wall beside the bed and picked up the metal pitcher there to give it a quick sniff. *Smells like water. Decent chance it's safe.*

She poured some into a copper cup and set that gently in the raug's open hand. He grasped the cup, his nails clinking on the metal, and brought it to his lips without lifting his head from the thick pillows. Water spilled from the side of his mouth and down around his shoulders. When it was empty, he tossed the cup away. Ember started at the harsh clang of copper bouncing on the stone floor.

The raug twirled a finger in the air before his hand dropped to the bed with a thump. "Get on with it. If I'm at the end, I'd rather get there sooner than later."

"You've got an awfully cheery view of things, don't you?"

He grunted and said nothing.

"Try to relax, I guess." Ember slowly reached out to hover both palms above the raug's broad, black-streaked chest. She focused on her healing magic, and a faint purple light glowed between her palms and the sick raug. After a full minute with no effect, she frowned. *I'm tasting bananas, so I know it's the healing and not the throw-things-across-the-room kind of magic. What am I missing?*

The raug wheezed. "See? No use for a fae."

"Shut up." Gritting her teeth, Ember placed her hands on the raug's chest.

He gasped and lurched, his orange eyes flying wide open as he gaped. Ember almost pulled away from the instant burning in her hands but forced herself to keep pressing on his chest. *I'm a full-blooded fae and the drow princess's goddamn* Nós Aní. *This is gonna work.*

The burning heat traveled slowly up her wrists and forearms, intensifying as it spread. Ember grunted against the pain and kept at her healing, even when the raug gasped again and started cursing in French. She would've laughed if she wasn't so focused.

An unseen force propelled her away from the raug. Arms flailing, Ember tried to keep her balance and focused on the levitation spell Corian had taught her, but it winked out the next second, and her feet dropped an inch to the floor. Her legs crumpled beneath her and she landed on the stone floor with a thud, shouting in surprise and pain.

The room was eerily silent.

Ember rolled as much as she could onto her side and pushed herself up to sit four feet away from the bed. She stared at her legs, willing them to move, and slapped a hand against her thigh for good measure. *Great. Almost no feeling. I'm right back to being a useless fae lump.*

A low chuckle came from the bed, and it quickly grew to a roar of laughter that made her want to cover her ears. The raug's hands shot into the air and he flipped them over and over again, staring at the scarred flesh free of black streaks. "*Hishmál.* Would you look at that?"

He bolted upright in the bed and swung his legs over the side, grinning at the space five and a half feet above the ground where he expected Ember to be. Then he looked down at the fae on the floor and cocked his head. "What's wrong with *you?*"

"Oh, you know. Just the usual."

"Let me see your hands."

Ember pursed her lips. "I didn't *take* your sickness if that's what you're wondering."

"Fae don't sit around on the floor, girl. Show me your hands."

Rolling her eyes, Ember lifted both hands and turned them back and forth as he had. "See? No black streaks. No blight. I'm just regular old me."

"Ha!" The raug leaped to his feet and smacked his bare chest, now gray again. "We *both* underestimated you. Vingat! De'garu!"

The heavy wooden door burst open on the other side of the

room, and the two raug guards thundered in. They stopped short when they saw the healed raug standing over the fae girl on the floor. "What is this?"

"*This* is your chief returned!" The raug pounded his chest again and spread his arms. "It's done."

The guards grinned at him and thumped fists on their chests in response. "It worked."

"What's this?" Foltr came into the room, his cane clacking across the floor. "What's all this now?" The same surprise and confusion flashed behind his widening eyes when he saw the raug and Ember, and he nodded. "Yes. Well done, girl."

"Just doing my fae thing, I guess." Ember patted the floor beside her. "Lost my mobility, though."

The healed raug laughed and stomped toward her. "We will fix that for you, Healer."

"I'm not really a healer. Wait, what are you doing?"

"Helping you." He bent down with a snort and scooped her up in his arms.

She tried to push him away. "No, that's okay. You don't have to pick me up."

"Ha! No fae enjoys the floor, and you most certainly do not deserve it. De'garu, find a crawler for this one."

One of the guards nodded and left the room.

"A crawler?" Ember stared at the raug's huge face right next to hers as he cradled her like a child in his bare arms.

"But you won't be doing the crawling." He chuckled. "What's your name, girl?"

She laughed and shook her head. *This is absurd.* "Ember."

"Ember. I am Cazerel. Welcome to my home."

"You were talking about yourself when you mentioned a chief, weren't you?"

"Ha. I thought I wouldn't be soon enough. Everything we have here is yours, Healer. You've done us a great service. Me, specifically."

"I figured I could help." Ember shot Foltr a nervous smile, and the old raug chuckled. "I don't need everything you have. Just the crawler, I guess."

Cazerel roared with laughter, bouncing her up and down. Ember tried to keep her arms from rubbing his rough gray skin but ended up laughing too. *Weirdest thing I've ever done. Cheyenne's gonna lose it when I tell her about this one.*

CHAPTER TWENTY-FOUR

Cheyenne folded her arms and watched the half-dozen raugs standing between L'zar's traveling band of rebels and the outer gates of Hirúl Breach. "Huh. Call me crazy, but this doesn't feel like a very friendly greeting."

The raugs prowled in the front of the massive gates, glowing eyes in various shades of orange narrowed as they scrutinized the newcomers. Most of them glared at General Hi'et, but some of their gazes turned toward Cheyenne and L'zar too.

"They're not doing anything," Corian muttered and glanced at L'zar, who was still sitting on the ground beside him. "And neither are we."

The drow chuckled. "I didn't say a thing."

Corian looked back at the agitated raugs. "You didn't have to."

Behind them, Maleshi had taken up pacing in jerking steps, occasionally stopping for five to ten seconds before she couldn't help but look at the raugs again. Then she'd walk three or four feet, pause, and do it all over again.

The next time she passed Corian, he reached out to touch

her forearm without turning away from the raugs. "You need to stop doing that."

Maleshi glared at his hand on her arm and brushed it off before continuing in her halting, irritated march. "Sure. *You* try being the target of all this hatred and standing still. Look at you, a perfect nightstalker statue, all proper and composed."

"Maleshi."

"I'm *trying*," she hissed, lunging toward him from behind to snarl in his ear. "You have no idea what this is like for me. I'm doing the best I can."

"It's not ingrained in you to kill them, and it's not ingrained in you to lose control of yourself when things get dicey."

Maleshi scoffed. "It is when I'm the one to blame for all of it."

Cheyenne caught the general's gaze and grinned. "I know exactly how you feel right now."

That caught the nightstalker woman off-guard, and she stopped to stare at Cheyenne. "Yeah, I guess you do." She picked up her pacing again.

One raug growled something in French, and Maleshi spun toward him and hissed.

"Okay, what was that?"

The general glanced briefly at Cheyenne and rolled her eyes. "More jokes about cats. Without claws."

Then the raugs switched to English and started pounding their chests. "The Hand of the Night and Circle couldn't push us all out, could she?"

"We stayed *true*, nightstalker!"

"Doesn't matter how long you've been gone, Hi'et. Our memories are *long*."

The raugs chuckled and snarled, stalking in front of the gates with their shoulders hunched and their hands outstretched to show how sharp their red claws were.

"Hey, maybe we'd be better prepared for this if we all knew

why they're so pissed off at you," Cheyenne suggested. When Corian and the goblins shot her confused looks, she shrugged. "Okay, I guess I'm the only one who doesn't know."

"They're the last of Gúrdu's tribe," Maleshi hissed. "I led a siege against Felagtrok under the Crown, and apparently, these are the ones I didn't manage to get my hands on before they fled."

Cheyenne narrowed her eyes. "What happened to the rest of them?"

"I gave Gúrdu the option to make the crossing. Perks of being an Oracle, I guess. And then I killed everyone else." Maleshi stopped, looked at the halfling, and shrugged. "It was a different time, kid. *I* was different."

"I sure hope so." Cheyenne watched the general pace, then had to look away. "You're making me nervous."

"I don't give a shit about your fragile composure right now. I'm too busy with my own."

Cheyenne and Corian exchanged quick glances, and the nightstalker man shook his head. "We'll hold right here. That's all there is to it."

"And if they attack us?"

"Relax." L'zar lifted his forearm from his knee to wave his daughter's concerns aside. "They're not going to attack."

"You want a sliver of your honor back, *nilsch úcat?*" The shouting raug thumped his fist on his chest over and over. "Let's see how you fight when I rip those fancy little whiskers right out of your coward's face!"

Maleshi hissed again and vanished in a flash of silver light. A second later, she'd stopped two feet from the line of raugs and snarled at him. "I dare you, grayskin. Anyone who holds onto the past this long has nothing else worth their time."

"Smashing you into the ground would be worth my time."

The raugs behind him chuckled darkly and snarled at the

nightstalker. Two of them stepped forward, and Maleshi cocked her head. "Don't."

"Why not, Hand of the Night and Circle?" The closest raug licked his gray lips with a shiny black tongue and sneered, eyeing her. "You look so *soft*."

The general lifted her arms away from her sides and extended four-inch claws from every finger. "Wanna bet?"

"Maleshi," Corian shouted. "Not here."

"This looks like the perfect place to me, *vae shra'ni*." The general spread her arms wider and lifted her chin at the sneering raugs in front of her. "Unless every one of you wants a repeat of the Felagtrok. I didn't tell anyone about the cowards who ran off and abandoned their tribe that day, but now we have witnesses."

Another raug hissed a bitter laugh. "I thought this was the General Hi'et who abandoned her post for a world full of weaklings. What a convenient way to avoid paying for what you've done!"

Maleshi snarled and took a step toward him, pulling her arm back and holding it there, ready to strike.

"I said, not here!" Corian came toward them in a flash of silver light and grabbed the general's shoulder. "If it comes to it, let *them* strike first."

The raug in front of Maleshi lunged forward and swung a powerful uppercut into the general's stomach. She flew across the stone courtyard, and in nightstalker fashion, landed in a crouch, sliding across the stone and glaring at the raug with a wild hiss.

The raug looked at Corian. "Thanks for the invitation."

The nightstalker glared at him. "That's not what I meant."

Maleshi flashed past him in a blaze of silver light and barreled into the raug, slashing across his chest with her claws. The other five gray-skinned magicals roared in approval, shouting insults at Maleshi and encouragement to their fellow raug as the two battled it out with their fists and claws.

"This isn't why we're here!" Corian shouted over the noise. "Maleshi, call it off."

She darted around the raug, who spun in the opposite direction and knocked her out of her enhanced speed when his left fist cracked into her jaw.

"Dammit, Hi'et!" Corian ducked when another raug swung at him. Then he hissed, rolled his shoulders, and blasted the attacking magical with a bolt of silver lightning.

"Jesus." Cheyenne jogged toward the nightstalkers, who were in furious single combat with two raugs. *It's gonna be two against six pretty soon. I thought I was the one who got pissed-off and stupid.*

"Hey!" She stopped four feet away from the cheering group of raugs and summoned a crackling black sphere of energy in one hand. "I know all of you can hear me. We have bigger problems to deal with right now, and this isn't helping."

L'zar stayed where he was, his forearms dangling over his knees, and chuckled.

"Fuck this." Lumil clenched her fists and summoned the red, spinning runes around them. "No way am I sittin' this one out."

"Nope." Byrd's hands filled with green flames, and both goblins raced toward the fight.

"You're all a bunch of idiots," Cheyenne shouted, trying to be heard without getting closer.

"Kiss my goblin ass, you beefy shits!" Lumil raced past the halfling and punched the closest raug where a human's kidney would have been. The raug stumbled forward with a grunt, whirled toward the goblin woman, and snatched the front of her leather jacket before tossing her away with one hand.

Byrd ran screaming into the fray, ducking huge, swinging gray arms and blasting green fire in all directions.

Every raug roared and focused on a new target. One of

them hooked a claw through the back of Byrd's collar and lifted the goblin off the ground, swinging him from side to side and grinning. The hulking magical beside him burst into thunderous laughter until Lumil launched at him and smashed her spell-enhanced fist into his mouth.

"Dammit." Cheyenne gritted her teeth and quickly scanned the fighting magicals. "Guess it's a full-on brawl now." She launched the crackling sphere of magic at the raug swinging both fists toward Lumil and knocked him back enough that he missed. Lumil cackled and dropped to her knees to bring her fist up into his muscular gut.

The halfling sent her lashing tendrils toward the raug dangling Byrd by the collar. Despite his odd position, the goblin man kept blasting green fireballs at the other raugs while he swung left and right. Cheyenne's black tendrils coiled around the raug's outstretched arm, and she pulled hard. Byrd's collar ripped, and he dropped to the ground and shot two fireballs into the huge magical's face. Cackling, he scrambled away and headed after someone else.

Blinking and snorting against the residual green flames, the raug's orange eyes settled on Cheyenne. He grinned and stomped toward her. "Shit."

Cheyenne slipped into drow speed and raced toward him. Just before she reached the gray-skinned magical, he turned with surprising speed for someone that size and lowered his shoulder toward her with a quick step forward. She couldn't stop in time and crashed into his muscular frame. It knocked her out of enhanced speed and sent her flailing across the stone.

He straightened and grinned at her. "Surprise."

Raugs don't have superspeed. How the hell do they move that fast? She cocked her head at him and spread her arms. "That all you got?"

The raug lumbered toward her. "No."

Metal hinges creaked at the base of the wall, and the smaller door opened. Foltr lurched through first, the clack of his cane unheard beneath the din of the brawl. "What is this? Not even an hour."

Cazerel ducked through the door with Ember in his arms and snorted, his eyes widening when he saw what was happening. "Excuse me, Healer."

Ember stared at the brawl. "For what?"

"What I am about to do." The raug chief stalked toward a short ledge of stone jutting from the wall of the canyon against which Hirúl Breach's outer wall was built and set her down with a firm nod. "My apologies."

He didn't wait for her to say anything but whirled and stormed toward the fight. "Enough!"

His booming voice cracked across the courtyard in front of the gates. At their chieftain's angry shout, every raug stopped immediately and straightened. The nightstalkers fell out of their enhanced speed with silver flashes. Cheyenne stepped away from the raug, who was no longer coming at her. Too far gone to her battle rage, Lumil charged her opponent with a roar. The raug reached out with one hand and wrapped his long gray fingers around the top of the goblin woman's head, holding her away from him at arm's length while she snarled and swung uselessly with her spinning red fists.

"Lumil," Cheyenne muttered. "Hey, cut it out."

The goblin woman grunted, then reached up with both hands and jerked the raug's palm off her head. "Get the hell off me."

The raug lowered his arm and stared at his chief, ignoring her like an elephant ignoring a fly.

L'zar finally stood and clasped his hands behind his back to watch the raug chief with a knowing smile.

"Who is responsible for this?" Cazerel boomed. None of his magicals replied, so he stalked down the line of raug men, who were all at least a foot shorter than him, thumping a hand against his bare chest. "You see this? Do you see your chief standing here before you? I lay ready to face the end, and I come to greet new friends, only to find you thick-headed beasts thanking them with your fists. Tell me what happened!"

"*Zokrí.*" The raug whose loose tunic was shredded to ribbons from Maleshi's claws stepped forward and pounded his chest. "This was vengeance."

Cazerel snarled. "For what?"

"Felagtrok." The raug gestured at Maleshi. "General Hi'et returns."

The chief turned toward Maleshi. Under his gaze and finally catching her breath, the general straightened and clasped her hands behind her back, lifting her chin.

"So she does." Cazerel nodded with another grunt of acknowledgment. "Felagtrok was a long time ago. Consider this battle the only vengeance you will have, Bru'uga."

The raug snarled at Maleshi but lowered his gaze when the chief looked at him. "I am not satisfied."

"Neither am I." Cazerel pounded his chest again. "See this! Your chief stands tall outside Hirúl Breach's gates because General Hi'et's party brought a fae to our door." His massive arm swung toward Ember, who was still sitting on the rock ledge beyond the gates. She coughed, then cleared her throat. "The healer has claimed victory over the deathflame for me. Maleshi Hi'et's debt to you has been paid with my life. Leave it."

"*Zokrí.*" Bru'uga dipped his head and stood perfectly still as Cazerel headed toward Foltr.

The chief leaned toward the aged raug and muttered, "You and yours are welcome in our city now, old one. Bring them. We have much to discuss."

"We do." Foltr nodded at the raug towering almost two feet above his shoulders.

Cazerel headed toward the open door at the base of the

gates and muttered something in French to a waiting guard. The guard nodded and disappeared inside, then the chief followed, stooping to squeeze his massive frame through the doorway.

Foltr cracked his cane on the stone floor and glared at the subdued raug warriors. His scowl turned on Maleshi and Corian next, and he moved slowly back through the open door, muttering and shaking his head.

"Well." L'zar chuckled and strolled casually across the small courtyard. "Hell of a welcome, huh?"

Grinning at the gathered raugs, he dipped his head and slipped through the door after Foltr.

Corian stepped away from the warriors and nodded before taking his leave. The raugs glared at him and then Maleshi when she followed Corian into the city.

Cheyenne nudged Lumil and muttered, "I'll go get Ember."

"Yeah. Get the chief-healing fae." The goblin woman scoffed at the warriors and stomped off, rubbing her hand vigorously through her mop of yellow hair until it hung over her eyes. Byrd jumped and headed after her, looking between the open door and the raug warriors growling at him.

Weird to not be the center of everyone's hatred, but I'll take it.

CHAPTER TWENTY-FIVE

Cheyenne headed quickly across the stone square toward Ember, who propped herself up on the ledge with her hands behind her and started coughing again.

"Hey." Cheyenne stopped beside her friend and turned to eye the raugs again, folding her arms. "Looks like you did it."

"Yeah, I did it." Ember sucked in a wheezing breath.

"You okay?"

"No." With another cough, Ember doubled over and shook her head. "I think I short-circuited my magic with that one."

"What?"

The fae looked at Cheyenne with a fiery violet gaze. "You think I'm just sitting here without getting up to follow everyone else for fun?"

"Shit. No floating spell?"

"Nothing." Ember snapped her fingers and opened her hands again. "Not even a spark."

"Must've been some seriously intense healing."

The fae girl scoffed. "He had the blight, Cheyenne. So yeah, it was pretty intense."

Nothing personal. I'd be pissed too if I couldn't walk after helping someone. Or float. Nodding slowly, Cheyenne sat beside her friend on the ledge and bumped her shoulder against Ember's. "Two good things out of this, though."

"Since when did you become the silver-lining drow?"

Cheyenne snorted. "Since the silver-lining fae went all dark and broody and could use a pep talk. Maybe."

"Whatever. Go for it."

The halfling watched the disgruntled raug warriors, who had gathered and were grumbling at each other, trying to find another outlet for their rage. "You saved a raug chief's life, apparently. And we were clearly only getting inside this place with the approval of a chief who doesn't want anything to do with Hangivol or the Crown."

"You mean, you couldn't have stormed the gates and blasted your way inside for another chat with a city leader?"

"Very funny." Cheyenne rubbed her hands up and down her thighs. "But we're in, thanks to you."

"No problem." Ember rolled her eyes. "I'm not accepting donations. You know, 'cause I can't walk *or* float around anymore. This is as good as it gets again."

"Nah. You still look like a fae. Your magic probably needs a reboot."

"It better come back."

"It will, Em. I still need you around, so you don't have a choice."

Ember snorted, and they both laughed softly. "Okay, so what's the second good thing?"

"Now we know it's possible to reverse the whole blight thing, at least when it's starting to take over magicals."

"Huh." Ember tossed a hand in the air. "Hope for healing Ambar'ogúl, right? I'd honestly settle for healing my own legs and leave it at that."

"You'll get there." They sat in silence for a moment, then Cheyenne slapped her thighs and leaned toward her friend. "If

I know those guys in there, they're probably *not* waiting for us to get started with their chief-to-chief chat, but I don't wanna miss it."

"By all means, drow." Ember gestured at the open door in the gates. "I'm not going anywhere."

"I'm not leaving you here. I was gonna offer to carry you with me. You know, drow strength and everything without having to worry about humans freaking out if they see it."

Ember grimaced. "I'm not a fan of being carried."

"Hey, I'm not a giant, bare-chested raug chief."

"Oh, jeez." The fae laughed and rolled her eyes. "That was one of the weirder things I've experienced. The guy's got, like, sharkskin."

Cheyenne snorted. "Sounds fun."

"At least he wasn't sweaty." Ember shrugged. "Dammit, just carry me."

"Yep."

Cheyenne stood and bent over so Ember could hook her arm around her neck. Before she could scoop the fae girl into her arms, a raug guard whistled sharply from the open door and shouted something at them in French. Cheyenne straightened again and shook her head. "English."

The guard frowned and banged the open door with another shout in French to someone up in the tower. "The healer's not forgotten, drow. Don't carry her. The *Zokrí* has a gift."

"A gift." Cheyenne turned toward Ember and raised her eyebrows. "From your hulking chief admirer."

"Shut up."

The grating creak and rumble of mechanisms turning in the huge metal gates echoed across the stone square, then a square section of metal at the base of the closest gate tower lifted like a garage door. The guard who'd called to them headed toward it and waited for a machine of black metal to fully emerge from the base of the tower.

"What the hell is that?" Ember muttered.

"I think that's your gift, Em."

"Oh, jeez."

The raug guard reached into the center of the old-school O'gúl tech machine and tapped the controls. Eight legs unfolded from the undercarriage with a clang of metal on stone, and the main body lifted three feet off the ground. When the guard headed toward Cheyenne and Ember, the machine scuttled after him like a giant headless spider with a depression in its huge abdomen.

Ember grimaced. "No. Please, no."

The guard stopped in front of them and offered Ember a sleek, two-inch bar of flattened black metal. "For you."

The fae took it and turned the item over in her hand. "Looks like the barrettes I used to wear in grade school, without the clip."

Cheyenne fought back a laugh and tapped behind her own ear. "Activator, Em."

"Oh." Ember lifted the piece of metal toward the raug and raised her eyebrows.

"Wear it." The guard looked at Ember and Cheyenne, his thick brow flickering in and out of a confused frown as he tried to keep a straight face.

He's gonna be wracking his brain forever, trying to figure out why a fae in Ambar'ogúl doesn't know how to use an activator.

"Behind your ear," she muttered.

"Yep." Ember lifted the metal piece to the back of her ear and gasped when the tech synced with her vision and her magic. Her eyelids fluttered, and when her violet gaze fell on the black metal machine behind the raug, her mouth dropped open. "Oh. My. God."

The guard grunted. "Until the healer regains her strength." Thumping a fist against his chest, he bowed and quickly spun to march back to the small door in the gate.

"This is *insane*." Ember studied the old-tech machine, her eyes flickering back and forth as she took in all the information the activator fed her.

"Told you you'd love it." Cheyenne folded her arms. "If that one came with the spider chair over there, I'm guessing it's one of the older models."

"I couldn't care less." Ember leaned over the edge of the rock ledge but caught herself before she fell off. "I totally get why you love yours."

"You haven't even tested it yet."

"I don't need to."

Chuckling, Cheyenne reached toward her friend. "Want a boost?"

"That's a seriously dumb question." Ember draped her arm over Cheyenne's shoulders and let the halfling pick her up and set her in the seat-shaped depression in the center of the machine. "Jeeze, getting in and out of your car would've been a hell of a lot easier if you could run around freely like a superdrow."

"Not an option back home, but yeah. Would've saved us a lot of time." Cheyenne straightened and gave her friend time to shift around and get comfortable in the machine.

Ember's gaze moved slowly across the smooth surface of the control panel at her fingertips. "I can't believe this. It's so easy."

"That's the point. Try it."

The fae girl swiped the panel, and the machine's legs lifted her higher off the ground before turning back toward the gate. Ember grinned, absorbed in the novelty of her first O'gúl activator.

Cheyenne snorted, tried to hold it back, then burst out laughing.

"What?"

"You." The halfling doubled over and howled with laughter,

stomping her feet. Every time she looked at her friend, she lost it all over again and had to turn away.

"All right, spit it out." Ember folded her arms and chuckled despite trying to look fed up. "What, am I doing it wrong?"

"No," Cheyenne squeaked through another laugh, waving her hand in front of her face. She sucked in a huge breath. "You're rocking the Doc Ock look like a pro!" She barely got the last word out before she cracked up all over again.

"Oh, so we watch one *Spiderman* movie, and now you're throwing around Marvel references?"

"I can't help it." Cheyenne wiped the tears from the corners of her eyes with the back of a hand and sniffed. "I totally blame you."

"He called it a 'crawler.'" Ember wrinkled her nose. "Does it really look like Doc Ock?"

Cheyenne pressed her lips together and nodded vigorously. Then she barked out another laugh. "Yeah, if he was sitting in a chair."

"Didn't you say you wanted to get inside and be part of the meeting with the chief?"

"Yeah, I do."

"You're wasting a lot of time laughing at me." Ember rolled her eyes and turned the machine toward the gates. "It's cooler than a wheelchair."

The machine lifted again on its mechanical legs, and with a swipe of her finger across the controls, Ember took off in the scuttling contraption. Cheyenne tried not to laugh and ended up laughing anyway as she followed her friend toward the gates.

Six feet from the small open door, Ember stopped, the metal legs clinking against the stone. "Crap. How the hell am I supposed to get through there?"

Cheyenne fell into another fit of laughter, holding herself

around the middle while Ember glared at her over her shoulder.

"You're not helping."

"I'm sorry, Em. Oh, man. I wish you could see what I'm seeing right now."

A raug peered out of the open garage door in the base of the tower and whistled sharply. He waved them toward him, and Ember lifted her chin. "Always a way, Cheyenne."

"Yeah, you have your own private entrance and everything."

The fae tossed her head and steered the crawler toward the beckoning raug. Cheyenne followed and finally managed to pull it together. *Just watch her head. Don't look at the legs.* Chuckling, she stepped into the base of the tower and pressed her lips together as the garage door groaned shut again behind them.

CHAPTER TWENTY-SIX

Cheyenne and Ember passed through the tower onto a wide stone walkway that ran around the perimeter of Hirúl Breach. The rest of the city was depressed into the canyon floor another ten feet, making the rising buildings of metal and stone even taller now that they could see their full height. The less-advanced metropolis was a quarter the size of Hangivol.

Most of the magicals here were raugs. The occasional goblin's green skin stuck out against so many hulking gray bodies, and as Cheyenne and Ember traveled down the stairs at the end of the walkway, the sound of steel pounding on stone grew louder from almost every direction.

The raugs gave them passing glances, but none of them stared at either the girls or the crawler. *This can't be a normal sight around here.*

The guard who'd brought Ember the crawler shouted from a doorway in the wall beneath the walkway. "Healer! This way."

They followed him through the door, which was thankfully wide enough for the machine to get through with only the occasional scrape into the long hallway beyond it. Ember gritted her teeth as she tried to guide the crawler in a perfectly straight line, her head jerking sideways when the wide base of her seat got too close to the wall and knocked her away.

"You good?"

"I'm fine," Ember hissed. "Still better than a wheelchair."

Cheyenne focused on the back of Ember's head.

The guard led them to another door on the left and stepped aside to let them enter. He had to press himself against the wall to avoid getting crushed by the scuttling crawler, but he nodded firmly at Cheyenne when she followed Ember into the room beyond and closed the door behind them.

The magicals sitting around an intricately carved stone table stopped the discussion when the clink and whir of Ember's crawler echoed along the back wall. The meeting included all of Cheyenne's party, the raug chief, and three older, skeptical-looking raugs taking up the chairs closest to their leader. Cazerel's orange eyes lit up when he saw Ember, his pointed teeth flashing in a wide grin. "Healer! Join us."

"Thanks."

"How does the crawler suit you, eh? You won't find the sniveling-fancy spark in Hirúl Breach like they have in Hangivol."

"It's great. Thanks." Ember steered the machine toward the corner of the huge table and positioned herself between Lumil and Corian.

"Good. *Good.*" Cazerel nodded vigorously and took a moment to grin at the fae.

Cheyenne headed for the empty chair beside Maleshi, gauging the others' reactions. *Nobody else thinks it's funny? Guess I'm the only asshole who laughs at a fae in a spider machine.*

She slumped onto the thick cushion lining the heavy wooden chair and gazed around the table. "What did I miss?"

"Not much," Maleshi muttered.

"Ah, yes." Cazerel turned his orange gaze onto L'zar. "I still do not understand why you need *our* help, Weaver. She's *your* kin."

"She's the worst part about me." L'zar set his folded hands on the table and leaned toward the chief. "Why do you think I've spent so much time away from her?"

Cazerel stroked his chin, his long red claws rasping his gray flesh. "Indeed."

"I know you lost all love for the drow when the last Cycle turned. K'laht did his part for you and Hirúl Breach in his time, did he not?"

"The Everbrite did more than *his part*." Cazerel sat back in his chair. "He was and is our Crown."

L'zar's eyes widened. "Sounds like you hate my sister as much as I do."

"I do not know the extent of your feelings, *Cu'ón*, but perhaps you are right."

"One has to know their enemies as well as their friends to protect themselves from that enemy." The drow spread his arms. "You've done well here in Hirúl Breach. I think you've also done well in drawing out as many dark truths about my sister as you possibly can. I need your help because I'm looking for the one thing that will make Cheyenne's terms of secession impossible for the Crown to refuse. I'm looking for leverage."

The chief's orange eyes narrowed. "I find it hard to believe the Weaver thief does not already have leverage."

"Oh, I have plenty, but it's not enough. If you tell me what *you* have, we can compare notes." L'zar grinned and sat back in his chair, feigning casual indifference despite how intently his golden eyes were fixed on the raug chief.

Cazerel studied the drow for a moment longer, then kept his gaze on L'zar as he turned his head toward one of the raug elders and muttered something in French. The elders shifted in their seats.

Cheyenne was acutely aware of the wary glances Maleshi and Corian exchanged across the table.

L'zar's eyes widened. "What don't I know?"

Cazerel growled and sat back in his chair, shifting his shoulders as if scratching an itch on his back. "Ba'rael Verdys has a child."

Cheyenne held her breath. *Holy shit.*

L'zar broke into a predatory grin and leaned forward. "Where?"

Corian shifted uncomfortably. "L'zar."

The drow cut him off with a raised hand without looking away from the chief. "Tell me."

"Somewhere not even the *Cu'ón* thief would find him," Cazerel replied evenly. "I expected you to know."

"Clearly I did not." L'zar set a slender slate-gray hand on the table and raised his eyebrows. "If you want to barter for this information, Cazerel, name your price. Whatever it is, you know I can and will pay it."

"Yes." The chief glanced at Ember and nodded. "I believe you paid in advance. It is no small thing to keep a healer at your side."

"I'm sure she's very good," L'zar muttered dismissively. "So, if the price has been paid, tell me where he is."

Corian hissed softly. "Don't you think the bigger issue is why we didn't know about him?"

"Not at all."

"If Ba'rael hears so much as a whisper about us going after her son, she won't wait for the rest of the fortnight, L'zar." Corian gripped the edge of the table. "She'll break as many of the old laws as she can to get to him before we do if she hasn't already."

"She has not." Cazerel dipped his head toward Corian and folded his arms. "And she will not. The child was sent away from her at birth. He has spent the first four hundred years of his life hidden, and not even his mother knows where to find him. On her own orders."

"Damn," Cheyenne muttered. "And I thought *I* had it bad growing up."

Ember snorted but immediately wiped off her smile when Corian shot each of them a warning look.

"The Olforím look after him now, or perhaps he looks after them. Either way, he is impossible to find." Cazerel's thick gray lips twitched into a grim smile. "But not for us."

A low chuckle rose from L'zar's grinning mouth. "That will work beautifully, *Zokri*."

"What? No." Cheyenne slapped her hands on the stone table and raised halfway out of her chair. "You are *not* gonna use her kid as bait or leverage."

L'zar turned slowly toward her and cocked his head. "I just want to *talk* to him, Cheyenne. I want to see this nephew of mine with my own eyes. A conversation won't hurt anyone."

"If he's sitting down to talk to you, L'zar, yeah, it might."

He chuckled and waved her off before turning back to the chief. "Will you take us to him?"

"L'zar, I'm serious," Cheyenne spat.

"Hush."

"Don't," she began, then Maleshi's hand clenched painfully around her wrist. The nightstalker woman nodded at Cheyenne's chair. The halfling seethed with contained anger, but she forced herself back into her seat.

Cazerel's tight smile widened. "If a new Cycle is to turn, I would say it's our duty to take you."

"Yes. We all have our own duties to perform, don't we?"

The chief stood, his chair scooting noisily across the floor. "Tomorrow, we will fulfill it."

The raug elders stood, quickly followed by L'zar and the rest of his party. "Thank you." He thumped a fist against his chest and nodded. "I look forward to it."

"I'm sure you do. You're welcome to stay in our city tonight." Cazerel walked swiftly around the table and stopped beside Ember. "If you think of anything else you need from us, Healer, my clansmen will provide it for you."

Ember stared up at him from her seat in the crawler. "Thanks."

He grinned at her, nodded brusquely, then pulled open the door and left, followed by the three raug elders, who didn't say a word.

When the door closed behind them, Cheyenne leaped to her feet. "You can't use this kid against his mother."

The drow brushed invisible dust off his shirtsleeve and rolled his shoulders. "I wouldn't keep calling him a kid, Cheyenne. He's *much* older than you."

"That doesn't matter. In a world where everybody lives practically forever, he's still a kid, and this is crossing a line."

"There *is* no line." L'zar stalked around the table. "If there were, I'd say *you're* crossing it right now. Don't speak against me like that again."

"I don't take orders from you."

"Oh, that wasn't an order." L'zar's smile faded as he pointed at her. "That was a warning. We do what we have to do, so my sister doesn't rip this world apart from the inside out. I'm not going to *hurt* him. He's family. Nothing better than family, isn't that right?"

Cheyenne scowled at him. "So far, my O'gúleesh family has been pretty disappointing."

"Aw." He cocked his head and winked. "We'll grow on you."

Without waiting for anyone else to share their opinion, the drow thief strolled past her and slipped into the hall. He was gone before the wooden door stopped swinging toward the wall.

Cheyenne looked at Corian. "He can't do this."

"I know. And so far, he hasn't," The nightstalker said, "It's the only option we have right now. He's right, though. Talking won't hurt the kid."

"It will if he's lived four hundred years, not knowing *anything* about this world."

"Can you honestly say living hidden and in ignorance is the better path, even when the truth is hard to swallow?"

She clenched her fists. "It's not the same."

"It's close enough, Cheyenne. Maybe you'll feel differently about it when you wake up in the morning."

Ember stuck a finger in the air. "Hey, does anyone remember we're on a time limit here?" The other magicals stared at her. "I mean, Cheyenne and I have a life to get back to Earthside. You know, after the weekend's over. Maleshi too, probably."

Maleshi gave the fae girl a sympathetic smile. "Time doesn't run quite the same way over here."

"No, but we have to go back, right?" Ember looked at the nightstalkers on either side of the table. "I mean, we *are* going back."

"Try not to worry about that right now, huh? We have slightly more important things to think about before we make another crossing. We'll make this as quick of a trip as we can." Maleshi exchanged glances with Corian, then the nightstalkers headed toward the door.

Corian paused when he passed Cheyenne, leaned toward her as if he wanted to say something, then nodded with a weak smile and stepped out of the room.

Lumil clapped her hands together and rubbed them vigorously. "All right. Time to see what kinda luxury suites these raugs are hiding behind all this dead stone, huh?"

Byrd chuckled. "I heard they're pretty good cooks."

"Not if we're talking about Foltr."

"I didn't say Foltr. Just raugs in general." The goblin man

pumped a fist in excitement. "I bet they know how to party, too."

Cheyenne stared at them. "You were just fighting them outside the gates."

"Yeah, that was fun, huh? Come on." Laughing, Lumil waved her toward the door before she and Byrd disappeared down the hall.

Cheyenne looked down at Ember. "We're running all over the place trying to fill in this hole, and it keeps getting deeper."

"Corian's right. Nothing's happened yet." Ember swiped the control panel on the crawler, the edge bumping against the table as the legs lifted in response. "Honestly, the only thing on my mind right now is finding something to eat in this place. I don't know if it's the long day or dumping all my magic into a raug chief, but I'm starving."

Cheyenne snorted. "One step at a time, huh?"

"Exactly." Ember slapped the side of the crawler, producing a metallic echo. "Or eight."

CHAPTER TWENTY-SEVEN

The raugs had given Cheyenne and Ember adjoining guest quarters that shared a central room and a small terrace overlooking the center of Hirúl Breach. Cool air spilled through the open stone wall connecting the terrace to the main room, bringing with it the scent of strange cooking spices, sweat, and ground stone.

Just as Cheyenne set Ember down on one of the giant cushioned lounges in the shared room, there was a knock on the door. "Yeah?"

The door creaked open, and a comparatively skinny raug with tattoos on his face bowed slightly. "The *Zokrí* sends a meal with his gratitude."

Ember grinned. "Food."

"I wouldn't get too excited until we see what it is," Cheyenne muttered out of the side of her mouth.

The raug flicked his clawed fingers into the room, and a metal table walked through the doorway on four mechanical legs, carrying a massive lidded tray, a pitcher of water, and two cups.

"Okay." Cheyenne hesitantly approached the table and

handed the cups and pitcher to Ember before grabbing the tray. "Thanks."

The raug nodded. "Anything else, Healer?"

"Oh. No, thanks. I think we're all good here."

With a final glance at Cheyenne, the raug recalled the table machine and waited for it to walk out ahead of him before he closed the door again.

Cheyenne sat on the low lounge stacked with pillows in front of the low table. "It's like they threw out the idea of wheels altogether."

Ember snorted and poured them each a glass of water before setting everything on the table beside the tray. "Why use wheels when everything you need gets up and walks on its own?"

"Not completely on its own." Cheyenne tapped the back of her ear, where her activator was placed. "It's a little weird."

"This whole place is weird. I like it." Ember leaned forward to remove the lid from the tray and paused. "Maybe I spoke too soon."

The dish was piled high with a steaming mix of what looked like rice and noodles with various colorful chunks layered throughout. Cheyenne leaned closer. "Huh. Smells like—"

"Chili dogs." Ember set the tray down and wrinkled her nose. "The kind you slop out of a can."

"Not the whole thing."

The fae playfully rolled her eyes and studied their meal. "Obviously just the chili, but *this* smells like the whole thing. Why are there chunks of glowing blue in there?"

"Oh, yeah. That's, uh…you know, I can't remember the name because it's weird, but my troll-neighbor friends cooked it for me one time. Some kind of plant, I think. It moves. Sometimes."

"Okay, so nothing with eyes, but the plants still move after they're cooked. Excellent." Ember shook her head. "I don't even care. I'm starving."

"Dig in, then."

The fae burst out laughing. "They didn't bring any silverware."

Cheyenne grinned. "Can you imagine raugs cutting into something like this with a dainty silver utensil in each hand?"

"No, but I can *vividly* picture them cramming handfuls into their mouths." Wrinkling her nose, Ember reached toward the steaming mound of raug delicacy. "We're going to eat this with our hands, aren't we?"

"I mean, you could always opt for the magical energy bar in your lunchbox."

Ember snorted. "I heard those were better to save for emergencies."

"Okay, then." Cheyenne plunged her fingers into the top of the pile. Thick, drooping noodles plopped back onto the tray when she tried to lift the whole thing to her mouth.

"Oh, jeez. Come on, I knew you had weird eating habits, but this is going a little too far."

The halfling chewed, nodding slowly, then swallowed and grabbed a cup to wash it down. "Okay. After a chaser, it's not that bad."

"Awesome."

"I'm staying away from that blue stuff, though."

Outside below the small terrace, raugs shouted at each other and knocked something over as the closest onlookers laughed and cheered on the fight.

Ember looked through the open wall toward the terrace. "These guys like their fights, don't they?"

"I hadn't seen raugs fighting before today." The halfling sucked leftover pieces of whatever it was off her fingers. "I mean, besides Gúrdu that one time. Those warriors outside the gates? They were pretty brutal and way too fast for something their size."

"What do you mean?"

"I mean, moving at superspeed isn't exactly an advantage." Cheyenne snorted and scooped up another bite. "Maleshi got punched out of hers."

"No way."

"They were all egging each other on. Hopefully, they got it out of their systems."

Ember laughed. "Listen to you, being all diplomatic and frowning at the brawlers in the streets."

"I mean, I ended up fighting them too, but you'd be proud of me, Em. I tried to break it up with words first."

"You're learning."

"I'm trying not to be that pissed-off drow who gets stupid when something goes wrong. L'zar doesn't lose it the way I do, at least most of the time, but spending so much time with him definitely makes me realize how much I *don't* want to be like him in a lot of ways."

"Was he fighting too?"

Cheyenne almost sprayed her next sip of water all over the table but managed to swallow it and laughed. "Are you kidding? He sat there and watched the whole thing like it was his own private show. Could've pulled out a bowl of popcorn, and it wouldn't have been weird."

"There's one thing you don't have to actively avoid not to be like him." Ember slurped a long, dangling noodle into her mouth, spraying sticky sauce all over her chin. She snorted, looked around for a nonexistent napkin, and used the back of her hand instead. "You've never been the kind of person who sees someone needing help and stands there watching."

"Not after the first time, anyway." Cheyenne buried her face in her cup for a long drink. *My friends get shot when I don't step up and do something.*

"L'zar could use some pointers from you that way."

"Right. Like he'd listen to them." The halfling shook her head. "I lost it on him when the capital exploded. He wanted to run away. That's all he ever does. And then he tried to stop me from helping a whole bunch of other magicals who would've been flattened by a falling building if I hadn't stepped in. I mean, I'm not saying I always make the best decisions, but at least I'm trying to be better about it."

"And you think L'zar's too stuck in his ways to even bother trying, huh?"

Cheyenne looked up from the tray and frowned. "He is."

Ember pressed her lips together and looked back down at the tray. "Maybe you're paying too much attention to what you don't like about him."

"Oh, come on. Don't try to tell me L'zar's a good guy with a big heart who had a rough time growing up, and all he needs is a little love."

"I didn't say that."

"That's what it sounds like."

Something heavy and metal clattered to the floor outside below the terrace, followed by cheers and snarls of encouragement.

"Okay." Ember leaned away from hovering over their weird dinner. "You guys had a little heart-to-heart after you got thrown out of that cave, right?"

"Just casually, huh? The *Sorren Gán* threw out the drow trash." Cheyenne laughed.

"Hey, that's an excellent description." Ember looked around unconsciously for a napkin again, couldn't find one, and settled for sucking the sauce off her fingers. "But I'm serious. A few weeks ago, you would've fought every single one of us to avoid sitting down with him like that. It looked like a pretty intense conversation, and no one left it bleeding or looking pissed."

"Yeah. I guess it was." *Pretty sure that's something L'zar wants to stay a secret. I can't believe I'm gonna keep it for him.*

"While you two huddled on the other side of that clearing, Corian had a lot to say about L'zar's sudden decision to start making better choices."

Cheyenne cocked her head. "Corian doesn't ever have a lot to say."

"It felt like a lot for him, okay?" Ember leaned back against the lounge. "He said he'd never seen L'zar show so much restraint toward another magical coming at him like you did."

"He was trying to protect himself, Em. Not by fighting me back, by trying to convince me I was wrong and he was right the whole time." Cheyenne shrugged. "Which might technically be true, but that goes back to the whole 'don't lie to Cheyenne if you want her help' issue. Which hasn't stopped."

"He explained everything to you, didn't he?"

"Yeah."

"And you didn't ask for it."

With a wry chuckle, Cheyenne folded her arms and stared at her friend. "You're diving deep into this, aren't you?"

"Hey, I'm not trying to convince you L'zar's a great guy. I'm not sure anyone believes that one hundred percent. I'm just saying he's changing. All the magicals who've known him forever can see it."

"They told you that explicitly, huh?"

"Yeah." Ember raised an eyebrow. "They were pretty worried about the whole thing."

"They shouldn't have been. I was pissed, but even if Corian and Maleshi hadn't gotten in the way, I would've run out of steam eventually. That tends to happen."

"Cheyenne, they weren't holding you back to protect L'zar."

The halfling wrinkled her nose. "What?"

"They were protecting *you*. Which apparently didn't need to happen because L'zar's been working on *not* killing the wrong people when he gets angry. You know, like his daughter."

"Huh." Cheyenne blinked at the pile of food on the table and shrugged. "I could still take him."

"Oh, my God." Ember laughed and rolled her eyes. "You're not even willing to say it's *possible* that he's trying to be better?"

"I don't know, Em. Not something I wanna think about right now. The guy basically killed himself for power no one else had, and I don't know what that says about how much he can change."

"What?"

Crap. "Nothing. It doesn't matter. I can't let my guard down around him, not all the way. I mean, however many thousands of years he's been alive, he's been Ambar'ogúl's trickster thief the whole time. Why would he stop that now?"

"Hmm. I hear people do weird things when they have kids."

Cheyenne snorted, then a cheer rose from outside, followed by a growling chant of, *"Cu'ón! Cu'ón!"*

"What the hell?" Cheyenne stood and quickly went out to the terrace. Below, a crowd of raugs had gathered around a cleared circle in the square. L'zar squatted on one side of the ring they'd formed, grinning at a huge raug sitting cross-legged on the other side. The raug cast some sort of spell, and L'zar copied the gestures almost exactly. Bright light strobed from their hands, and Cheyenne blinked against the glare before heading back into the room.

"Okay, you can't stand there watching without telling me what's going on down there. Immobile fae girl, remember?"

"He's down there competing in some kind of spell-off with a raug. I have no idea what they're doing."

"Oh." Ember perked up. "That sounds cool."

"If your magical battery recharges before we leave, I'm sure you'll have a chance to try it out for yourself." Cheyenne plopped back down onto the lounge, then turned and kicked up both feet to stretch them out in front of her. "I'm totally fine with sitting here and doing nothing for a while. Things feel okay right now, you know? I mean, if we ignore the whole part about this entire world falling apart under the Crown's shitty ruling habits."

"Ha. Delicately phrased."

Cheyenne widened her eyes and shrugged. "You know *me*, Em. Super-eloquent halfling."

"I know what you mean, though. Not always running around trying to fight off the next thing coming for you. I mean, I don't know what it's been like for you, but I can imagine."

"It is what it is. It's kinda nice to sit back and know that at least right now, nothing's coming after me, and no one's gonna open a portal into our apartment and tell us to get ready for something *right now*."

Ember glanced around and grimaced. "I'd knock on wood right now if there was any."

"Not trying to jinx it."

"I know."

"Don't get me wrong. I know how much work it's gonna take before anything in this world looks even *half* right again. I don't think I can even say things have ever been right with a drow on the throne."

"Maybe not *our* version of right." Ember sipped at her water. "But right for this world. Like the fighting pits."

"Oh, yeah. Everybody goes crazy for the chance to smash each other up for fun and call it honor and glory." The halfling chuckled and closed her eyes. "Not to mention purposely slicing each other to the brink of death."

Ember laughed. "Can't say a little fun never hurt anybody anymore, can we?"

"Not in Ambar'ogúl."

"No, I'm talking about the deathflame and the healing part.

This place runs on violence. That's obvious. But it seems to balance itself out, you know? Violence as a way of enjoying peace. Or getting seriously fucked up for a purpose. Get healed in the fighting pits and spread more life magic to this entire world."

"Hey, good idea." Grinning, Cheyenne swept her hand in a wide arc around the room. "Let's set up a giant fighting pit and have everybody go at each other at once. Giant deathflame bonfire on millions of dying bodies, and *bam*. All the blight gone, everybody healed and happy, and we go home."

"In theory, that sounds like a promising solution." Ember refilled her copper cup and sat back again, cradling it in both hands. "Not sure how great it'd work out, though. That's a lot of deathflame torches on a lot of bodies."

"We could figure it out."

They were silent for a moment, then Ember added, "You planning on going back home and picking up right where you left off after all this is over?"

"Probably. I mean, no, not *right* where I left off. That'll be impossible after getting the Crown to step down. L'zar said I had two options: stay as the Crown here, or go back home and be Earth's drow royalty there instead."

"Everybody needs a leader, right?"

Cheyenne said, "Not everyone, but all those O'gúleesh who made the crossing to get away from this mess? Probably. The FRoE isn't enough to handle things over there anymore. They don't even know *what* they're handling, or how to help those magicals beyond sticking their names in a stupid database and giving them a tiny house until they think they're ready to move into the brave new human world on their own. But they're not. They're missing huge pieces about how to get by over there, and they don't have anyone there to show them. The FRoE doesn't give a shit what they do after they leave the reservations."

"Sounds like you've already made your choice."

"Not quite. I'm hyper-aware of what those choices are. I mean, there *is* a third choice, which is going back home without being the Earth-drow monarch but still knowing what I know. It won't be the same as before, but I won't be wearing a damn crown, that's for sure."

Ember laughed. "Now *that* I'd like to see."

"Sorry, Em. Not gonna happen." Cheyenne looked at the ceiling and brushed loose hair away from her face. "The only thing I know is that I'm not gonna be the Crown here. That's just too much. I don't want it, and I can't leave my mom behind."

"What, you don't think she'd follow you across the Border and find herself a cozy little tower?"

They burst out laughing. *At least we can still find the parts of this to laugh about.* Her smile faded.

"I still need to find someone to be the new Crown over here. I'm not leaving this place in a giant power vacuum, and I have less than two weeks to figure out who the hell that's gonna be."

"Maybe your cousin will want the throne."

"My what?" Cheyenne sat up and frowned at her friend, then made the connection. "Oh. Jesus, that's weird."

"Should I call him Ba'rael's secret heir instead?"

"Very funny. I don't know what's gonna happen with him, Em. If he's anything like me, he won't want to be a part of this either, and if he's anything like either of our parents, he's not the right drow for the job."

Ember leaned sideways against the lounge and pursed her lips in thought. "Or maybe the right drow for the job isn't a drow."

"What, do *you* want it?"

"Ha. Nice try."

"Didn't think so." Cheyenne kicked off her black Vans and

crossed one ankle over the other, lacing her fingers behind her head. "I guess we'll just have to find out."

"You don't seem like you're in much of a hurry."

"I'm not. Not right now. Tomorrow's a whole different story." *And L'zar sure as hell better keep his word. A talk, or I don't think I'll be able to hold back.*

CHAPTER TWENTY-EIGHT

Maleshi poured herself a glass of Bloodshine and took a long drink. The fizzing bubbles made her swallow quickly before she let out a satisfied sigh. *Totally worth arguing with three different raugs to get a bottle. Nobody ever said I wasn't persistent.*

Sitting in the large pile of cushions that served as a raug armchair, she dropped her head back and enjoyed the relative silence. She could still hear the cheers and laughter from the square outside and briefly imagined herself out there with the crowd. *Nope. I have everything I need right here, though a bath with hot water would be excellent.*

A gentle knock sounded on the door to her guest quarters.

Frowning, Maleshi set her cup on the low table and stood. *I told them to leave me alone for the night, and I know how good raugs are at remembering.*

She went to the door and pulled the iron-ringed handle. "If you're here to get the Bloodshine back, it's already gone. Oh."

Corian stood in front of the open door, his hands in his pockets, and cocked his head. "I always knew you could handle your booze, but that seems a little excessive."

Maleshi gave him an exasperated look. "It's a lie. I just

opened the damn thing, but the raugs in charge of guarding the alcohol supply here take their jobs seriously. Why are you here?"

He shrugged. "I was hoping you had time for a chat."

The general frowned and shifted her weight onto one hip. "Why?"

"Oh, I don't know. Not having had the chance to talk to you about anything without interruption for the last few centuries feels like a good place to start."

"Hmm." Maleshi leaned into the hall and quickly glanced up and down. Then she shrugged and pulled back in. "Close the door behind you."

"Yes, General."

"Cut that out, huh? The loyal soldier crap is getting old."

Corian closed the door behind him and stood in front of it, his hands in his pockets again.

Maleshi flopped onto the mound of pillows and picked up her cup again, then saw him standing there and snorted. "You're obviously not standing at attention, so what are you waiting for? I already invited you in."

"I'm giving you enough time to change your mind."

"Change my mind." She snorted and took a long drink of Bloodshine. "I know exactly what I want, not that I'm gonna get it here. Duty before desire, right? And the way I remember it, you're the one who had problems making up his mind."

Corian chuckled and dropped his gaze to the floor. "All right. I suppose I deserved that."

"That's the least of what you deserve, *vae shra'ni*." She studied his bowed head. He still hadn't stepped farther into the room. "I'm not going to change my mind. Come sit."

Glancing at her briefly, Corian moved swiftly across the room and pulled an extra-large cushion toward the low table.

Maleshi grabbed an extra cup, filled it to the brim with bubbling Bloodshine, and handed it over. "What's going on?"

"I'm concerned." Corian took the drink and held it over his crossed legs, frowning at the golden liquid.

"Interesting."

"Ha. That's all you have to say?"

"I didn't come here to talk to myself." She eyed him with a smile. "What task did L'zar give you that you can't figure out this time, huh?"

Corian shook his head. "Not a task. I'm concerned about him and where this is headed."

"And you came to *me* for advice?"

With a self-conscious smile, Corian dipped his head and stared at the cup as he raised it to his lips. "More like comfort, honestly. I'm starting to think I knocked on the wrong door."

Maleshi swallowed and watched him try to hide his embarrassment behind the cup. *After centuries,* now *he needs comfort from me. Something's wrong.* "Where is he right now?"

"In the square playing king of spells with the raugs."

"Are you sure?"

Corian looked at her, his jaw clenching. "Maleshi, I wouldn't have come to you like this if I didn't know exactly where he was and what he was doing. I don't want him to know I'm here."

"Neither do I." She set down her cup and sat up straighter on the mound of pillows. "But you obviously need to get something off your chest, and I think you should stay to do that."

"Thank you."

"You're welcome." She spread her arms and gestured to the pile of cushions around her. "I *am* very busy right now, so just know this bottle of Bloodshine is going to feel particularly abandoned until I can give it my full attention again."

He snorted. "By all means, drink while you listen. We might both need it."

"Corian."

"Yeah."

"You're stalling."

Corian took another drink and reached for the bottle to refill his cup. "All this about Ba'rael having a child and us going to find him. It doesn't feel right."

"I thought you agreed we should speak to him?"

"I do. Cazerel didn't say a thing about where he is. About where we're going."

"You don't trust the raugs?"

"No, I do. I don't think they trust us. We only got into that meeting because of Ember, and that says enough on its own. I'm not worried about the raugs, but L'zar seems way too excited for a family reunion and a quick chat about the future." Corian rubbed the back of his neck. "He won't tell me what he plans to do with this newfound nephew of his, and I'm not sure I can predict his intentions anymore. Not as well as I used to, at any rate."

"You think he's lying to you?"

"Lying and avoiding the whole truth are one and the same for him. You know that."

Maleshi frowned. "I do. I also don't see a reason why he'd keep anything from you. Not now, when we're so close to finishing all this."

"Neither do I, but I can *feel* it." He rubbed a hand over his mouth and stared at the ceiling. "Now I know how Cheyenne felt before she learned the rest of what she needed to know."

"You're comparing two very different things, *vae shra'ni.*" Maleshi dipped her chin and stared at him from beneath her darkened brows until he met her gaze. "Neither of them knows how to fulfill their role with the other. Is it strange to see L'zar Verdys loosening up around the halfling daughter he's known for all of a month? Absolutely. Can we trust that he's trying to do all this for her and for the world he despises as much as some O'gúleesh despise him? Maybe."

"That's the thing. I thought I did." Corian bit his bottom lip, his nostrils flaring as he tried to put his thoughts into words. "I'm not sure I do anymore. I think he's hiding things from me *because* we're this close to the end, and he no longer thinks it's necessary to keep me informed."

"That's not the way you two operate."

"Yes, I'm well aware."

Maleshi scooted closer to the edge of the pillows. "Do you think he's noticed that you feel this way?"

"No. He knows I agree with Cheyenne that using Ba'rael's son against her is not the route we want to take. He also knows I stand with him in heading out to wherever they're keeping him to see him for ourselves and make our judgment call then."

"Then leave it at that. Make the judgment call then, and don't spend time worrying about it until we get there. That won't do any of us any good."

Corian closed his eyes. "I can't lie to him, Maleshi."

"You have to. If L'zar thinks you're questioning him, you know how he'll react. He hasn't had nearly enough time to recover from the Weave he spent all that time cloaking around himself, and then he returned to the *Sorren Gán*. If I had to guess, I'd say he's as unstable now as he was the first time he made that journey. Don't set him off."

"You think I want to?" Corian set his cup on the table, rubbed his lips, and stood. "It was a mistake to come here. I'm sorry."

"Corian, you brought me into this by coming to talk to me *now* of all times. Don't walk away from this conversation before it's finished."

"Why, because you're the only one who gets to do that?"

Maleshi leaped from the cushions and hissed, "Don't you dare compare that to *this*! I told you exactly what was happening. I laid everything at your feet. All her plans. All the orders I'd been given to carry out. Every single speck of information, yours and L'zar's to do with however you saw fit. You had a *choice.*"

"I know." Corian stared at her and raised both hands in submission. "I know. I'm sorry."

"No, sorry isn't good enough, especially not now. He *told* you to leave. He saw what you wanted, and he handed it to you on a fell-damn tray. You turned away from all of it."

"Maleshi."

"Don't do that." She pointed at him and shook her head. "Don't try to talk your way out of this. You've been skirting around it for centuries, Corian, and you're trying to do the same thing again, right here in front of me! L'zar *knew* he'd be going Earthside again. He *knew* he'd be spending as much time over there as he did, and he told you to come with me. You turned against *both* of us when you stayed here, and then what? You made the crossing centuries later, settled into a world full of humans, and didn't once try to find me? I am *here* for you now, *vae shra'ni*, and you still owe me."

"You're right."

"I know I'm right!" Maleshi balled her fists, glaring at him and breathing heavily through her clenched teeth. "Don't talk to me about walking away like you know what that means."

His jaw clenched, Corian stepped toward her and paused. "I should have come with you. I didn't have all the pieces before you left, and L'zar didn't give them willingly to me then. That's what I'm afraid of, *ma gairín*. It feels like it's happening all over again, only this time I know the consequences of *not* seeing what he sees." He took a sharp breath and grimaced at the ceiling. "Maybe the consequences of knowing what he plans to do are even worse."

"Maybe they are." Maleshi smoothed her dark hair away from her face and regained her composure. "There's a good chance that if he hasn't told you to do something, there's nothing to do but wait and watch. And if he *does* give an order, no matter how insane it is, I hope you follow it. Sometimes I want to rip that drow limb from limb, but as long as I've known him, he's never been wrong."

"*I* was, though." Corian slowly approached her and lifted a hand toward her face. Maleshi tilted her head away slightly and stared at him. He nodded, ran his fingers briefly along her cheek, and dropped his hand. "And I *am* sorry."

"So am I." Maleshi closed her eyes and took a deep breath. "I think we're finished with this conversation."

"Right." A pained frown creased his eyebrows, and he nodded. "I'll let you get back to your drinking."

"I didn't tell you to leave." When he turned back toward her, she gave him a soft smile. "You said you came looking for comfort, didn't you?"

A wry chuckle escaped him. "That's not what I found, but I'll be fine."

"Or you could stay. Find comfort without L'zar Verdys being at the center of it." Maleshi nodded toward the bottle on the table, still three-quarters full. "That Bloodshine won't drink itself."

The corners of Corian's mouth flickered into the hint of a smile, and he turned to eye the bottle. "Are you sure?"

"As I said, I know what I want. Just waiting for you to make your decision."

He studied her silver gaze, then dipped his head and returned to the table to fill both their cups. When Maleshi joined him, Corian handed her a drink and raised his for a toast. "To Maleshi Hi'et, who always gets what she wants."

"And Corian Vedi'im, who somehow always wants what he gets."

They knocked their metal cups together, staring at each other, and drank.

Get sneak peeks, exclusive giveaways, behind the scenes content, and more.
PLUS you'll be notified of special **one day only fan pricing** on new releases.

Sign up today to get free stories.

CLICK HERE

or visit: https://marthacarr.com/read-free-stories/

AUTHOR NOTES - MARTHA CARR

I've been working with my old trainer from Chicago – over Zoom. One of the strange benefits of a very strange year. Laura was my favorite trainer I've ever run into because she bothered to research physical hindrances I had with credible sources and came up with creative solutions. They were challenging without being dangerous and lead to progress. Never had anyone before or since tailor something to me that much and so effectively. Also, she's got a wicked sense of humor, which is a big plus.

It turns out Laura has added a new element of mindfulness around exercise. I've been practicing mindfulness around food for a couple of years now and it's changed the way I eat in ways I didn't think were possible. Basically, the short version is that I became more aware of whether I liked what I was eating or not (you'd think that would be obvious but turns out, nope) and whether I was hungry or full.

I wondered when I started that journey just how much it could change decades old habits. Turns out, it could change them to the point where I can actually eat just one. And I quit doing the old seesaw of eating perfectly or throwing caution to the wind.

How do you do all that with exercise? When we started, I had no clue.

I'm kind of all or nothing with exercise too and generally, I don't like it most of the time. There are aspects of it I like and certain exercises I like more, but how do I get to mindfulness? (Laura likes to say there are certain exercises I dislike less. Semantics.)

Some of my instructions have been to use a short meditation before I start working out. To take an approach of building at a moderate pace to something. To make up a list of ways to blow off steam – the naughty list – so I already know what I'd like to do on days that running seems like too much. (Actually build in that there will be those days and be ready, instead of acting like maybe this time that won't happen). And to make a list of the exercises I like – or dislike less till there are sixty or more for me to choose from.

Mind blown. So obvious but I never saw any of this before. Makes me think that there's a chance I could learn to incorporate regular exercise in my life without long stretches of doing nothing but walking the dog. I'll let you know. More adventures to follow.

AUTHOR NOTES - MICHAEL ANDERLE

Thank you for allowing me to work in a profession that feeds my need to be creative. That is to you the reader, and companies such as Amazon (and others such as Apple, Google, Kobo, Barnes & Noble etc.) which have created the distribution methods we indie publishers use today.

Without readers such as yourself willing to take a chance, I wouldn't have the honor to chat (even in the back of the book) with thousands of people.

So, I just got off the phone and did something I've NEVER done before. I reached out to Martha and asked her to add to her author notes.

I had to explain that mindfulness (the concept) is something my brain doesn't understand (nor the corollary be-in-the-moment.)

I heard the term hundreds of times, but never have I had someone explain what the @#%@# it meant in a way I could grasp.

And Martha did it.

But, I couldn't follow all of her comments without trying

two or three times to unpack her thoughts. So, I reached out and asked if she would EXPAND her author notes.

You know, to author block me because she needs my help to accomplish that little feat (she does not.)

I appreciate her explanation for a concept I am going to be able to use. I'm 52 years old. Maybe I've got 10 years, maybe I've got another 50 years (my grandmother was 100 when she passed) but I now understand when someone tells me to be in the moment.

Don't even ask what I said to those people in my head after about the 10th time. Even Bethany Anne might be impressed with the purity of the cursing.

Since I didn't say anything out loud, I nodded my head politely and still went away confused. So, if you haven't read Martha's author comments in this book (and don't understand 'mindfulness') go back and give it a read.

It's pretty freaking useful as a core tool to use to help you make your life better.

I'm looking forward to another chance to talk in the next book!

Ad Aeternitatem,

Michael Anderle

CONNECT WITH THE AUTHORS

Martha Carr Social

Website: http://www.marthacarr.com

Facebook: https://www.facebook.com/
groups/MarthaCarrFans/

Michael Anderle Social

Website: http://lmbpn.com

Email List: http://lmbpn.com/email/

Social Media:

https://www.facebook.com/LMBPNPublishing

https://twitter.com/MichaelAnderle

https://www.instagram.com/lmbpn_publishing/

https://www.bookbub.com/authors/michael-anderle

OTHER BOOKS BY MARTHA CARR

THE LEIRA CHRONICLES
SOUL STONE MAGE
THE KACY CHRONICLES
MIDWEST MAGIC CHRONICLES
THE FAIRHAVEN CHRONICLES
I FEAR NO EVIL
THE DANIEL CODEX SERIES
SCHOOL OF NECESSARY MAGIC
SCHOOL OF NECESSARY MAGIC: RAINE CAMPBELL
ALISON BROWNSTONE
FEDERAL AGENTS OF MAGIC
SCIONS OF MAGIC
THE UNBELIEVABLE MR. BROWNSTONE
DWARF BOUNTY HUNTER
MAGIC CITY CHRONICLES
CASE FILES OF AN URBAN WITCH

OTHER BOOKS BY JUDITH BERENS

OTHER BOOKS BY MARTHA CARR

JOIN THE ORICERAN UNIVERSE FAN GROUP ON FACEBOOK!